Ordinary Mr. Billionaire

THE BILLIONAIRE ROMANCE COLLECTION

GIGI SLOAN

Copyright © 2023 by Gigi Sloan
All Rights Reserved.

No part of this book may be reproduced in any form or by any electronic or mechanical means, including information storage and retrieval systems, without written permission from the author, except for the use of brief quotations in a book review.

ISBNs
Paperback: 978-1-961595-06-4

Cover Designers: Mia Kiely@MiaKDesign and Anees Ahmed@Aneesdesigner7
Editors: Lisa Sargent@Upwork
Logo: Flower Image by jcomp on Freepik.com
Chapter Image: Mansion by Anees Ahmed@Aneesdesigner7
Format Designer: Dawn Baca

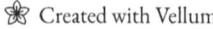 Created with Vellum

For my family and friends who had patience and love for me while I wrote this book.

I love you all!

*Above all, thank you to **God** for giving me the ability to accomplish this.*

Atticus

PROLOGUE

"Dad, you can't be serious." I rub my forehead where the early signs of a headache form, the echoes of my misadventures from last night still fresh in my mind.

My parents have been relentless lately, insisting I "get my life together." But today's approach is different and absurdly dramatic, a *literal* wake-up call that no one needs.

Why they roused their heartbroken 30-year-old son, who had just stumbled home at four a.m. — with an *air horn* — is a mystery. Where did they even get an air horn? With one look at my dad's face, I bite back the urge to comment on their choice of alarm clock.

Dad's pained expression dares me to speak, and that is enough to make me hold my tongue.

"I'm serious, Atticus. Your mother and I have been lenient with you for as long as we could, but this can't go on!" Dad shouts and then coughs roughly. "You're putting the Winslow name in jeopardy!"

Mom's expression is more anxious than angry, an unwilling participant in this morning's theater, as she rubs

Dad's shoulder to calm his heavy breathing. She would never go against his wishes, and today is no exception.

"Your father is right, Atticus. First, you mess up *embarrassingly* at the company—so bad that we have to pull you from the business. Now, all you do is spend your days sleeping and your nights partying and, well, whoring about." Mom blushes when she says the words. "I can't bear to watch it anymore." Her quivering voice bears the profound weight of emotion.

"It's disgraceful!" Dad chimes in again. "All of this happened because of your girlfriend leaving? It's been six months!"

A frown forms on my face before I can help it. "We were together for five years, Dad! Five years of thinking I was in love with someone I could have a future with! And then I find out I was never in her plans at all? *You* were the one who introduced me to Heather! This whole thing is *your* fault!"

"Atticus!" my mother says. "Please! Don't talk to your father like that. He's only trying to help you."

"Heather ran off with *your* friend, Dad. Some friend, stealing your son's girlfriend!" I blurt.

Dad narrows his eyes at me. "That's enough. I don't need to listen to this."

My dad looks behind him and pulls my mom to the side. Confused by what's happening, I see two security guards approach me after my father waves his hand at them.

"What's going on?" I ask, glancing from my mother to my father.

"Like I told you, Atticus. I'm *done* with this. You need to leave and start your own life. It isn't a suggestion. It's an order." Dad places his arm around my mother's shoulder, his face like stone, as two hefty men I've never seen before grab me by the arms and usher me toward the door.

"Wait! Dad, what—"

"You get nothing but $6,000, the clothes on your back, and the car outside." Dad is unyielding as I'm dragged outside. My mother's face looks like she's watching a horror film.

My parents follow us downstairs. I'm sandwiched between the guards, each holding fast to an arm. My parents stop at the doorway once I've tugged my arms from the guards who have deposited me at the bottom of the front stairs to the house. Dad squeezes Mom's shoulder, pulling her to him. Mom looks like she wants to throw up.

"I can't do this, Raymond... he's still my baby." Mom buries her head in his chest and sniffles.

"This is the only way to help him, Carol. We talked about this. You need to be strong."

My mother lifts her head and speaks. "Your father and I agree." She clears her throat and glances at my dad, who is staring at me. "You can return when you've got your life together, darling. Your father wants you to have an apartment, never miss a bill payment, and start a business grossing $100,000 by the end of its first active year." Mom takes out a tissue from her pocket and wipes her eyes. "You can do that, baby. I *know* you can."

"You have one year." Dad's voice holds finality. "Oh, and one more thing. Don't you dare tell *anyone* who you are. Don't expect to use our reputation and good name to your advantage. I want you to do this on your *own*. Do you understand? Use your middle name, James, and tell *no one*, and I mean *no one*, who you are!"

Stunned, I stare at them as the realization hits me they aren't trying to intimidate me into compliance this time. They're kicking me out.

"The clothes on my back? Mom! Dad! I'm in my pajamas!"

My parents have turned and started back into the house, but my dad stops and pushes the door open just wide enough for me to hear him when he yells, "That's unfortunate! You would have been in better clothes if you'd gotten up before noon." He slams the door shut.

The guards hand me an envelope full of cash and car keys before taking their place by the front door, guarding it like sentries with their arms folded, staring straight ahead. Still in disbelief, I turn to the baby blue Prius parked in the driveway that's supposed to be mine.

"Oh, come on! No way! This ugly thing is my car? What am I supposed to do with that?"

The thing doesn't even look like it belongs on my father's property. Dad did this on purpose. I've never driven anything like this, not even when learning to drive.

It quickly dawns on me I don't have a roof over my head for the night. I don't even have *my phone*. I only have pajamas and a baby blue Prius.

My disbelief quickly turns to anger and spurs me into action. So what if I've been a little out of it for a while? Treating me like this? I'll show them! My anger is soothing to the rapidly growing anxiety threatening to break me down.

I drive to the only other place I can go for the night — my best friend Archie's house. He's going to have a field day when he sees my Prius.

Determination burns inside me. I have one year to prove my parents wrong.

Charlie

PROLOGUE

"Did you seriously quit your job at GGBuff, Charlene?" My boyfriend, Mark Benson, asks, his voice tinged with disbelief.

I frown, feeling my frustration rise as he uses my full name. He argues that it's necessary to show seriousness sometimes, but that explanation doesn't sit well with me. He treats me like a child. The only time I heard my given name was during my younger years when my parents wanted to convey their sternness. Despite already feeling on edge, I mentally coach myself to remain composed and avoid reacting impulsively.

"Yes, Mark. I had to quit. Obviously. Have you not been listening to me for the past few weeks? I need to care for Ronny during the day and can't afford an in-home aid. That's why I quit GGBuff and now have to find a night job. What's so hard to understand?"

Mark regards me as if I'm speaking in a foreign language. "I hear you, but what you're saying is ridiculous. GGBuff is a good job, Charlene. Have you thought this through? You won't make that kind of money at some night job."

I groan and slip my hand out of his. "Ronny... needs... my... help." I emphasize each word, wondering why such a straightforward concept seems so hard for him to grasp.

He raises a skeptical brow and glances over my shoulder. He smiles, still looking past me, and then signals for our waitress. She approaches, her hips swaying from side to side. Mark smiles at her, looking her up and down, and then orders another vodka martini, neglecting to ask me if I want anything.

I can feel smoke steaming out of my ears, and it takes all my willpower to avoid an outburst. I notice Mark's gaze lingering on the waitress as she walks away. His blatant ogling makes me laugh, despite my irritation.

Mark turns back to me, unfazed by the distraction. "I won't lie to you, Charlene. I think it was foolish of you to quit your job."

I bristle, feeling like someone has slapped me in the face. "What? I feel like I'm talking to a wall."

"Stop being dramatic, Charlene." He pushes his chair back, screeching it on the floor, and his tone grows colder. "Ever since Ronny's accident, it's been all about Ronny. I'm so tired of it, and now *this*!" He lifts his napkin from his lap and throws it on the table.

The dining hall falls silent as Mark's voice echoes. He's created a scene.

I struggle to respond, but Mark doesn't seem interested in listening to me. "You're only thinking about yourself. What about me, huh? When do you think about me?"

His words cut deep, and my mouth goes dry. Tears well up as I try to form a response to defend myself. I've never asked Mark for a dime, and while I don't expect him to help with Ronny, if he's so upset and adamant that I keep my job, why doesn't he offer his help financially?

The waitress returns with Mark's martini, appearing

embarrassed for me. I glance away, although that's no better since everyone is staring at us.

Mark stands, taking the drink from the waitress, and drains the glass in one chug. He sets the glass on the table. "It's over, Charlene. I can't continue dating a woman with such wildly off-kilter priorities. We're done. Don't call me."

He tosses a hundred-dollar bill in front of me and storms out without looking back.

As the room returns to life around me, I'm left sitting alone at the table, the ruins of my five-year relationship starkly evident, and my face drenched in tears.

CHAPTER 1
Atticus

"I tell you, Archie, I'm not sure if I'm up for this. Perhaps my parents were right in pushing me to face the world," I confess, my voice a whisper against the game or whatever he has blaring on his TV. I'm too nervous to pay attention. The weight of recent decisions and a gnawing emptiness have settled in my chest, making it hard to breathe. "I was sick of being holed up in my room, anyway."

"Oh, dude, come on! Where's the Atticus I know? You're not going to let a little thing like poverty get you down now, are you?" Archie, my closest confidant since we were kids, chuckles. But his typically infectious laughter does little today to soothe my nerves.

I've always admired and envied Archie's laid-back, carefree attitude. His short, spiky, blonde hair gives him a perpetually youthful look. He's tall, like me, but he doesn't share my enthusiasm for the gym. He laughs off the idea of working out like it's a foreign concept. And now, it's his unwavering support that keeps me driving forward, contemplating the leap I'm about to take.

"You're getting a kick out of this, aren't you?" I say. "Some friend you are." I get up from his sofa, a 1970s model, I'm certain, and switch off the TV, of the same decade, I'm sure.

"Oh, relax, Att, I'm just teasing you. You're a smart guy. You'll figure it out. Besides, you always have me, you know that." His reassuring smile helps soothe my nerves, but just barely. "You can stay here," he says, motioning to the antique couch. "I've got extra blankets, and I'm sure I can scrounge up a pillow."

As I take a right at a busy intersection, I'm reminded of the past few weeks I've spent on Archie's couch, grateful for his support but feeling like a burden. Not to mention that sleeping on his couch is grueling. One night was all it took for me to start apartment hunting, and I don't know what he stuffed in that pillowcase, but I'm sure it wasn't an actual pillow.

I had imagined that securing a new place would be a breeze, given my background, but the reality of my financial constraints hit hard. My parents' estate in Saratoga Springs might as well be on another planet from this humble basement apartment in Albany, where I'm about to begin a new life with six thousand dollars to my name. Now minus my first month's rent and security deposit. I never thought the NY Capital District was an expensive place to live until now.

The apartment is far from perfect, but it's what I can afford. The prospect of sleeping on the floor pushed me to choose a furnished place. And, with no job yet, my dwindling allowance is taking a hit.

Thank God Archie offered me some clothes. He's a bit bigger than I am, but nothing a belt didn't remedy. The only things I had to buy were shoes to wear for interviews. I can't show up in shoes that are clomping off my feet. Archie has enormous feet. I also bought a pair of sneakers and a few groceries.

Working at my father's company had made me complacent about job hunting, and I hadn't foreseen the challenges. With Archie's help, I'd created a resume, something I'd never actually done before, and landed a job at GamesMade, a gaming company. It's a programmer position, and it pays pretty well. I start today, but I have to admit I'm not feeling it.

I'd scoffed at the idea of Archie helping me prepare for my interview, recalling the numerous interviews I'd conducted at my father's company. "I've interviewed plenty of people. I don't need to go over the interview questions," I'd told him.

Archie's concern is touching, but returning to his place isn't an option. I've already imposed too much on him. My goals are clear — save money and start my own company. It's not about proving my parents wrong. It *is* about fulfilling *my* ambition.

"Hey, Atticus, you there?" Archie is on the phone, talking me off the cliff as I drive to my new job. I don't know why I'm nervous, but I am. It's probably because this is an unfamiliar experience for me. I've never had to work for anyone but my father before.

"Yeah, buddy, I'm here. I'll be alright. I know you're worried, but I have it all figured out." This job is a means to an end. But now the tables have turned. I'm lower than I ever thought I'd be, and Archie is looking out for me now. I honestly don't know what I'd do without him.

I approach the security booth and offer a friendly smile as I introduce myself. The guard reciprocates with a nod and hands me a visitor's pass, along with helpful directions to the underground parking lot. Pulling into a parking spot, I pause for a quick second to gather my thoughts and remind myself that this position at GamesMade is a step toward owning my own company one day.

That was always my plan, anyway, even before this fiasco. Working for my father was only supposed to be temporary. Things were going great until Heather took off on me. Then I just lost it. I hadn't intended to mess things up, but I did, royally, and now my parents think I'm a screw-up.

The journey ahead may be riddled with challenges, but it's a path I need to tread to prove my worth, not to my parents, but to *myself*. As the elevator moves, I wonder if the excitement of my new life — or let's call it my new adventure — will ever replace the emptiness that still lingers in my heart over Heather.

In the lobby of GamesMade, I'm met by a dozen eager faces. Most of them look to be about my age, mid to late 20s or early 30s. They stare around with wide-eyed wonder, the massive lobby something out of their wildest fantasies. The space exudes an air of potential and opportunity. It's different from my father's company, grand in its own way, but not as grand as Dad's. But it's just a stepping stone on my path to independence. Everyone is chatting excitedly, but I keep to myself.

A tall man stands before us. "Welcome to GamesMade," he announces, his voice nasal and grating. His questionable fashion choices make him look odd, but I try to push the judgment aside. He must not have received the email I received about dressing in business casual. He's disheveled, and he's wearing a red vest with a paisley print and a large purple silk tie.

"My name is Todd Brierly," the tall man continues, "and I can be your best friend or your worst nightmare. You will address me as Mr. Brierly at all times."

He smiles a smug smile, and his teeth are a disgusting shade of yellow. His eyebrows shoot straight up from his eyes like he's put some kind of gel in them, and I wonder why the company would ever put him as their first point of contact for recruits.

"As you know, this is an opportunity of a lifetime." The nasal quality of his voice makes him sound funny and annoying simultaneously. "To most of you, this will be the first day in a step towards greatness, but to others, this position will expose your mediocrity."

When he insists on being addressed as Mr. Brierly, it's clear he enjoys playing the authority figure. He makes a point about this being a pivotal moment, but I can't help but snort at his theatrical villain-like laugh. Judging from the frowns and glares directed at me by the other recruits, I wasn't as quiet as I thought. It appears I am now the center of attention.

"Ah, the back-row snorter," he says, pointing at me as his face turns red. I curse myself for drawing attention but act as casually as I can when he asks me, "What's your name?"

I curse under my breath and step forward. All eyes are on me as I boldly say, "Jimmy." He continues to glare, saying nothing. "Jimmy Winslow," I conclude.

Some recruits chuckle, and Todd's irritation becomes clear. My first impression of Todd is less than favorable, but I refuse to let it get under my skin. He's just a minor distraction. I appear, however, to have made an enemy at GamesMade.

He shakes his head, and the orientation continues as Todd leads us through the building. He provides details about our workstations and the training process, droning on about every little detail. I struggle to remain engaged as *Mr. Brierly's* words become a background noise to my drifting thoughts.

"Let me reiterate," Todd says, snapping me from my thoughts. The man is staring at us like we're on trial. "You are *NOT* to fraternize with any of the maintenance people. Not the security, not the cleaners, nobody. Doing so is grounds for *immediate* termination. Am I understood?"

He looks around the entire group surveying to be sure we

all heard him. I see several confused faces alongside mine. What is he rambling on about? We can't talk to the cleaning staff? Just when I think no one is going to question this ridiculous stipulation, a hand shoots up in front of me.

It's Tiffany, the ever-enthusiastic one of the group, who questions the rule. "I'm sorry," she says. "I was wondering. Ending someone's employment for talking to the service people seems...unusual. Any reason for such an extreme punishment? Also, why would it be wrong to talk to them in the first place?"

There are several nods from the newbies and all eyes turn to Todd expectantly. His smile suddenly doesn't look so wide anymore. Instead, it looks like he's trying a little too hard to keep it in place.

"Good question, Tiffany." Todd clears his throat, and it's apparent he's a smoker because he coughs and coughs as we all look around at each other. When he's finally done, he continues. "We had an issue where one of the cleaning staff accused a *top* professional here of inappropriate behavior. *Of course*, it wasn't true, but it turned into a tremendous scandal, and the effect on our image was catastrophic. Any other questions?"

The recruits murmur and glance around at each other. I can't help but wonder whether Todd wasn't the 'top professional' involved in the alleged scandal. The recruits fall into silence, and Todd quickly moves on, resuming the orientation.

CHAPTER 2

Charlie

As I pull into the dimly lit parking garage of my workplace, I come to a stop in front of the security checkpoint. By flashing my identification card, I catch the attention of the security guard, who has his eyes glued to a recap of the game between the Jets and the Buccaneers. After a moment, he nods lazily to signal my passage, and I slowly drive past him.

In the elevator, headed to the maintenance floor, my thoughts drift to the night ahead. I'll head to my locker, change into my gear, the blue cleaner's jumpsuit that's so attractive — not — and start my shift. This place has become my second home.

Changing into the jumpsuit, I sit in the maintenance lounge with time to spare, way earlier than my shift. It's become a precious pocket of solitude before the grind begins. I sit on the bench and lean my head back on the wall, closing my eyes.

Tonight, as with every night, I left Aunt Debbie with the monitor for Ronny, her unwavering promise to keep an ear out. No need for promises, though. Aunt Debbie has been the anchor, the rock, and a mother when ours abandoned us. She's more than family. She's my savior.

Aunt Debbie, my father's sister, stands a little over 5'2", but her presence is much larger than her petite frame. Short, curly brown hair hugs her round face, and her big brown eyes glisten with kindness and love. There's an undeniable strength beneath that gentle exterior. Her grace carries her through the most challenging days. Aunt Debbie is a constant reminder of the importance of family, love, and sacrifice.

She had assumed the role of a parent long before my parents skipped town to Mexico. After Ronny's accident, she took the reins fully. She didn't need to be asked. She just stepped in, a maternal force to be reckoned with.

Our duplex, with Aunt Debbie's apartment on one side and mine and Ronny's on the other, is a physical representation of the way she's always been there. There may be a dividing line between us, but we're united under one roof from the harsh world beyond.

My brother, Ronny, sleeps through most nights, which is a blessing. I wouldn't want Aunt Debbie to lose any sleep helping us. She's a teacher, and she gets up early for work. But she's there if Ronny needs help. She's become his lifeline — a constant source of comfort.

In the maintenance lounge, memories of Mark Benson flood my thoughts. I try to push them away, but they linger, casting shadows on my heart. The night he walked out of the crowded restaurant, I sat there, tears streaming down my face, and he didn't look back. Five years meant nothing to him.

Hatred simmers within me now — hatred for him and the privileged world he represents. I don't like feeling that way, and I fight myself to forgive him somehow. But that's one perk of my job, one of the few positives of working here. In this world, I don't have to see the likes of Mark and his kind, those who reek of entitlement.

My lip quivers as I think of him. He's nothing to me now, merely a bitter memory, and a lesson learned. And I know that soon I'll move on, and he won't matter anymore.

He was wrong, you see. Wrong about me and my priorities. My family, and especially Ronny, are everything. I've always tried to help Ronny, even before the accident that left him paralyzed. Growing up, he was a troubled kid, and I was the only one who ever seemed to care about him. He's a sweet guy, and intelligent, and there's nothing I wouldn't do for him.

After his accident, he had to lean on me. He had no insurance, and there was no money for his care. I get meager tokens from my parents occasionally, but they are hardly enough to cover the bills.

I won't pretend it's easy. It's not. Caring for a grown man who weighs 160 pounds and has no use of his legs is difficult. Aunt Debbie spent a chunk of her savings buying two hydraulic patient lifts, one for upstairs and one for downstairs. I use them to transfer Ronny into the bed, into the tub, or onto the couch. She also purchased us a stair lift to get him upstairs and had it installed. I wish I had more help, but at least Aunt Debbie didn't bail on us like my parents did. I plan to pay her back someday.

I glance up at the clock. My shift starts in five minutes. Other employees are filtering in, and I greet them warmly. I get up and gather my supplies. My supervisor will fine me if I'm still in the lounge when my shift begins.

As I make my way through the upper floors of the building, the sound of my trolley echoes off the walls. They polished the floors to a shine, and the smell of furniture polish is almost overpowering. The offices are empty, and the only sound is the soft hum of the air conditioning. I pull out my cleaning supplies and get to work, the sound of the vacuum drowning out my thoughts.

I go through the first two hours of my shift in a typical fashion. I've learned which offices still have occupants when I start my shift, and I give them a wide berth, saving them until the end of my shift when I typically do the restrooms. I still occasionally run into a few people while I work, but I might as well be invisible to them.

When I first started here, I'd say a polite greeting when I passed people who worked here. After getting ignored quite a few times, I'd learned to stay quiet while I worked. *They're a bunch of snobs, apparently.*

I've been working here for a little over a week, and I've settled into a pleasant rhythm. I give Ronny his dinner and help him get ready for bed. I don't have to bathe him. He does that on his own. I have to help him get into and out of the bathtub, though. It's no easy feat, but the hydraulic lift is a lifesaver.

I help him get dressed in his pajamas, get him into his bed, give him his remote, his gaming controller, a drink of water with ice, and leave for work. I ring Debbie when I'm on my way out the door, and she turns on her monitor so she can hear if Ronny needs any help.

I ignore the man banging ferociously on the copy machine and make my way to the men's bathroom at the end of the hall. It typically needs little work done, but as strange as it sounds, I enjoy spending time there. I can take a quick break where there are no cameras. I can scroll through my social media on my phone and then go through the motions, cleaning the stalls and urinals, shining the massive mirror on the wall, and mopping the floor.

When I finish, I think of Ronny. He's probably asleep now, but I'd still like to confirm. I push my trolley into the handicapped stall and lock the door behind me. I get comfortable on the toilet seat and then get my phone out to call Aunt Debbie.

"Hello, Charlie?" Aunt Debbie says after the second ring.

"Hi, Auntie. I'm sorry. Did I wake you?"

"Not at all, Dolly. Is everything alright?"

"Yes, everything's swell," I say. "I was just checking in. How's Ronny? Is he sleeping?"

"Actually, no. He's right here. We're watching a movie together."

"Really? How come? Is he alright?" It surprises me he's not asleep.

"He's fine, sweetheart," she says. "He had to use the bathroom, and when I came over, he told me he was having trouble sleeping. Turns out I was, too, so we decided to watch a movie together."

"Hey, Charlie?" Ronny's voice sounds over the receiver. "Don't be mad. I promise I'm gonna go to sleep soon, and I won't give you a hard time tomorrow."

"It's fine, Ronny. You'll just have to take your meds a little late if you don't get up. Don't worry about it."

"So, how's work?" Ronny asks.

"Not bad. Uneventful." There's a silence on the other end of the phone that stretches on a little longer than is normal. "You still there?" I ask.

"I'm here," he says. Another brief pause. "I just feel bad you have to do this."

"Don't feel bad, Ronny. None of this is your fault. We're family, and family sticks together. Besides, this job is just temporary. We'll figure it out. Okay?"

"Alright then." He sounds so defeated. It breaks my heart.

"Listen, you, I love you so much. We'll get through this, okay? I promise. Now get to bed soon, you got that?" I laugh.

"I will. I love you, Sis."

After the call disconnects, I stare at the dark screen for a long time. It saddens me that Ronny feels responsible for my resignation from my previous job. His accident was not his fault. Tears stream down my face, and I pull out some toilet paper, wipe them away, and blow my nose.

Suck it up, buttercup! My Aunt Debbie always says that when I complain about things I can't control.

The bathroom door squeaks open and shakes me from my gloomy thoughts. I freeze. What the—? My guess is it's the same young man I saw assaulting the copier earlier. Ugh. I push my cart out of the stall, pretending I was in there cleaning.

It's someone else. He jumps in surprise when I step out of the stall. He places a hand on his chest and takes a deep breath. His eyes are wide, and it looks like I scared the heck out of him.

The first thing I notice about him is how handsome he is. Ooooh. He had rolled up the sleeves of his crisp white shirt, revealing strong, muscular forearms. His hair is a ruffled mess, dark and sleek, but it makes him look even more handsome. His five o'clock shadow along his firm chin line quickens my pulse more than the shock of his entrance.

He doesn't have the archetypical look of a game developer, whatever that is, and there's something different about him. He doesn't seem as stuffy as the other *suits*. It's almost like he doesn't belong here. People probably thought that about me when I worked with GGBuff.

"Holy crap!" he says. "You scared me to death. I wasn't expecting anyone to be in here. Certainly not a *woman*." His widened eyes return to their normal size. I definitely frightened him. His brow furrows, and again, I can't help but notice how *gorgeous* he is.

I tap my forehead in mock frustration. Maybe a joke will lighten him up. "Ugh, you caught me. This is my secret hiding place. Promise not to out me?"

He raises a brow and then laughs. *Phew, it worked.* He raises his hands. "Don't worry. Your secret is safe with me." He glances at the trolley and my uniform and sucks air through his teeth. "I take it you're the cleaning staff?"

"Yes, and my primary job is to terrify unsuspecting men by appearing out of nowhere."

He laughs again. "Well, you're doing a fine job, then." His eyes sparkle when he laughs, and though he looks young, he has slight creases at the sides. Maybe he laughs a lot.

"You bet," I tease. "Good thing you caught me. My magic powers only come alive after dark."

"Ah… I see." He taps his super sexy jaw that I can't stop staring at with a manicured finger. "So, you must be the one responsible for the disappearing toilet paper trick. You're a being of lore."

I laugh, not a polite laugh, but an honest belly laugh. He's kind of funny.

He smiles and wags a finger in my direction. "They've warned me about you guys. I was told we can't talk to the maintenance people. It must be all that magic you wield. It made no sense to me, but now, I'm glad I had prior warning."

I raise a brow. "Wait, what? You've been told you can't talk to us?"

He sighs and then shrugs. "Yes. Apparently, somebody from my company was inappropriate with somebody from your company, so now we have to stay on different sides of the playground. Strange, right?" Seeing my confused look, he adds, "You didn't know?"

"Ah," I say. "No, they did not inform me of that." It finally makes sense why the staff has been so cold and indifferent to me. It's not *me*. They avoid associating with me because of my position. Because I'm a 'cleaner.' I nod. "And yes, it *is* strange."

Chatty and witty as he has been since we met, I imagine even he would have walked past me if we met in the halls, subject to dozens of CCTV cameras and several more pairs of eyes.

"Yes, a very unusual rule," he says, nodding.

"Well, I don't care if you don't care," I say. "My name is Charlie. Short for Charlene. Charlene Welsh."

"Well, Charlie, short for Charlene. I don't care either. My name is At — Jimmy."

I look at him. "At — Jimmy? That's a funny name."

He laughs and runs a hand through his beautiful, messy hair. "It's just Jimmy. Jimmy Winslow."

"Okay, well, it's a pleasure to meet you, *just Jimmy*."

This job just got a lot more interesting.

CHAPTER 3
Atticus

I've been at GamesMade for three weeks, and while I like the work, I'm nowhere near where I was at my dad's company. Adapting to being a newbie is tough after managing multiple departments. Until, of course, my father asked me to step down.

I'm still a long way off from having enough money to start my own business and grossing $100,000 in income. Patience is not my strong suit, so I started working overtime.

Fortunately, all my time spent partying and club-hopping has left me quite resistant to sleep. Ironically, the very thing that led to my exile could now be a major advantage for me.

As soon as I laid eyes on Charlie last night, I knew that my life was about to change. It's strange our paths have never crossed, considering how much time I spend at work and how often I take breaks, thanks to all the coffee I douse myself with. Perhaps fate brought us together last night, but more likely, it's just a coincidence.

She and I share the same opinion about the senseless divide between the maintenance crew and regular staff. Her willingness to bypass company rules without a second thought is both bold and intoxicating. As I reminisce about our conversation now, I realize it stirs within me a desire for her that unsettles me. She's *hot*. My father had given me quite an ultimatum, and a woman like Charlie, with her captivating presence, could be a big distraction. But try as I might, I've thought of little else since we met.

I stare at my screen, but it's pointless. My mind is elsewhere. I'm too distracted to be efficient right now. My thoughts are a jumbled mess, and I can't tell my left from my right. I know I won't be able to produce anything of value in this condition.

I grab my stuff and head for the elevator. My heart rate picks up a bit as I near the restrooms — maybe Charlie is in there? Slowing down, I keep an eye out, hoping to catch her before leaving. I pop into the men's room, but it's empty. It's odd, but when I don't see her, disappointment creeps in.

Even in her goofy coveralls, she's a stunner, and so funny. I want to see her again. It's non-negotiable. Hanging out near the men's restroom might seem ridiculous, but right now, my entire existence feels just on this side of absurdity. The current circumstances are shaky, at best, and laughable, at worst. But amidst all this chaos, she's a bright spot, and I need that right now.

I shake my head to clear out my mind as I unlock my car. The parking lot is empty, except for a handful of vehicles.

As I pull out onto the almost empty streets of Albany, a gentle drizzle paints the windshield in hues of grey. Albany is not a large city by any means, even though it's the capital of New York. There isn't much nightlife here, and the city is a ghost town after dark unless there's a concert at the arena.

As I begin my not-so-long journey back to my tiny apartment, I ponder whether it's deserving of the title "home." But I suppose, for now, it's the only place I can call my own. Meanwhile, my parents are probably enjoying a nice bottle of wine that costs more than my rent. But I refuse to let such comparisons bring me down. My current financial struggles may seem bleak, but a little poverty won't stifle me.

I notice the flicker of lights still on in several buildings as I pass through the business district. It's probably the cleaning staff, but something about the sight makes my heart flutter as my thoughts turn to Charlie. I wonder if everything is going to remind me of her now.

Coming to a stop at a red light, I drum on the wheel to the beat of the song streaming from the radio. On the opposite side of the street, a billboard perches atop a five-story building, an advertisement for eyeglasses. The glow from the massive screen fills my tiny car, creating a serene atmosphere.

When the billboard screen changes, the next image makes my stomach turn. On the big screen is the woman who singlehandedly destroyed my perfect life, beaming from ear to ear while her pearly whites fill the screen with a blinding light. I can't help but clench my fingers around the wheel as the bile rises in my throat.

Heather Masterson is wearing a tight-fitting T-shirt with the words "Flash White Teeth Whitening Strips" written in bold letters across her chest. I can't help but roll my eyes at her. She loved showing off her D-cups.

Despite how badly I want to tear my eyes away, they're glued to the screen, watching Heather's perfect teeth sparkle. It's as if she's taunting me from beyond the ruins of our failed relationship.

The green light comes as a relief, and an advertisement for a special at a local supermarket takes the place of the one that held me hostage. I turn up the radio, trying to drown out the thought of Heather.

She must have gotten a very lucrative deal with Flash White. Good for her. She was always very materialistic, even though she never had to worry about anything. When we were together, I bought her whatever she wanted if her parents didn't buy it for her first.

I thought I was doing okay, moving on from her. Yet, her perfect smile, with those big white teeth, is all I see now. Her smile used to be one thing I loved about Heather, but now it only reminds me of her betrayal.

The Mastersons are well-off, but not as wealthy as my family. Heather's dad, Tyler Masterson, and my dad are close friends, with connections to the same country club cronies. I steer clear of the place myself, preferring a low-key bar with Archie over rubbing shoulders with the rich and famous.

Heather's family spends Sundays at the racetrack, where her dad's horses compete. Our mothers don their biggest hats and join them every Sunday for the entire month of August at the Saratoga Race Track — the "August place to be." I wouldn't be caught dead there. Running into her family is not something I'm interested in.

Heather and I knew each other from childhood, but it wasn't until we both landed at Syracuse University that our paths crossed again. Our parents, in their infinite wisdom, plotted to set us up. I wasn't thrilled, but my parents insisted we attend the Mastersons' dinner during Christmas break.

Heather and I hit it off from the start, though, and ended up dating throughout college. Looking back, I cringe at how over-the-top it was.

After we graduated, I proposed to Heather. How foolish I was. I think I made such a display of the whole thing because I knew deep down Heather didn't love me. The signs were there, but they were too painful to accept, so I chose not to see them.

I had been hoping for an ecstatic reaction. "You're kidding, right?" Heather had said instead when I held out the ring, down on one knee in an extravagant upscale restaurant.

Upon realizing I was serious, she'd laughed. "Oh, get up, Atticus. You're making a scene."

I stood up, feeling embarrassed and disappointed. It felt like all the eyes in the restaurant were on us as she held her hand over her mouth, laughing. I glanced around at the people gawking at us, relieved that I hadn't chosen one of my favorite restaurants to propose to her in. I knew I wouldn't be able to go there again without feeling the sting of rejection.

My heart sank when I glanced back at Heather. She looked ugly, sitting there rolling her eyes and flicking her hair. Had I really just proposed to her? Her laughter pierced my heart, and a lump formed in my throat as I put the ring back in my pocket. I remember clenching my fists so tightly that my knuckles turned white, and my temples pulsed with anger.

"Listen, Atty," she'd said, catching her breath. She'd stood up, placing her napkin on the table and grabbing her purse from the back of her chair. Then she'd rested her manicured hand with her long red nails on my wrist, and I'd recoiled at her touch. "What we had was fun, and I loved it. But that was college, babe. Everyone was having a little fun."

Fun? We'd been together for over four years! How could she dismiss our relationship like that? I had to struggle to keep my emotions in check.

"I think you're amazing, but I don't want this," she'd continued. "At least not right now. I want to be an actress, babe, and let's face it, it ain't gonna happen in Saratoga Springs, is it?" She'd cleared her throat and finished the drink in her hand, placing the glass on the table.

The check arrived then, and I'd handed my card to the waitress. Despite the air conditioning, I was sweating profusely and had to remove my suit jacket. I gulped my glass of water on the table and noticed that people were still watching us.

"I got an offer from one of Dad's friends to go to California, babe! I'm going to star in a commercial!" She'd picked at her nails, which was a sign that she was nervous. She'd smiled at me like I should join in her revelry. "I accepted the offer, Atty. Aren't you happy for me? I mean, I've got a real shot here. A big break. I wanted to tell you sooner, but I wasn't sure how you'd take it and all."

I tried to be understanding, but it was hard. As I stood up, my heart was pounding so hard into my chest that it felt like there was no air left in the room. I bit my tongue, swallowed hard, and blinked rapidly to hold back my rage.

"Yeah, sure, I understand," I said, not trusting myself to say anymore.

Heather had clapped and smiled. "Great! I guess this is goodbye then, babe. I leave in two days, and I've got a *ton* of packing to do."

My mouth still hangs open when I think about it. It burns holes in my mind whenever I remember, searing me with fresh pain, forcing me to relive that horrible moment. She had flicked her hair nonchalantly as she turned to leave, saying to me over her shoulder as she walked, "Toodles, Atty." The little wave of her hand is my last memory of her.

I might have been able to move on, but then I'd discovered the truth. Heather's father's friend, who was also *my* father's friend and a man twice her age, had been her *lover* for over two years! The betrayal was too much to handle. It felt like my world was falling apart. She had lied to me and been with another man and was going to California with him to boot.

After Heather left me, I refused to date any woman more than once. I went on a string of meaningless dates that left my parents shaking their heads in disappointment. The media caught wind of it and made a mockery of me, which made matters worse. But I couldn't help it. Heather had broken my heart, and I didn't know if I could ever trust anyone again.

The once stellar work I'd done at my father's company

faltered. Badly. I was no longer disciplined enough to handle the myriad of responsibilities I had, reeling from heartache, and not myself. I messed up projects, took time off from work without permission, missed important meetings, and danced around the company's rules and policies.

Eventually, my father had to make the tough decision to let me go to avoid further embarrassment. I left the company feeling bitter, betrayed, and blaming everyone but myself for the decision. After that, all I wanted to do was hole up in my room and play video games. I didn't care about anything.

I inhale a deep breath and try to calm my racing thoughts. It's hard to admit, but thinking back, my parents did what they had to do. My reckless behavior was bringing everyone in my family down with me, and I know my parents were terribly worried about me.

I park across the street from my apartment building and let out a long sigh. Stepping out of my car, I check the locks twice. The neighborhood is not the safest, and while my baby blue Prius is not the most attractive car, losing it would be devastating.

As the rain stops, the moon peeks from behind the clouds, as if asking for permission to illuminate the night with its radiant glow. I stare at it in awe, admiring its circular shape and natural beauty. I can't help but wonder if Charlie is out there somewhere looking at it, too.

I toss my bag onto an armchair and sink into my well-worn sofa. With a steady stream of income now, I've been considering giving this place a bit of a facelift. Nothing too extravagant, of course — most of my earnings are being tucked away for the future — but a few new pieces of furniture would undoubtedly do the trick. A new couch would be ideal, along with a comfortable bed for a good night's sleep.

I close my eyes and picture Charlie smiling as she rolled her trolley out of the restroom. The memory of meeting her in the men's room brings a smile to my face. She looked so cute in those blue coveralls. That thought of her is enough to melt away every feeling of pain and anger I feel towards Heather. *Heather who?*

Unfortunately, Charlie only works the evening shift, which means I'll have to continue working overtime if I want a chance to see her again. I don't mind working overtime, but I have to be careful. I'm not supposed to fraternize with the cleaning staff, and I don't want to risk losing my job.

A realization hits me that sours my mood. I want to see Charlie again, but I can't ignore the reality that my parents will never approve of me dating a 'cleaner.' Suppose I start a serious relationship with Charlie and they find out? In that case, I might as well kiss my chances of getting back in their good graces goodbye.

Despite my concerns, I can't get Charlie out of my mind. I don't want to hurt my parents, but I can't live for them. I *need* to speak to Charlie again. That silky blonde hair, her beautiful smile, and the way her nose crinkles when she laughs...

I grab my video game controller and headset from the nightstand next to my bed and turn on the console. It's the one major purchase I've made since my exile, and I consider it job research. But in reality, it's my way of staying sane.

Since there's nothing I can do about my worries tonight, I kick off my shoes and cross my legs in front of me on my bed. It's time to shoot lots of aliens in *Pirates of Starcrest*. That should keep me preoccupied for the next few hours, at least.

CHAPTER 4
Charlie

As I approach the men's restroom on the tenth floor, I feel a sense of anticipation, and my heart beats a powerful tune. I can't stop thinking about Jimmy. The man I met in the restroom last night has been on my mind ever since, and I find myself drawn to the possibility of seeing him again.

After Mark, I promised myself I'd stay away from men, especially white-collar types, so I don't know why I'm even entertaining thoughts of Jimmy. Besides, I doubt he's even given me a second thought. Nevertheless, I circle back to the men's restroom on his floor, hoping for another 'chance' encounter.

I wonder what I would do if he asked me out, anyway. Would I be ready to risk being in a relationship again? I think about the responsibilities I have for the care of my brother. I wonder if Jimmy would stay once he learned about my life. I can't help but compare him to Mark, who was only interested in his investments and wealthy acquaintances.

Mark never offered to help me with my brother's care, and I can't help but think that Jimmy would be the same. But then

I'm reminded that I shouldn't judge Jimmy based on his high-paying job. When we met, he seemed so nice and *hilarious*, and I found myself drawn to him immediately. Perhaps he could differ from the other white-collar men I've encountered. Only time will tell if he is truly genuine or just another snob.

Plus, Jimmy's the only member of GamesMade who has ever spoken to me despite the company's policy of ignoring the maintenance staff. He didn't seem to care that I was cleaning the bathroom. He talked to me anyway. Yes, it was out of the camera's view, but he still seemed genuinely interested in what I had to say.

I regret not asking him more about his work at the company. His floor, which is the tenth floor, is massive and divided into several departments, and I'm curious about which one he works in and whether he always works late at night. My role is now limited to taking care of the hallways and restrooms on the ninth, tenth, eleventh, and twelfth floors. Tracy has now taken on the responsibility of cleaning the offices, so I have no reason to enter them.

I stow away my cleaning equipment and quickly change out of my work overalls. I've finished 15 minutes earlier than usual. I wait patiently, excited to clock out for the evening. When it's finally time, the other members of my shift and I clock out and head toward the elevator together, ready to call it a night.

After saying our goodbyes, we go our separate ways. I walk toward my old, beaten-up sedan, a car that has seen better days. It has a few dents that are quite embarrassing, but I haven't had enough money to fix them yet. A while back, someone hit my car while it was parked in front of my dry cleaners. Of course, they had no cameras outside. I had intended to fix it, but then Ronny had his accident, and I couldn't spend my savings on my car when I needed it to contribute to Ronny's equipment.

With the car windows rolled down, letting in the sweet, crisp New York air, I begin my drive out of Albany. It's my favorite time of the year — fall, late September. It's still pretty warm during the day, but the cool air of evening is a welcome change from the stifling summer heat. As I turn onto the main drag running north, my stomach growls. The only place open this late is Juan's. I've gotten to know the owner, Carlos, whose Mexican burger is to die for.

I pick up my food from the pick-up window and drive straight home. I unlock and enter my side of the duplex quietly. The house is quiet, so I figure Aunt Debbie has returned to her side for the night.

Tiptoeing up the stairs to Ronny's room, I find him sound asleep under his covers. I peek at him through the crack in the door, feeling my heart break. I hate feeling sorry for him, and he hates it, too. But it's hard not to when I see him like this.

Quietly, I close the door behind me, tiptoe back downstairs, and collapse onto the couch, taking a big bite of the spicy cheeseburger and washing it down with soda. I take a handful of fries, shove them into my mouth and lean back, enjoying the quiet of the house. I sit for a while eating and unwinding after a long shift. Finishing my burger, I grab my game controller and headset from the side table and settle in for an hour or so of gaming.

My thoughts drift back to Jimmy Winslow. It's ridiculous, really, to allow him so much space in my head, but I can't seem to stop thinking about him. I actually looked forward to work tonight in the hopes I would see him. I don't remember ever feeling like this about Mark. I know I loved him, but I never obsessed over him. Not like this. Not even at the beginning of our relationship.

I stuff the last of my fries in my mouth with reckless abandon. I was hungry, apparently. The salty taste is a perfect match for the sweet soda, and the bubbles burn my nose. I quickly undo the button of my jeans and wiggle around until I'm more comfortable.

"Okay, *Starcrest*. What do you have for me tonight?"

I've learned that patience is key when it comes to the loading sequence of the heavily packed games. Better graphics equals longer load time, but it's worth it. Finally, the icon on the screen flashes 100%, and I crack my knuckles before picking up my controller.

Pirates of Starcrest is hands down one of the best games I've ever played. It's a futuristic, sci-fi, fantasy game. The graphics are breathtaking, and the combat scenes are masterful genius. The tasks require a certain level of skill and intelligence to unlock, and it takes forever to finish a level.

I usually play with a team, but since I started working late at night, I've had to deal with playing alone or finding someone here or there to navigate the open world of the game. I've been stuck on the sixth level for a while now, *Techno Metropolis*.

Playing games helps me take my mind off things like constantly obsessing about my career as a developer. Returning to where I was will be difficult, and sometimes it feels unfeasible. So, for now, I'm going to focus on the game and put my troubles on pause, as well as my thoughts of Jimmy Winslow.

The space shuttle transports my avatar, *MysticSorceress222*, to the game's central lobby. I wait to see who's available to team up with, if anyone. I'm about to exit the lobby when a second player lands, *ChaosMaster518*.

As I enter the virtual world of gaming, I can't help but notice the unique outfit of *ChaosMaster518*. Unlike other gamers, his avatar is sporting knee-high combat shorts with Air Force sneakers, a sleeveless vest that showcases his heavily tattooed arms, and a pair of aviator shades. He even has a chain of bullets slung across both shoulders and a massive rifle as tall as him. I can't help but laugh at the ridiculousness of the outfit, although I find myself oddly intrigued. Before I can even request to join his game, he invites me himself.

I accept and am taken aback by his first chat. "Hey, lady. Ready to kill some alien terrorists?"

"How do you know I'm a woman?" I ask as a shuttle launches us toward the game.

"Pretty awkward if you're not, to be honest," *ChaosMaster518* replies. "Your avatar looks pretty female to me."

I chuckle. "Well, yeah. Turns out I am a woman."

"Alright, so are you ready to play? I've waited for this all night," *ChaosMater518* says.

"Sure am."

ChaosMaster518 is an amazing player. He takes the lead, and I follow behind him. It's as if he's played the level before with the skill and precision he displays.

"How many times have you played this level?" I ask.

"Enough times to know that you're alien chow without my help," he replies smugly. "Big, bad alien on your left in about fifty meters. Aim for the head. Needs about four shots to drop it."

True to his word, a massive alien roars and breaks through a wall, lumbering in a destructive run straight for us. I take aim and fire multiple times, dropping the alien just a few feet away.

"Great shooting, lady," *ChaosMaster518* chats as we move up. "Only took you about two magazines."

I roll my eyes at his comment and follow his lead, taking a quick sip of my soda as we round a corner to meet an alien ambush waiting for us.

CHAPTER 5
Atticus

"You're working late again tonight?" Tiffany's voice echoes through the bullpen.

I glance up from my computer and see her standing at the door, her satchel hanging across her shoulder as if she's set to leave. She's always been the class favorite, but tonight, she looks different, like she's concerned about something.

"Looks like it," I reply, focusing on my screen.

She steps back into the room, her face contorting into a worried expression. "I'm sorry, Jimmy. I don't mean to upset you, but perhaps you should be less harsh toward Todd."

I raise my brow in surprise. "What?" I laugh. "Where's this coming from?" Is Tiffany standing up for Todd now? I explain my point of view. "You need to learn, Tiffany. Jerks will always be jerks, no matter how nicely you treat them. They may pretend for a while, but trust me, it's pretty easy to see through."

"Still," she says, "I think you could make things easier for yourself."

"I'll try, Tiff, I promise," I say. She's a sweet girl, just trying to look out for me, and I appreciate it.

Tiffany hesitates at the door, tucking a lock of hair behind her ear. "Do you... need some help or anything?"

I turn away from my computer to look at her. "No, no. Thanks, but I've got this. No worries. You get home. It's late."

She nods understandingly.

"Thanks for offering, though. I appreciate it," I add.

She smiles and nods. "Good night, Jimmy."

"Night, Tiff."

If Tiffany had rounded my desk and looked at my screen, she would have caught me playing Spider Solitaire and wondered what the heck I was doing.

I check the clock on my screen — eight forty-five p.m. Charlie's shift started fifteen minutes ago. With a smile, I lean back in my chair, swiveling as I toss and catch a tennis ball absentmindedly.

After my first encounter with Charlie, I returned to the restroom at the same time each night, hoping to see her again, but it wasn't until three nights later that luck was on my side.

On that third night, I'd entered the restroom to find her backing out of a stall, mop in hand, obviously pretending to be working. Our eyes met, and we both burst out laughing.

"Were you really working?" I'd asked her, smiling. I'd narrowed my eyes, pretending to be onto her game.

"Honestly?" Charlie had said. "I wiped that stall five times, waiting for you." Then she chuckled before continuing, "I was worried you got fired. I haven't seen you around."

I'd scoffed at her suggestion. "Me, fired? Never! I'm a *wiz* at my job. They'd *never* fire me. Besides, I've been around. It's *you* who's been doing the disappearing act. I thought maybe you were avoiding me."

"Why would you think that?" she'd asked.

Scratching my chin, I'd pretended to think for a

moment. "Well, for starters, magicians are known for their disappearing acts. And second, I wasn't sure you were interested."

"Interested in what?" Charlie asked, a sparkle in her eyes.

I hadn't been able to hold back my smile. "Why, *me*, of course." I'd taken a bow, which made her laugh.

We'd spent the next half hour bantering back and forth before going our separate ways. Every night since then, we've met in the men's restroom, enjoying each other's company and sharing stories. But tonight was going to be different.

I've decided to ask Charlie out. Not a formal date, but just a chance to meet outside of work. Outside of the men's restroom, for sure.

I glance at the clock again, watching as the time inches toward our agreed-upon time for 'running into each other.' With over an hour to burn, I return to the card game on my computer screen.

"Took you forever," I say as Charlie pushes her cart into the restroom.

She breaks into a wide smile that spreads across her face. "I guess you missed me, then," she replies playfully.

"Kinda, did you?" I narrow my eyes and give her a grin.

"Miss me?" Charlie repeats, her eyes shining with amusement.

"Funny girl," I say, chuckling. "Should've been a comedian."

Her infectious and genuine laughter makes my heart flutter.

"Hey," I say, hoping I don't appear nervous. "You up for breaking the law?"

Charlie's eyes widen with curiosity, and then a playful

smile tugs at her lips. "Sounds intriguing, but I thought we already were," she remarks, her voice laced with humor.

"We are, I suppose," I say, "but how would you like it if I took you out sometime?"

Her expression shifts, and I can't quite read it. My nerves intensify as I hold my breath, waiting for her response.

"Not like a date-date," I add quickly, hoping to clarify my intentions. "Just a couple of friends grabbing a bite to eat."

"Awww, the knight wishes to break the lady from the tower!" Charlie exclaims. She giggles and curtsies, and then she says, "Yes, please, m'Lord. The lady grows tired of the smell of antiseptic."

I can't help but smile at her response. She's so freaking cute. "To be honest, same here," I say. "Is tomorrow too soon?"

"Tomorrow?" she repeats. "Uh, well, it depends on what time."

"How about six-thirty?" I suggest. "We could meet at the Capitol House Chinese restaurant about two blocks from here. It's right on North Pearl Street. If that works, you could head to work right after."

"Oh, yes, I've seen the Capitol House. I haven't been there yet, but I'm a big fan of Chinese food. Yes, that could work for me."

"Great," I say, taking a deep breath and feeling relieved. "Most people from here will be long gone by six-thirty. Those who are still around would be working overtime and not heading to the Chinese restaurant. But just to be safe, I'll go to the restaurant first and make sure no one from the office is there." I glance around the men's room, leaning in to whisper, "You can never be too careful."

Charlie giggles again, her eyes sparkling with mischief. "Yes, we need to play it safe. Can't have the cleaning staff corrupting the office staff, now can we?"

I scoff, nodding in agreement. "Dumbest rule on the planet, but I can't be giving Hot-Toddy any reason to fire me."

"I love you call him that," Charlie says. "I don't even know the guy, but I can't stand him, anyway." She shakes her head in amusement. "Hot-Toddy," she repeats.

We both laugh, and a sense of warmth and contentment overwhelms me. Being around Charlie always has that effect on me. That, and a few other effects as well.

"So, we'll meet there?" she asks.

"Yes. It's a date," I say.

"But it's not a 'date-date,'" Charlie adds, a twinkle of mischief in her eyes.

"Definitely not," I agree, and she smiles the most beautiful smile I have ever seen, sending a jolt of electricity through me as I realize I'm falling for this woman. Bad.

I can't believe the time is almost here! I barely slept last night, tossing and turning about tonight. My 'not a date-date' with Charlie is just a few hours away, and I'm practically busting open with excitement. Anticipation has made work difficult, and Hot-Toddy is in a mood. He's been hovering over my desk all day, making snide comments that only he thinks are funny.

Tiffany stops by my desk shortly after four p.m., a curious look on her face. "Care to share?" she asks.

I raise a brow at her. "Huh?"

"Well, you've been glowing like a gas giant all day," she says. "What's making you so happy, if I may ask?"

"Oh." I laugh nervously. "Nothing. Just looking forward to the weekend." I realize it's a stupid response as soon as it comes out of my mouth.

Tiffany shakes her head and walks away. She says over her

shoulder, "Today's Wednesday, but enjoy the *weekend*." I cringe at my stupidity.

As soon as the clock strikes five-thirty, I practically run out of the office. Todd is still in his office as I head out. He doesn't look up when I pass by, and I say nothing. Avoiding Todd has become my favorite pastime.

I arrive at Capitol House twenty minutes after six and grab a table in the corner. We'll be able to have some privacy in the scarcely populated restaurant, but if anyone from work shows up, we will be in clear view. I doubt they will, though, so I'm not overly worried.

As I wait for Charlie to arrive, I fidget nervously, running my fingers through my messy hair. I'm more nervous about making a good impression on Charlie than about getting caught.

When Charlie finally walks in, my heart skips a beat. She's wearing a beautiful white summer dress that flows around her like an angel, with a denim jack thrown over it. Her face lights into a broad smile when she catches my eye, and I stand up as she approaches.

"Charlie," I say, moving her chair out so she can sit. "You look amazing."

She grins a sly smile. "You can close your mouth now, drool-boy." Her laughter fills the empty restaurant.

"I can't help it. *Look* at you! That dress is... *nice*. I've just never seen you dressed up."

"Thanks," she says, glancing up at the menu on the wall. "Did you order anything yet?"

"No, not yet. I was waiting for you." I can't stop staring at her. If I thought she was beautiful before, wow!

She glances back at me from the menu and catches me staring at her. Blushing, she says, "You weren't expecting me to show up in my coveralls, were you?"

I laugh. "Oh, no way! Although I must say, you look pretty cute in those, too."

We head to the counter to place our order. Charlie orders a beef and broccoli dinner with fried rice and an egg roll, and I order the same with two bowls of hot and sour soup. After we get our drinks, I pay for the food.

As we wait for our food, we chat easily, like we always do during our nighttime restroom meetups. The conversation flows naturally, and we laugh a lot. Charlie's funny, and it feels like a long time since I've laughed so much. Even though we haven't known each other long, it feels like I've known her forever.

I explain to Charlie a problem I was having with my car last week. "The darned thing kept misfiring." I still don't know why my parents would get me such a hunk of crap. I guess they wanted me to make it on my own, car repairs and all.

"Did you have to take it to a mechanic?" Charlie asks, her eyebrows raised.

I laugh. She never met my dad. He loves to tinker with cars, and he taught me a lot about fixing them. He might have billions, but he always taught me the value of hard work and doing things on my own. "No," I tell her, "I figured it was a spark plug."

"So how do you change a spark plug, or is that a stupid question?"

"That's not a stupid question at all. Not everyone knows how to work on cars. I just learned at an early age. All you have to do is use a spark plug ratchet to remove the bad plug, check the new plug's gap to make sure it matches, hand-tighten it, re-attach the wire, and Bob's your uncle."

She laughs and shakes her head. "You say that all the time. What does that even mean?"

"Bob's your uncle? It's an English expression I picked up

during my time in London with my family. Simply put, it means 'ta-da!' or 'there you have it,'" I explain. "Let's say you ask me how to make chocolate milk. I would say to you, 'Put milk in a glass. Add chocolate syrup. Stir it around, and Bob's your uncle.'"

Charlie laughs. "Oh, I get it. So, let me try it." She thinks for a minute. "So, let's say I wanted to meet a cute guy who's hilariously funny. All I'd have to do is go into the men's room, hang out in a stall, pop out and scare the first unsuspecting guy, and Bob's your uncle!" She beams.

I burst out laughing. "That's about it." I loved she referred to me as 'cute' and 'hilarious.'

"You remind me of a guy I used to work with at GGBuff. He had a weird expression, too. He would say, 'You can't put lipstick on a pig, sweetheart.' It always made me laugh."

"Oh, you cleaned over at GGBuff?" I say.

Her expression changes. "No. I was actually a game developer for them."

"Wait. I don't understand. If you were a programmer, how'd you end up cleaning at GamesMade?" I blurt out the question without thinking and wish I could shove it back into my mouth.

Charlie doesn't flinch. Instead, she looks like she's about to explain when I hear a laugh behind me. A voice I know all too well — a voice I despise. My blood runs cold and I stop breathing for a few seconds as realization sets in. I spin around to find Todd standing over me.

"Well, well, well. And what do we have here?" Todd crosses his hands over his chest and beams at me. He looks from Charlie to me and then back to Charlie. "I know you," he says to Charlie. "You work at GamesMade, don't you?"

Charlie scowls at Todd. They've never met, but from his tone, it's obvious he's no friend. I want to introduce him to her as Hot-Toddy, but I don't.

Todd smiles at me, flashing his yellow teeth, and pats my shoulder with an annoyingly condescending air. "Oh, Jimmy, Jimmy, Jimmy. You were never that smart, were you? No. You were never that smart at all."

I stand up, ready to give him a piece of my mind, but before I can even open my mouth, he turns around and leaves without another word. I watch him go, his step bouncy and carefree. He didn't even order food, the weirdo. He likely knew I was considering punching him when I stood up. As he leaves, I unclench my fists.

I look down at Charlie, and my heart sinks. The cold, angry indifference she had been wearing like a mask on her face has disappeared, replaced by worry.

"Who was that?" she asks.

I exhale deeply. "That would be Hot-Toddy," I say. "My lovely boss."

"Ugh." Charlie lets out an exasperated sigh. "So, now what? He's going to cause trouble for you, isn't he?"

Charlie already knows the answer, but she needs to hear it spoken to have it resonate with her. I scoff and turn to her with an air of finality. "Yes. He's going to cause trouble, alright. I hate to say it, but I probably just lost my job at GamesMade."

CHAPTER 6
Charlie

Jimmy was sure his boss would terminate him for finding us together, but I refused to believe it. I remember when he'd mentioned the company policy to me the first time we'd met in the men's restroom, and we'd both laughed about it. It had seemed like such a silly rule.

However, after three consecutive nights of Jimmy's absence from our designated meeting spot, it's clear that something is wrong. Each night, I wait anxiously in the stall, scrolling through my phone, waiting for the door to squeak open. But it doesn't. I think I have to admit that Jimmy got fired — because of *me*.

I can't shake the feeling that I'm cursed. I experienced my parents abandoning me, my brother getting paralyzed in an accident, and the end of my five-year relationship with Mark. Now Jimmy has lost his job. I'm thinking that maybe it's best for everyone if I avoid close relationships altogether.

That I kept my job while Jimmy lost his only adds to my guilt. Although a formal complaint was received by the servicing company that owns my contract — probably by Mr.

Hot-Toddy — I only received a stern warning and a strike on my record.

It's been seven long days since Jimmy's abrupt termination. I try to go about my daily routine as usual, but everything in the office reminds me of him. The men's restroom, once a peaceful hideaway for me, now feels like a constant reminder of Jimmy's absence.

Going to dinner with Jimmy was a terrible mistake, especially since it was near our workplace. I should have known better than to get involved with a co-worker, but I already lost my heart to him. The company's absurd policy of discriminating against cleaning staff is unjust, and I can't believe it's even legal.

My heart aches. I miss Jimmy more than I ever thought possible. He made me feel special, even in hideous blue coveralls. Not to mention, he's *gorgeous*. He has an air of mystery about him, and his unkempt hair and dangerous eyes could make any girl weak in the knees.

As much as I hate to admit it, I'm pining over him and hoping to find a way to reach out. But he's disappeared without a trace. I've tried searching for him on social media, but it's been hopeless. There are too many Jimmy, Jim, and James Winslows, and none of them seem to be him.

I hate it that I fell for Jimmy, knowing about the stupid company policy. But now that he's gone, I can't help but wonder what could have been.

The sound of my watch beeping interrupts my miserable thoughts. It's a familiar sound, informing me that my shift has ended. I join the rest of the unit in the service lounge, change into my regular clothes, and head home.

I'm not hungry, so I decide not to stop by Carlos' for

dinner. I drive back home in silence, savoring the cool breeze that seeps in through the cracks in my windows. As I enter the house, it's dark and quiet, just like always.

I make my way up to Ronny's room as is customary and pause for a moment, watching him sleep. He's snoring softly, bundled up under his blankets. I feel a sense of comfort as I realize I'm not alone. I still have Ronny, and he has me.

I walk over to his bed, lean down, and softly kiss his forehead, careful not to wake him. Leaving his room, I shut his door and head down to the kitchen. I grab some water, chips, and dip and plop down on the couch in the living room.

As I'm about to dig into my snack, Aunt Debbie gently knocks and walks in through the front door.

"Hey, Auntie! What are you doing up so late?" I ask, surprised to see her.

"I heard you come in," she says, making her way over to me. She sits down close, and I lean my head over onto her shoulder.

Uncertain whether I should share with her the issues that are troubling me, I hesitate. But Aunt Debbie is my best friend, and I know I can always count on her for sage advice.

"It's been a long night," I say, finally breaking the silence. "Work's not much fun anymore since they let Jimmy go."

"I know, sweetheart," she says, giving me a comforting side hug. "It's not your fault, you know."

I feel the tears prickling at the corners of my eyes. I try to hold them in, not wanting to worry Aunt Debbie. "Yeah, I know. I just miss him. He made the job fun."

"I'm sorry, honey," she says, hugging me tight, her arm around me comforting and warm.

"I'm okay, Auntie. I'm going to shower and get some rest," I say, pulling away from her embrace.

Taking a hot shower helps me clear my mind and wash away some of the stress. I don't like feeling sorry for myself, so

I remind myself to *suck it up, buttercup*. Jimmy was a pleasant addition to my life, and a bit of raw excitement, but I only just met him. My priority is Ronny, and that's where my focus needs to be.

As I crawl into bed, I feel the exhaustion take over. But my mind won't let me rest. I toss and turn, trying to find a comfortable position, but sleep doesn't come. Giving up, I throw my blanket aside and head back down to the living room, where I know the only thing that can cheer me up is waiting for me.

The *Pirates of Starcrest* gameplay loads as I slip on my headset, eager to dive into the virtual world. I'm hoping to find *ChaosMaster518* in the game. It's been a while since I last saw him online.

As I sit down and pick up my controller, a notification pops up on my screen. *ChaosMaster518* has invited me to join a game. *Speak of the devil.*

I smile when I see his avatar dressed in its punk outfit. "Hey, thanks for joining," he says.

"Sure thing," I respond. "Where have you been? I've been trying to find you on here for some days. I was afraid you gave up and quit."

ChaosMaster518 falls silent for a moment, and then he speaks up again. "Yeah. Just had some issues that needed sorting out, that's all."

I can tell something is bothering him. "Hey, are you alright?" I ask tentatively. We've never really talked about personal stuff before, but there's something about how he's acting that concerns me.

Another pause. "Yeah, I'm fine. Just had a rough patch at work, you know?"

I nod sympathetically. "I hear you. Well, you're in good company. Work's been a real pain for me lately, too."

"Sorry to hear that," he says.

"Wanna play a level?" I ask, shaking off my sad thoughts.

"Naah. Not feeling dangerous tonight." Another silence. "There's this amazing side mission on Planet Soros, though. We can explore the open world and play the side mission together. What do you think?"

Frankly, I'm not enthusiastic about playing the more challenging levels inside, but I want to play with him, so I say, "Lead the way, captain."

We descend into a hush as the mission begins, and I don't mind one bit. My mind drifts to Jimmy again, and I wish I could tell him how sorry I am. As I rappel down a rope with a space suit on, I wonder if Jimmy and I will ever cross paths again.

I feel like I'm to blame for him getting fired. He had so much to lose, while I, on the other hand, had little at stake, apparently. Jimmy put his job on the line for that date. Non-date. Whatever it was.

He probably hates me.

CHAPTER 7
Atticus

'*Jobless in Seattle.*' Well, technically, Albany. This whole 'me out in the world' thing isn't going so well. It would surely disappoint my father, as is usual. I've never been one to follow the rules, constantly pushing the limits. But I'm a fighter, and I'm confident I'll emerge victorious.

I'm glad he can't see this minor snag, though. I sometimes feel like he loves to cut me down. I think it's his way of trying to strengthen me or something.

I sit on my couch, a beer in my hand, and mull over the situation.

Losing my job hurts, but losing Charlie hurts even more. I don't even know where she is or what she's doing. I can't help but wonder if Charlie even wants to be with me now that I'm unemployed. And a liar — she doesn't even know my real name is Atticus. She doesn't know who I really am, and now I'll probably never get the chance to tell her.

Taking a sip of my beer, I try to push the thoughts from my head. I can't let myself slip into a funk again. I have to keep fighting and pushing forward. But it's hard when I feel like I've lost everything — again.

I think back to the day Todd fired me, the day after he saw me out with Charlie, and it makes my blood boil. I had gone to his office to resolve things, but it had only made matters worse. Much worse. Todd had a smug smirk on his face, and I had wanted to knock him out right then and there. But I knew I couldn't.

Todd's words had dripped with sarcasm as he spoke first, reminding me of my high school principal. It was as if he had been waiting for me to mess up so he could pounce on me. "Well, hello, Mr. Winslow," he'd said, his tone grating on my last nerve. "I would be lying if I said it surprises me to see you in my office. Have something you want to say to me, do you?"

I couldn't help but feel like a schoolboy being schooled by a teacher. But I'd known enough to keep my cool about me. I had gone there with a purpose, and I wasn't going to let Todd's condescension impede that. So, I took a deep breath and kept my voice steady as I spoke. "Listen, Todd, I know there's a rule about not talking with the maintenance staff, but Charlene and I—"

"Ah, yes, *Charlene* is it? Thank you for that." Todd picked up a pen and wrote her name on a notepad on his desk. My blood pressure rose as he looked up at me again with a smirk on his face. "I suppose you're going to tell me you just happened to run into her at the restaurant? Care to explain?"

I remember my face growing hot with anger, but I'd remained composed as I replied through gritted teeth, "There's nothing to explain, and I don't know why you're writing her name down. We're just friends."

Todd's smirk had grown wider. He was enjoying himself. "Now, Mr. Winslow. We both know *that's* not true. I wasn't born yesterday."

"And I'm telling you, nothing was going on."

He'd laughed right out loud, a sneering laugh, and I'd

wanted to punch him. "Oh, Mr. Winslow," he'd said, shaking his head. "There was *definitely* something going on."

"I don't know what you think you saw," I said, my voice getting louder, "but Charlie and I are *just friends*." I wanted to add, "*Do you need a damned hearing aid?*" But I refrained.

He'd laughed again. "Oh, *Charlie*, is it, now? How sweet. Hmmm. Let me think about this for a minute."

"Think all you want to, Mr. Brierly, but we both know the rule is ridiculous. You can't dictate who I have dinner with on my off time." He was making me so angry, and I had all I could do not to reach over the desk and lunge at him.

He'd ignored me and continued with his snide comments. "Tell me, Jimmy, did you miss the orientation? I made it very clear. Stay away from the maintenance staff! Eating dinner with one of them seems like the opposite of staying away. Or, am I mistaken?"

I had gritted together my teeth so hard my jaw ached. The man was a broken record.

He got up from his desk and walked toward the door of his office. Without turning around, he'd said, "Mr. Winslow, would you follow me, please?"

I'd followed him, reluctantly. Anxiety had churned in my gut, as I wondered what he was up to as he led me into the bullpen. A hush came over the room when people noticed his presence. All eyes were on him and then on me.

I had no idea what Todd was planning, but I'd braced myself for whatever was about to happen. Whatever it was, I knew it would not be good.

"Can I have everyone's attention?" Todd's voice had boomed. "I'm sure you all remember the one rule I gave you when you joined this company. Would anyone care to refresh Mr. Winslow's memory on what that rule was?"

Everyone had looked around at each other, and, of course, Tiffany's hand shot into the air.

"Yes, Tiffany," Todd had said, a smile beaming across his face.

"Um, we can't talk with the maintenance people," Tiffany had said hesitantly, glancing over at me.

Todd's smile grew wider. "Yes!" Todd had said. "Thank you, Tiffany!"

Todd had wrapped his arm around my shoulder, and an overwhelming urge to push him away and knock him down had consumed me. I could have easily done it. Instead, I'd taken a deep breath and forced myself to remain calm.

Pulling me closer, he'd said, "Our Mr. Winslow here took it upon himself to break that rule. I caught him having dinner in public with a member of the cleaning staff. I don't think he realizes how serious we are about this policy, do you, Mr. Winslow? So, therefore, an example is required."

He had released my shoulder as the room erupted in whispers and murmurs. Todd raised his voice to silence them.

"Quiet!" he'd bellowed, the room returning to silence. Once again, he turned to me. "Mr. Winslow. You will exit this building and never return. You, my friend, are *fired*."

Todd had relished that moment, savoring every syllable of the word "fired." He'd pointed to the door like an actor on a stage and then turned to face the stunned crowd.

"Let this be a warning to anyone who's thinking of following in Mr. Winslow's footsteps," Todd had said, pointing around the room at the wide-eyed faces. Then he'd shouted, "Get back to work!"

As people scurried away, Todd looked at me and repeated, "Mr. Winslow, *get out*."

Only Tiffany had looked back as she walked. Silly girl. I knew she would soon learn the truth about Todd Brierly.

As I walked to the elevator, Todd had followed close behind me, his presence looming over me like a dark cloud. I'd pressed the down button, hoping to escape the situation before I lost control, but Todd had leaned in close and whispered, "Don't worry about your little friend. I'll let her boss know about her behavior. And check your mail. We'll be sending you your personal effects."

My heart sank as I heard his words, and I couldn't help but react impulsively. I'd grabbed Todd's arm, gripping it, and blurted out, "Charlie knew nothing, you little weasel! You leave her out of this!"

Todd's face had twisted in anger as he pulled his arm from my grasp and yelled back, "Let go of me! Clean Rise will take care of her." He brushed his arm off, dramatically, like I'd had some disease.

As I made my way down in the elevator, I hadn't been able to shake off the guilt gnawing at me. What if Charlie loses her job because of me? I couldn't bear the thought of it.

My doorbell jars me from the memory of my last moments at GamesMade. I wonder who this could be. I rarely have visitors. I chug the rest of my beer, setting the empty can on the table next to me where three others sat.

I take my time getting up from the couch and heading toward the door. It's probably a salesperson or something. I don't feel like seeing anyone.

The doorbell rings again, followed by loud knocking. I groan inwardly. "Coming!" I yell as I make my way to the door.

Archie is waiting outside, leaning casually against the door frame. "Took you long enough," he says, bringing me in for a hug.

I can't help but smile. It's good to see his familiar, dependable face. "Nice to see you too, Archie," I say, stepping aside to let him in. I'd called him the day everything had gone up in smoke, but he'd been in Europe on business. I'd told him I was having trouble at work and would catch up with him when he got home.

He looks exhausted, as if he got off the plane and came straight to my apartment. I'm grateful for his presence, though. I need someone to talk to — someone who won't judge me for the mess I've made of my life.

Over the next ten minutes, I catch him up on everything that happened. He knew about Charlie and our evening meet-ups, and he thought, like I did, that the whole fraternization rule was ridiculous. He derived great amusement from our meeting place — the men's room at work.

One time, a while ago, he had asked me, "What will you say if somebody walks in while you two are hanging out in there?"

I had laughed. "Nobody's around that late, and besides, it's not like we're *kissing* or anything. We're just talking. She's the cleaning staff. She's supposed to be in there."

"So, question for you, ol' boy," he'd said, patting me on the back.

"Yeah, what's that?"

"Why *aren't* you kissing her?"

Good question, I had thought. Why wasn't I kissing Charlie? It's not that I didn't want to. I wanted to, alright, but I didn't want to spoil a good thing. Besides, how lame would it be to remember our first kiss happening in a men's restroom?

As I finish recounting all the miserable events of the last few days, Archie's eyes widen in shock. "Wow... that's a lot to unpack," he says, clearly taken aback. "I've got to say, I'm surprised you didn't punch Hot-Toddy out. It sounds like you wanted to."

I nod, still feeling the anger simmering just below the surface. "Believe me, I wanted to. But I knew it would be pointless."

It would have been satisfying, though, especially after his comments about trying to get Charlie in trouble.

Archie walks over to the fridge. "Please tell me you haven't been lying in bed, beating yourself up? Please say you're out looking for another job."

I laugh without humor and roll my eyes. "I wish. I haven't left the house in days. Everything happened so fast. One minute, I had it all figured out, and the next minute, I was back to ground zero. I just need time to regroup, you know?"

He nods, opening the fridge. "I get it, man. But you can't stay cooped up forever. You should start looking for another job." He looks in the fridge and shakes his head as he reaches inside.

He shuts the refrigerator door, two beers in his hand. "Dude," he says, "Don't you ever buy groceries? Your fridge only has two more beers and some half-eaten Chinese food. You don't even have milk."

"Shut up and give me that beer," I say to him, smiling, but snatching the beer from his hand. We sit on the couch, and I see Archie eyeing the three empties on my table.

I take a swig of my beer, relishing the bitter taste. "I know. It's just hard to muster up the motivation." I say.

Archie pokes me in the chest. "You've got bills to pay, Atticus. You can't just sit around feeling sorry for yourself. Besides, I can lend you a hand if you need it."

I nod gratefully. "Thanks, man. I appreciate it."

He reclines on the couch, beer in hand, and says, "So, spill the beans. What's up with this girl, anyway? You've been looking pretty lovesick since you two crossed paths."

I feel a flush creep up my neck. "I don't know, man. There's just something about her. I can't stop thinking about her."

Archie grins, obviously relishing my unease. "So, what's the holdup? Haven't you called her yet? Please don't tell me you didn't even get her number."

I shake my head, feeling foolish. "No, I didn't. I didn't

want to appear too eager. Asking her out to dinner was hard enough."

Archie's eyes widen in disbelief. "Dude, you're slipping! What are you going to do? You can't just let her get away."

I know he's on point, but the idea of contacting her fills me with dread. "I don't know, man. I'm just scared of making a mess of things." Besides, how dumb that I never even asked her for her number.

He sets his beer down, his expression thoughtful. "Well, you're definitely going to mess things up if you never see her again. So, make a plan to find her."

He has a point.

"I know, Arch, but it might be better if I don't communicate with her. I don't want to lead her on. Spending half an hour at work was fine, but she might read too much into it if I try to contact her."

"Dude!" Archie picks up his beer again. "What are you even talking about?" He looks at me incredulously, making me feel even more foolish.

"She's a cleaning lady, Archie. A *cleaning lady*." I chug my beer, finishing it.

"Yeah? And?" Archie raises an eyebrow, waiting for me to continue, chugging his beer as he does.

"Dude! You *know* my father. He'll have a fit if I bring home a cleaning lady. A cleaning lady named *Charlie*." I scoff loudly.

"Oh, Atticus, come on, man. When are you going to realize you're your own person? Your own man? You're 30 years old! Your father believed you needed to be on your own feet. So, stop worrying about what *he* thinks or what *he's* going to say. It doesn't matter. You gotta do *you*!" Archie's tone is firm, but I know he's just looking out for me.

I remain quiet for a while, letting his words sink in. He's

right, of course. I don't know why I'm suddenly worried about my father's acceptance, anyway. There's been plenty of disappointment where I'm concerned, obviously, since he threw me out. His *only* son. His *only child*.

"I think you should go for it," Archie says, breaking the silence. "Think about it. If you're successful with your bills and you set up a successful business like your dad wants — and we all know you *will* — then your parents might just be willing to overlook the whole 'commoner' thing."

"Yeah, maybe," I say. "But it's not a 'commoner' thing. It's a 'gold digger' thing. They only want me to date within the circle to ensure someone isn't just trying to get after our money."

"Your father instructed you to keep your identity a secret, correct? He didn't want you riding on the family coattails, so to speak. So, if Charlie is *unaware* of your identity, she can't be a gold digger, right?"

"You have a point, but it's irrelevant if I can't get ahold of her."

He thinks for a minute, sipping his beer. His eyes get big. "You know where she works," he says. He squints his eyes and beams at me with the silliest, most infectious grin.

I sit up. "I *do* know where Charlie works, but—"

"But *nothing*, dude! Stalk the place and talk to her after work. Nobody's going to see you. By then, everyone you know will have left."

"She's going to think I'm creepy," I say. *I just don't want to push her away.*

"Do I need to smack you? Atticus, go see her after work!" Archie's frustration is evident.

He gets up, picks up our empty cans, and takes them to the kitchen. He opens the fridge and grabs my last two beers. He opens my cupboard and grabs a bag of chips. Upon reentering the room, he hands me a beer and throws the chips onto the coffee table. "So, it's settled then. You're going there tonight when Charlie gets off work."

"Tonight?" I want to argue.

"Tonight, Atticus. There's no time like the present."

He scoops up a handful of chips and shovels them into his mouth, half falling to the floor. Then, he snatches the remote and points it at the TV, announcing, "The game's about to start."

I take the bag of chips, still unsure about the night ahead.

Tonight.

I'm going to see Charlie *tonight*.

"I've got to jump in the shower," I announce, but Archie's engrossed in the game.

This whole nervous edge I'm experiencing is new to me. The tight knot in my stomach constricts my breathing, causing discomfort. Countless what-ifs are racing through my mind as I get into the shower.

What if she doesn't reciprocate my feelings?
What if she's mad that I got her in trouble?
What if she calls the police? No, she would never do that.
What if she finds it creepy that I'm waiting outside her job for her?

I dress casually in a white sweater and jeans. I don't want to spook her, so I'm unsure how to get her to stop her car. I consider parking outside and doing a "psssst" out my car window as she drives by, but she might have her window up and would probably not even hear me.

It'll be dark, but if I try to shine my flashlight on my face, she'll probably scream and speed away.

I decide I'll pull by the garage exit and park under a street lamp. Then I'll get out and stand by my car. I'll watch for her to come out of the parking garage and wave to her as she pulls up toward me. She'll probably think I broke down or something, but it should get her to stop.

It's the perfect plan.

CHAPTER 8
Charlie

The men's room is empty once again, and I can't help but feel a sense of longing for Jimmy. It's been weeks since he's been gone, but the ache of his absence continues to linger. It's like a phantom limb, a part of me that's missing but still feels present.

Aunt Debbie called me earlier to tell me that Ronny wanted to stay up late again. I don't mind. When he sleeps in, I get to sleep in, too. When he gets up early, I have to get up with him, and sometimes, it's rough.

As I finish up my shift, I make my way to the service lounge and take a seat on the bench. It's quiet, and I close my eyes momentarily, trying to relax.

But my thoughts keep drifting back to Jimmy. He was the reason I used to look forward to coming to work, but now it feels empty and boring. I'm sure I'll get back in the rhythm eventually, but for now, it's just not the same.

A stiff breeze blows as my coworkers and I make our way through the parking garage. I wrap my jacket tight around me and wave goodnight to the others as I jump in my car.

As I leave the parking garage, I notice a man standing in

front of his car, parked across the street under a streetlight. It takes me a moment to realize that it's Jimmy. My heart skips, and I can't believe what I see. He's leaning on the door of his Prius, grinning at me.

A blaring horn behind me reminds me I should move on, so I put on my blinker and pull my car in front of Jimmy's.

He walks up to my car as I park. "Are you alright in there?" he teases. "I didn't know you were the type to create road rage." He laughs. The car behind me roars away, trying to make a point.

I jump from my car and grab Jimmy for a hug. The force of the hug throws him backward, and he staggers as he finds his balance, but he holds me tight, wrapping his arms around me.

"Jimmy! I thought I'd never see you again!" My heart is racing, and I'm thinking I should pinch myself. *Is he really here?*

I inhale deeply, taking in his scent. It's a familiar fragrance I've smelled on him before, and it's so intoxicating I can't help but feel drawn toward him. It's a clean scent, like freshly laundered linen, but with a masculine twist. Whenever I catch a whiff, my heart races in my chest, and all I can think about is... well...

"What are you doing here?" I ask. I know why he's here, but I want to hear him say it.

"I came here to see you, silly. Why else?" Jimmy smiles that smile and runs his hand through his messy hair. "How about you get in my car so we can talk?"

He doesn't have to ask me twice. I follow him to the passenger side, and he opens the door for me. As soon as I'm settled, he takes his place behind the wheel and glances around, checking to see if anyone's watching.

"Should we go somewhere else?" he asks, concern etched on his face. "I don't want you to get into trouble."

"It's okay," I reassure him. "I got off with a warning. Besides, you're not an employee anymore."

"Right," he says.

I can't believe he's here, sitting next to me. I've missed him so much. "How have you been?" I ask, desperate to catch up on everything that's happened since we last spoke. "I've been so worried. I wanted to talk to you so badly, but I had no contact information and nobody I could ask."

"I've been worried about you, too," he says, "which is why I decided just to show up here. It's the only way I knew to get ahold of you. I don't know what I was thinking, not asking you for your phone number."

My heart skips a beat at his words. "I'm so glad you're here," I say. "I feel so guilty about what happened."

He shakes his head. "Oh, no, you don't. I won't allow it. I asked *you* out. I knew the rules, and I made my own decision. You have nothing to feel guilty about."

"I know, but—"

He puts his fingers to my lips. "Shhh," he says. "I don't want to argue about this."

He removes his fingers from my lips and gently cups my face in his hands. I'm momentarily stunned, not knowing what to expect, but anticipation courses through me.

Is he going to kiss me? I've fantasized about this moment countless times, but never thought it would actually happen.

"My life was better with you in it, Charlie," he says, his voice low and serious.

I stare at him, trying to process what he's saying. Is he really saying what I think he's saying?

"I know we haven't known each other very long, but I can't help how I feel about you," he continues, his eyes never leaving mine. "I have to admit, I feel lost without you."

I can feel my heart racing in my chest as he speaks,

pounding in my temples. I want to tell him my feelings, but the words won't come.

"My life's a mess," he admits. "I'm a bit of a mess. I wasn't even sure you wanted to see me."

I take a deep breath and reach for his hand. "Of course, I wanted to see you," I say, my voice laced with longing. "I've missed you so much. Why would you think that?"

Relief floods his face, and he smiles at me briefly. Then he scoffs. "I don't know. I'm unemployed, for one."

I can't help but laugh out loud at his comment. "That's hysterical," I say. I don't know if he was going for comedy, but regardless, it was funny.

He laughs. "So, you're alright with guys who have no money?"

"I'm better with guys who have *no* money than guys who have a *lot*, that's for sure."

He shifts a bit and lets go of my face. His eyes leave mine, and he sits back in his seat.

"What's wrong?" I ask.

"What do you mean about not being alright with guys who have money?" he asks, his brow furrowed. His change in demeanor confuses me.

I try to explain. "I mean, people who have a lot of money are greedy. Why do you think they have a lot of money?" I thought everybody knew that.

"That's kind of a general statement," he says, looking over at me. "I have a lot of friends who have money. They're not greedy."

I feel embarrassed about putting my foot in my mouth. "I didn't mean to offend you. I'm sure they're great people. I'm just talking in general."

"Alright, let's just drop it," he says. He takes my hand in his and changes the subject. "How's the men's room?" It's so cute how his eyes squint when he makes jokes, and that dimple that flashes sets me on fire.

"It's not the same without you," I say, grinning. "I don't clean very well in there. It's too lonely now."

He laughs. "We're crazy. You do know that, right? Everyone else can tell their kids they met online, but we'll have to tell ours we met in the men's room."

My heart skips a beat. "Our kids, huh?"

"Yes, all eight of them," he says.

"Well, that's too bad," I say. "I always had my heart set on *ten*."

He laughs. "I've missed you, Charlene Welsh."

I chuckle back. "I've missed you, too, Just Jimmy!"

He hugs me tightly, and I feel a warmth spread through my body. Electricity seems to crackle in the air as we sit there, lost in each other's embrace. I can't help but wonder if he's *the one*.

He breaks the comfortable silence with a nervous laugh. "Charlie, could I have your phone number? Maybe we can start seeing each other now that work policy isn't an issue. Would you like that?"

"Seeing each other? Like...a... relationship?" I'm stuttering, but he's taken me by surprise again. *Did he just ask me to be his girlfriend?*

His intense gaze locks onto me, and I feel myself getting lost in the moment. The windows are fogged, creating our own little world. As I look into his eyes, anticipation pulses through me. Everything's tingling.

I can feel my heart race as his fingers suddenly slip under the hair tie that's holding my hair back, freeing my hair from its constraint. His rough fingers wrap around my hair, holding it tight on either side of my head. I gasp at the suddenness of it, feeling goosebumps rise on the back of my neck. I look at him, silently pleading with my eyes, but his gaze is unyielding.

I'm frozen, unable to move or look away, as my breathing quickens.

I can feel his lips getting closer, and my heart pounds so hard he has to hear it. The sound of our breathing drowns out any traffic outside the car. Its rapid and harsh rhythm makes me squirm with a desire I haven't felt in a long time. Maybe never. Not like this.

He gently pulls my head back by my hair, and I can feel his warm breath on my neck. "You didn't answer me, Charlene." His voice is low, almost a growl, and it commands my attention.

My heart flutters when I hear my full name on his lips, and I'm taken aback by its impact on me. I used to hate when Mark called me Charlene, but hearing it from Jimmy in that commanding way sets me on fire.

"Answer you?" I ask, my voice barely above a squeak. His mouth is hovering over my neck, and he tugs on my hair.

"I *said* I'd like to start seeing you and asked you if you would like that. You didn't answer me." He leans in, his face inching closer to my neck. His warm breath gently tickles my skin, and I'm relieved that one of us can still breathe. He licks my neck and I gasp out loud.

He continues breathing on my neck, his lips grazing them slowly. I moan, held captive by a desire so intense it's immobilized me. I long to scream 'yes,' but the words are trapped within me, as if longing has imprisoned me in silence.

"Answer me," he commands, his voice demanding my response. He yanks my hair to one side and nibbles my neck. Then he brings his face up, hovering dangerously close, his lips mere inches from mine. So close. I can now feel his breath on my lips, but he doesn't kiss me. "Open your eyes," he says.

I open my eyes, and his gaze burns into me. I'm torn between the desire to comply and the fear of surrendering to this attraction. My racing heart and the war of emotions within me make it impossible to answer, but I hope he can read my silent plea, my desperate longing for his kiss.

"Uh!" The sound of my moan reverberates in the silence. It's the best I can do. My neck pulses with the rhythm of my heartbeat as my blood rushes through my body. He releases my hair and strokes it softly, bringing his hand down and grazing the side of my face, still holding my gaze.

"Oh, what's the matter, Charlie?" His voice is a seductive whisper as he barely brushes his lips across mine. My entire body shivers in response to his touch, and a gasp escapes my lips again. I want him desperately. I lean forward, hoping to close the gap between us, to press my lips to his, but he grabs my hair again, yanking my head back, asserting his control.

"Oh, no, no, no, you don't," he playfully scolds, a mischievous smile playing on his lips, making him even more irresistible. "Bad girls don't get kisses. Now, be a good girl and answer my question. Would you like to see me?" His teasing tone and that enchanting grin have me yearning for more.

My breaths come in short, desperate pants. "Yes," I say, breathless.

"I'm sorry," he says, a smile exposing his dimple again. "What was that?" He winks at me, knowing how much I want him.

"*Please*," I plead, frustration and longing blending into my voice. I want to pull Jimmy closer, to taste his lips, but I can't move. "Yes," I pant, my desire laid bare. "Yes! *Please!*"

He releases my hair, his fingers gentle as he cradles my face. I don't dare move, my entire being focused on him. In an agonizingly slow motion, he pulls me to him and presses his lips gently to mine. But I want more. The sparks between us demand more, and I respond eagerly, pressing myself against him.

Our kiss becomes passionate and fiery. Yearning bursts within me. Jimmy bites my lip, and I let out a surprised squeal.

I part my lips, inviting him in, and he accepts, running his tongue around the outside of my lips, around and around.

I cry out, unable to contain my need. The world around us disappears, and our burning desire is the only thing that exists.

"Oh, Charlie," he whispers against my mouth. "I've wanted to do this for so long."

He leans in harder now, his lips molding to mine, a passionate, urgent kiss that engulfs me in the depths of his yearning. As my lips part in surrender, he claims me in a way that is both intoxicating and possessive. His fervor defies restraint, and his tongue explores my mouth as I willingly release myself to him.

I've been kissed many times before, but this kiss is different. I can feel the depth of his affection in the way his lips touch mine and how he holds me. He's kissing my lips, my cheeks, and even the tip of my nose. As his lips retreat, he pauses, and our eyes lock in a magnetic gaze. My breath catches as he gently brushes my hair behind my ear.

I try to blink to regain my composure, but I can't escape his intense gaze. A torrent of electrifying sensations courses through my body, every nerve alight with desire. I hear his low, appreciative groan, deep and guttural, and my heart races. I gasp, my lips parting as I surrender to the overwhelming intensity of the moment.

His fingers gently follow the contours of my ears, playfully exploring their shape. I shut my eyes and let out a soft moan, unable to hold back the pleasure surging within me. How does he understand how to arouse me like this?

"Oooh," he says. "You like that?"

I see him smiling a mischievous smile as I open my eyes, his dimple deepening with every passing second. I'm completely at his mercy, unable to form coherent thoughts or speak. My breathing is ragged, and I'm pretty sure my face is giving away how much I want him.

He moves his mouth to my ear, and he's breathing rapidly. I'm not sure how much more of his teasing I can take. He stays there for a few moments, just breathing, and I'm about to lose my mind.

"Something tells me you like it," he says into my ear. His low, deep voice is like a drug, and I crave more. I can hardly contain myself as he runs his tongue along my ear. I feel like I'm on fire and my heart rate soars. He grabs my hair and pulls my head back, diving into my neck. Goosebumps burst through my skin, and I tingle from head to toe.

"Mmmm," he moans again as he nibbles my neck. His touch confirms everything I've felt for him.

I never thought I'd be able to feel this way after Mark, but with Jimmy, everything feels different. I'm willing to cast my reservations aside and try again. I know it won't be easy, but I'm willing to take that risk.

As we reluctantly break apart from the kiss, I secretly yearn for more. But Jimmy leans back, his chest rising and falling as he catches his breath. I sit back and take a deep breath, trying to calm myself down.

"That was intense," he says, and I can't help but agree. It was so much more than just a kiss. It confirmed everything I've been feeling for him.

We sit in silence for a while, holding hands and breathing. All the loneliness and worry I've been feeling disappears in Jimmy's presence. It's like he's my anchor in this stormy sea of life.

For the first time in a while, I experience a deep sense of tranquility. I close my eyes, wishing this blissful feeling could continue indefinitely. Yet, beneath it all, I know nothing is eternal. So, I cherish this moment, replaying it in my thoughts before safeguarding it like a precious gem in the vault of my memories.

"Hey, are you alright?" Jimmy asks. He furrows his brow with concern.

I smile weakly. "Yeah, I am. I'm just very overwhelmed," I admit. "I feel better now, though, Jimmy. I'm still trying to wrap my mind around you being here."

"I'm sorry it took me so long," he says, gently smoothing my hair back from my face. He smiles, causing my breath to catch in my throat again. I can't help but smile back, feeling shy under his gaze.

I take a deep breath, trying to regain my composure. "Have you started searching for a new job yet?" I ask, hoping to change the subject.

He shifts in his seat uncomfortably. "Not really. I've been trying to process everything. But I was planning on getting started this week, though. Why?"

I hesitate a moment, but then I decide to take a chance. "Remember, I told you I used to work at GGBuff?" I ask, watching as his eyes widen with interest. "Well, I still have great ties with the team over there. I could probably get you a job if you're interested."

Jimmy sits up straighter in his seat, his eyes shining with excitement. "Yes, absolutely, I'm interested," he says. "They designed the *Final Empire* game series." His smile is as wide as his eyes.

Of course, he knows their most successful product. "I'll let you in on a little secret. I was one of the lead developers of the third installment." I grin proudly.

His eyes widen further. "You're joking! That's the best in the trilogy!"

"Not joking, I assure you. You can check the game credits if you still have a copy. It's a great company, and I think you'd fit right in. What do you think?"

Jimmy shakes his head. "Charlie, you amaze me," he says. "I would love to work at GGBuff. Thank you so much!"

I grin, a wave of relief flooding through me. "No worries at all. Consider it my way of making things right," I say, my guilt at his situation still weighing on me. "And I believe you'll love the place."

He's quiet for a minute. Then he says, "Look, it's none of my business, and you don't have to talk about it if you don't want to, but why did you quit such a good job to work for a cleaning company? I mean no disrespect, but what happened?"

I pause for a minute, then open up to him and share everything about Ronny. I hold nothing back and even mention that my parents live far away, but I choose not to go into detail about how they up and moved to Mexico right after Ronny's accident.

Nor do I share with him the burden my good ol' mom and dad put on my Aunt Debbie and me to care for Ronny. It's a sensitive and embarrassing topic to talk about. However, I do mention my Aunt Debbie to him and how she's been my rock-solid support. I tell him how she's been available for Ronny whenever I need to work and how we even share a duplex, Ronny and me on one side and Aunt Debbie on the other.

"Why don't you just hire someone during the day?" Jimmy asks.

It's a simple question, but the answer is, again, embarrassing. "Ronny had no insurance," I tell him. "We simply can't afford to hire help. My aunt teaches during the day, so she can't watch him. So, I had to find a night job so I could be with him during the day."

"But I don't mind so much," I add. "I mean, Ronny's my brother. He needs me, so here I am, cleaning an office building. It pays the bills."

I quickly suppress the tears welling up in my eyes. I'm usually good at hiding my feelings, but there's something about the way he looks at me that makes it difficult to hide anything. The concern etched on his face and the gentle squeeze of his hand show that he genuinely cares. It's a comforting feeling, but one that also makes me feel vulnerable.

There's *no way* I'm going to cry in front of Jimmy, as it seems foolish to cry over my current situation, anyway. I don't want to scare him off with an emotional outburst. Besides, Ronny and I are managing fine, although I wish my parents would send more money to help us. But I know I can't do anything about that. Sometimes we have to accept the cards we're dealt and count our blessings.

An odd sense of relief washes over me as I unpack my truths. For so long, only Aunt Debbie and Ronny knew even a fraction of the turmoil inside me. I have to appear strong, even with them, hiding my vulnerabilities like a seasoned actor. I don't want Ronny to see me upset and keep blaming himself.

With Jimmy, I feel like I can share almost anything. It's a strange feeling, but it's there. And in that moment, it feels right to tell him about Ronny. I take a deep breath.

"So, he has no insurance?" Jimmy asks, his eyes fixed on mine.

"Well, Ronny has health insurance now. Aunt Debbie helped me get that for him, but it doesn't cover a home aid or anything like that. All that falls on our shoulders."

Jimmy's face falls. I don't want his pity, but I'm grateful for his empathy. He's the real deal.

"I'm so sorry," he whispers.

I shake my head. "Don't be sorry, Jimmy. Not for me. It's just life."

He nods, his eyes still fixed on mine. I can tell that he's processing everything I've just said. I've known him a while, but he's never known this side of my story. It has to be a shock.

"I think it's time I headed home," I say, punching a hole in the silence.

Jimmy nods. "When can I see you again?"

I pause, thinking of a way to tell him about my limited availability without sounding like a burden. "That depends. I'm only available to go out on Saturday or Sunday evenings. Aunt Debbie will be there for Ronny, and I don't work weekends."

"Of course, that's fine," he says quickly, before pausing again. I can feel my nerves lighting up. *Is he going to tell me it's all too much?*

"Charlie," he says, his voice soft but serious. "I just want to clarify. I want to see you, but I'd like it if we took things slow, okay?"

I feel my heart race as I listen to Jimmy's words. My worst fears are coming true. He's going to bolt, just like Mark did, now that he knows about Ronny. I try to keep my composure as I respond, "Yeah, sure," and step out of the car. "See you around, I guess. It was so nice to see you again, Jimmy."

Tears threaten to spill from my eyes as I walk toward my car. But before I can even reach the door, I hear Jimmy's voice calling out to me. "Are you really about to leave without giving me your phone number?"

I turn around to face him, surprised by his sudden change of heart. "Oh, I'm sorry. I just thought—"

"You just thought you wanted to give me your phone number." He hands me his phone, and I enter my number. "Now, let me open your door. You know I'm a gentleman, right?" A hint of humor peppers his voice, the humor I've so sorely missed.

I let him open the door, feeling comforted by his chivalry as he takes my hand in his and plants a soft kiss on the top of it. His lips linger, and my heart flutters. When he releases my hand, I climb behind the wheel, and he closes my door.

I roll down my window to say goodnight. Jimmy leans down and kisses my lips with a soft peck. "Goodnight, gorgeous," he whispers. I start my car and drive away.

But as I drive home, my mind is in a jumbled mess. I can't make sense of the mixed signals Jimmy gave me. He wants a relationship, so he says, and he even *kissed* me, but when I opened up to him about Ronny, he pushed me away.

I hate men.

CHAPTER 9
Atticus

It was a nerve-racking four days before the email from GGBuff finally arrives, inviting me to interview for a position on their development team. As soon as I see it, I know I have to call Charlie. I dial her number, my heart pounding in my chest.

She answers the phone, sounding breathless, and I wonder if I've interrupted her. "Did I catch you at a bad time?" I ask, hoping I didn't.

"Jimmy?" she says, a hint of surprise in her voice.

"Yes, it's Jimmy."

"Sorry, you took my number, but I didn't take yours. I was just doing some cardio. What's up?"

"I just received an email from GGBuff. They'd like to meet with me today! Thank you for wielding your magic wand."

"Oh, I didn't know *what* was going on. I hadn't heard from you." I can hear a bit of annoyance in her voice.

"I'm sorry," I say, my emotions jumbled. "I've been... swamped."

"Oh," she says. There's a pause on the other end of the line, and I hold my breath, unsure what to say next.

I'm grateful when she breaks the silence. "It's alright, but don't be nervous. You have nothing to worry about. I said only great things about you, and you'll impress Lindsay. I know it." Her voice is reassuring.

"Lindsay?" I ask, curious.

"She's the head of Programming," Charlie says. "She's got clout at GGBuff. Everything runs through her. And she just happens to be my good friend."

I mentally note that, feeling thankful for any inside information I can get. "Anything else I need to know before I walk in there?"

"She hates fake," she says. "She can smell fake from a million miles away. Whatever you do, don't embellish. Just be yourself. Call me back and let me know how it goes — if you want."

"Yeah, for sure. I can't thank you enough."

"Sure, no problem." She hangs up. I had hoped for more conversation, but I guess she's busy. I take a deep breath, attempting to steady my nerves.

While talking to Charlie felt incredible, anxiety twists my stomach in knots as I realize I hadn't called her since I saw her that day outside the parking garage. That was *four days ago*. She didn't sound too thrilled to hear from me. I've probably messed everything up.

I sit on my couch, my phone still in my hand, and stare at it, lost in thought. My mind drifts to that kiss — how Charlie's lips felt on mine, the smell of her skin, and how she melted in my arms. I can't help but smile as I reminisce about teasing her and how she appeared to enjoy it. But I wonder if I might have gone too far by expressing my desire for a relationship. I hope not.

The truth is, I like Charlie. I mean, I *really* like her. But there's this nagging feeling of dread that won't go away. Every time I thought about calling her these past few days, I froze up. I knew I should call her, but my fingers wouldn't dial. *It's ridiculous.*

I put my feet on my coffee table and lean back on my couch. Life was so much easier when I didn't care about a woman the way I care about Charlie. I used to date girls once or twice and then move on to the next one. No strings. No mess. *No heartache.*

But when I'd brought up the idea of taking things slowly, Charlie had appeared to be upset. When we chatted on the phone just now, she seemed somewhat distant. But honestly, who can hold it against her? One minute, I'm all over her in my car, and the next, I'm hitting the brakes. She's probably confused about my intentions.

I run my fingers through my hair, trying to tame the wild mess atop my head. With a resigned sigh, I give up and make my way to the kitchenette in my tiny apartment. As I open the fridge, I can't help but hear Archie's voice in my head, telling me to go grocery shopping. I rummage through the drawers and find a container of cream cheese I picked up from the corner deli and a bagel to spread it on.

I find a toaster tucked away in the cabinet. This small, furnished apartment may not be much, but at least it has the basic creature comforts.

But as I take a bite of my bagel, my thoughts drift to Archie's advice about Charlie and my parents. I know he's right, but it's not that easy. I don't want to hurt my parents any more than I already have. They've always been good to me, and even though I hate my current situation, I know it's partly my fault. Maybe *mostly* my fault.

My fingers itch to call my mother. I know she's probably worried sick about me. I pick up my phone, hands trembling slightly as I press the screen. But of course, she doesn't answer. She probably wants to, but she knows my father would blow a fuse if he found out. It goes to voicemail.

I take a deep breath and leave a message. "Hi, Mom, it's Atticus," I say, trying to sound casual. "Just wanted to let you know things are going well for me. I've got an apartment in Albany, my car is still running, and I have an interview at a big company this afternoon. I didn't want you to worry."

I pause and then add, "I love you, Mom. Don't tell Dad I called, okay? I'll check in with you soon."

I take another nibble of my bagel as I sit down at my small kitchen table. The old metal table with its red accents looks like something from the 1950s. Sometimes, I feel like I'm living in a sitcom surrounded by relics from the past.

Charlie. She forces her way back into my thoughts. She's been through a lot, and yet she remains incredibly resilient. Her revelations about her brother and her situation sit in my gut, churning without relief. I picture her face, so bright and lovely, and I can't help but wonder how she keeps it together.

Then, like a slap in the face, I remember Heather. Stupid Heather, with her pearly white teeth. That breakup was tough. I know Charlie is *nothing* like Heather, but the thought of another heartbreak is enough to make me want to give up before I even try.

I think about Charlie's kindness — the way she stuck her neck out for me with her former employer and the way she believes in me. It gives me hope, even when I have my doubts. For the first time in a while, I'm starting to believe that maybe, just maybe, things could work out.

The interview with Lindsay lasts all of thirty minutes. As I nervously fidget in my seat, Lindsay's smile only seems to amplify my anxiety. When she finally asks, "When can you start?" I'm momentarily taken aback. But I quickly regain my composure.

"I guess as soon as possible," I say, my face breaking into a wide grin as I shake her outstretched hand.

"Great. See you tomorrow then?"

"I'll be here," I reply, still smiling. "Thank you."

Lindsay smiles back. "It was a straightforward decision. You got a shining recommendation from Charlie."

The elation I feel is palpable, and if I knew how, I'd jump up and kick my heels together. This is a job I can sink my teeth into, and I can't wait to tell Charlie. As I return to my car, my heart pounds hard with excitement. I immediately dial Charlie's number, eager to share the good news.

"I got it, Charlie! I got the job!" I say excitedly when she picks up the phone.

"I knew you would," Charlie replies, her voice filled with pride. "You deserve it, Jimmy."

Our conversation quickly turns to celebrating. "How about dinner?" I ask. "We can celebrate. Saturday?"

Charlie hesitates. "I thought you wanted to take things slow?"

"I don't think we can go any slower, Charlie," I say. "I'll pick you up at seven."

She pauses for a while as I hold my breath. "No, I don't think so. I've got a lot going on."

She doesn't sound like she's kidding, and she doesn't laugh. I knew I upset her when I said we should take things slow, but I didn't mean *this* slow, like non-existent slow.

"I thought you said you could go out on the weekend evenings?" I push.

"I can, but—"

"But nothing," I say. "I'll pick you up at seven."

"You don't even know where I live," she says. She makes a noise, but I can't tell if it's a scoff or a laugh. I'm hoping it's a laugh.

"That's no problem because you're going to tell me," I say. She hasn't learned yet how persistent I can be.

"No, I think you were right about taking it slow. I've got a lot going on with Ronny, and it's kind of hard to—"

"Charlie?" I cut her off.

"Yes?" she says.

"You need to tell me where you live because we *are* going out on Saturday, and I'm not taking no for an answer."

She pauses. "Fine," she huffs after what seems like forever. "I'll give you the address."

After hanging up with Charlie, I make a reservation at Druthers, a new Clifton Park restaurant just north of Albany. It has a gorgeous outdoor area and will be perfect for our date. The anticipation of being close to Charlie again is almost unbearable.

As I walk into GGBuff, I can't help but feel a wave of apprehension wash over me. The memories of my previous job at GamesMade still haunt me, and I can't shake off a strange feeling of impending doom. Ah! I'm just being ridiculous. I've landed a dream job!

I'm greeted by a group of young men and women scattered throughout an entire floor. They welcome me warmly but quickly return to their tasks, leaving me standing alone amid their buzzing activity.

Throughout the onboarding process, I can't help but feel the nagging sensation of PTSD from my previous job. But gradually, I realize things are different here. No one is out to get me, and there is no hostility in the air. The atmosphere is relaxed, not charged with tension, and no Hot-Toddy breathing down everyone's neck. I let out a sigh of relief, realizing my fears were for nothing.

This job is my chance to show my worth and earn my father's acceptance. The pay is excellent, which will help me save toward my goal of getting back to who I *really* am.

Getting back to who I *really* am. The words echo in my head, and an overwhelming wave of guilt washes over me.

The truth is, I've been living a lie. Charlie, who helped me get this job, knows nothing about the real me. She's been nothing but honest with me, open like a book. Yet all I've given her in return is a series of practiced lies, a complete fabrication of a person who doesn't exist. Despite her honesty and openness toward me, I've deceived her with a false name and sense of who I am. She has no idea about my family or my past.

I call Archie on my lunch break, feeling a tight knot of anxiety in my stomach. I need his advice and perspective on this situation, which is weighing me down.

"Hey, man," he says when he picks up. "How's the new job?"

"It's amazing," I tell him, my voice brightening. "I honestly didn't expect to love it this much. I think I'm going to thrive here."

"Right on," he says, his tone genuinely pleased. "So, what's on your mind?"

"Listen, I need to talk to you about something important." I'm hoping he's not in the middle of a project at work.

"Where are you?" he asks.

"I'm in my car. I'm on lunch."

"Your car?" He laughs. "Dude, really?"

"I didn't have money for lunch, so I brought some stuff from my house. I felt weird going to the break room, so I came down here."

"Meet me at Off Shore across the river. I'll buy you lunch. How long you got?"

"I get an hour, but I only have 45 minutes left."

"Not enough time. I'll bring lunch to you. Send me your location."

Archie arrives twenty minutes later with Wendy's hamburgers and fries. I laugh. "I was looking forward to a fish fry," I say.

"Shut up and tell me what's going on. I could tell from your voice something's up." He throws me my bag of food and places two sodas in my drink holder.

I steel myself for the conversation ahead and jump right in, opening my bag and grabbing the burger. "It's Charlie," I say, taking a huge bite of my burger and shoving a handful of fries into my mouth.

"Relax, Att, you'll choke." Archie laughs.

"No, really, Arch, I'm sick about this." I take a big gulp of my soda to try to wash down the food.

"Alright, sorry, go ahead." He says.

"I can't keep lying to her about who I am," I say, my mouth still full of food. My blood pressure is going up just by talking about it out loud. I take another sip of soda.

"What do you mean, lying?"

I swallow, finally. "You know what I mean." I shove more fries into my mouth. I guess I was hungrier than I thought. I hesitate, unsure how to articulate the complex webs of half-truths and omissions I've woven around myself. "I mean...I haven't told Charlie about my family or who I really am. And I feel like I'm running out of time."

"Okay, so you haven't told her you're from a wealthy family. So what?" he asks, a cluster of fries poised in his hand. "Is it that important? Besides, your father told you that you can't tell people who you really are. Remember, *Jimmy*?" He smirks, shoving the ridiculous amount of fries into his mouth, and he was worried about me choking.

I feel my frustration building up inside me. "See? That's what I mean. My name's not Jimmy."

"It's your middle name, so technically, it *is*." He takes a sip of his drink, looking at me like he just beat me at chess.

I roll my eyes. "You're not helping. I need to tell Charlie about my situation. If I pursue an actual relationship with her, I need to tell her who I am. What if she accepts the truth? Then I have to hope my parents will accept her."

"Look," Archie says to me, his tone serious now. "You said it yourself that you didn't want your parents to think she was a gold-digger, right? She doesn't come from money. I've said this before! How can she be a gold digger if she doesn't know you're wealthy? Hmmm?"

Finishing my burger, I can't help but admit that he has a point. Charlie can't possibly be after my money if she doesn't know.

"I just worry she'll be devastated when she eventually finds out," I mumble, my mind racing with doubts. I shove the last bit of fries into my mouth.

"She'll be fine," Archie says, reassuring me. "It's not like you're telling her you're rich only for her to find out you're broke." He laughs.

"Yeah, I guess." I'm not so convinced, but I push my fears aside.

"Don't you need to get back?" Archie reminds me, crinkling up his bag and grabbing his soda.

"Oh, shoot. Yes. Thanks for lunch, Archie. Thanks for everything."

We jump out of the car.

"Sure thing, Att. See ya."

I lock my car and rush back to work.

This afternoon, Lindsay leads me through the labyrinth of corporate offices to introduce me to the top executives. We stop in front of a white-haired man with dancing eyes. Lindsay introduces him as Jonathan Tomkins, the vice president of operations.

I shake his hand. "Nice to meet you, sir."

Jonathan chuckles. "Please, call me Jonathan," the older man says. "Nice to have you aboard, Mister..." he tilts his head to the side, waiting for me to offer my name.

I hesitate for a moment. "Uh, Winslow, sir. Jimmy Winslow."

He squints at me, studying me carefully. "Are you related to *Ray* Winslow?"

My heart skips a beat at the mention of my father's name. I try to keep my face neutral, but I can feel the sweat beading on my forehead.

I give a nervous chuckle. "I'm no spy for the competition," I say, my voice shaking slightly. My parents always taught me not to lie, and then my father sent me away, demanding I keep my identity hidden. It's beyond frustrating.

He scratches his white hair, looking thoughtful. "Huh... I see. I could have sworn, though. You sure look like Ray."

I force a laugh again, hoping to ease the tension. "Yeah, I get that a lot. But I promise, I'm here to work hard and make a difference."

Jonathan nods. "Anyway, Jimmy, welcome to the team. It's good to see another fresh, young mind join our team."

As we continue the tour, I can't shake the feeling that it's only a matter of time before I meet someone who will connect me to my father. If that happens, it could destroy my chances of getting back in the good graces of my family.

My father had made his instructions clear. No one can know he's my father until I succeed in the tasks he gave me. I push the thoughts of my father out of my head and focus on getting through the rest of the welcome tour.

Saturday night arrives faster than I could have hoped, and with it, the anticipation of taking Charlie to Druthers. As I pull up to her duplex, I can't help but feel a sense of excitement mixed with nervousness. I step out of the car, and to my surprise, she is already standing outside waiting for me.

Seeing her standing there, looking so stunning in that dress, I am already floored. She's dressed in a delicate yellow floral dress that complements her figure, and she had styled her silky blonde hair in an updo that enhances her natural charm. A few bouncy curls frame her beautiful face, but what grabs my eye is the string of pristine white pearls gracing her neck. I almost can't resist the urge to feel her soft, perfect neck against my lips again.

As we get into the car and start driving to Druthers, I can't help but feel nervous. The last time we went out to eat, Todd Brierly had caught us, and it left a sour taste in my mouth. But this time, everything is different. There are no rules or overzealous jerks to prevent us from enjoying each other's company.

Seeing how beautifully Charlie's dressed, I wish I could have worn my beige suit. It's my favorite, perfectly tailored to me, and would have matched her dress perfectly. Unfortunately, it's hanging in my closet at my parent's house with everything else I own. I had to borrow a suit from Archie, and it's a little big.

By the time we arrive at Druthers, my nervousness has turned to excitement. I made a reservation on the patio, and as the hostess leads us to our table, I can't help but notice the heads turning to look at Charlie. She has a beautiful smile on her face, and it's contagious.

As we approach our table, Charlie looks at me with a smile. I say to her, enamored by her beauty, "Well, Charlie, you sure know how to make an entrance." I hold her chair for her while she sits, and then I take my seat across from her.

Candles flicker in the center of the table, casting a warm glow over the patio. White lights twinkle in the surrounding trees, creating a magical atmosphere. Nearby, patrons pepper the low hum of conversation with laughter.

"Nice restaurant," Charlie says, raising a brow. "I see why Aunt Debbie likes it."

The waiter arrives and takes our drink orders. Charlie orders a white Russian, and I opt for a Merlot. It's a far cry from the Château Pétrus I'm used to, but that's out of the question with my current budget. I secretly want a beer, but I don't want Charlie to think I have no class.

I couldn't help but hear my mother's voice in my head while I contemplated my drink choice. "Atticus!" she used to scold me if I tried to order a beer. "Save that for your *buddies*. Order wine like a normal human being." I smile, thinking of her. I sure miss her.

Archie was kind enough to lend me some money until payday, and though it's not ideal, I'm grateful for the help. If someone had told me a few months ago that I'd be borrowing money from Archie, I would have laughed out loud.

The waiter sets down two menus in front of us, and we take our time perusing the entrees.

"Wow, this menu is stacked," Charlie says, flipping through the multitude of pages. Her expressions are adorable.

"Tell me about it. I must be hungry because everything looks amazing," I reply.

We both order steak when the waiter returns with our drinks. As we sit and wait for our dinners, I turn to Charlie and say, "I can't thank you enough for getting me a job with GGBuff. Working there has been great. I love it."

Charlie's eyes sparkle. "Come on, Jimmy. It was the least I

could do. I'm glad you've enjoyed the experience so far. They're a great bunch."

As we sip our drinks, the conversation flows easily. I tell Charlie all about work and everything that's been going on since I joined. I leave out my conversation with Jonathan Tomkins. She tells me a few antidotes about Ronny and Aunt Debbie, speaking lovingly about both of them.

The food arrives, and the aroma is heavenly. We both dive in hungrily, barely speaking as we savor every bite. It's a moment I'll always remember — the warmth of the flickering candles and the sound of Charlie's laughter. I could sit here all night with her.

Charlie's hand grazes mine as we both reach for a roll, sending a subtle yet electrifying thrill through my veins.

"Tell me more about Ronny," I say after the waiter clears away the dishes and brings two cups of coffee and chocolate mousse for dessert. "What happened?"

Charlie's gaze drifts into the distance, and a faint shadow passes across her eyes. "Ronny had an accident a few years ago," she begins, her voice tinged with sadness. "It left him with a spinal cord injury, and he's been in a wheelchair ever since. I've had to step up as his caregiver. Aunt Debbie helps when she can, but she works as a teacher and is very busy."

My heart aches for Charlie as the weight of her responsibilities becomes clear. "That must have been incredibly tough on you and your family," I say, unable to imagine the trials she's faced.

She nods, her eyes misty. She pours cream into her coffee and picks up her cup, blowing across the top before taking a sip. "As you know, my parents moved away shortly after Ronny's accident. They now live in Mexico." Her voice quivers with a hint of betrayal. "I guess they couldn't handle it or didn't want to. It's just Aunt Debbie and me now."

I can't believe what I just heard. I poise my spoon of

chocolate mousse in mid-air. "They moved *after* his accident? I don't know what to say."

Charlie slumps her shoulders, and her voice carries a sense of resignation. She rolls her spoon around in her mouse, playing with the whipped cream on top. "Yes, they did. It's been a challenge, but it also opened my eyes to the struggles people with disabilities face every day. I've become Ronny's primary caregiver, and it's a role I wouldn't trade for anything. But it made me realize that there's still a lot of room for improvement in enhancing the lives of people like him."

I lean in, my curiosity piqued. "How so?" I say, taking a sip of my hot coffee.

Her eyes light up, and she draws closer, her passion radiating from her very being. She lowers her voice and glances around. "I'm currently working on an app for people with disabilities. The software would help people like Ronny to lead more independent lives. I want to make a difference, not just in Ronny's life but in the lives of other people who face similar challenges."

Charlie shrugs and takes a bite of her mouse. "It hasn't been easy with the late nights and caring for Ronny, but it's a project that I believe in." Then her eyes get wide, and she says, "Mmm, this is delicious."

Her passion for Ronny's plight is inspiring, and I admire her even more. "That's an amazing mission, Charlie. Anything I can do to help? This kid's a wiz at programming if you haven't heard." I grin, putting my thumbs through imaginary suspenders and sitting up straighter.

She laughs, the tension easing. "I have heard that," she says. "Honestly, though, I've never shared this with anyone, but yeah, I could use your help, if you mean it." She takes another sip of her coffee.

"Of course I do," I reply eagerly, the idea firmly taking root in my mind.

Returning home a few hours later, the first thing on my agenda is calling my father. I want to run a few things by him. His voice, gruff and impatient, answers after a delay.

"Yes?"

"Hey, Dad. Sorry to call you so late," I begin, anxiety creeping into my voice.

"We're still up, but why are you calling? Have you made that first $100,000 yet?"

I clear my throat nervously before responding. "No, not yet, but I think I found a way to accomplish that. I met someone recently who could use some help. There's this girl at the office, and her brother—"

My father's impatience cuts me off. "Two things," he says. "One, don't call me again until you've completed your tasks. Two, don't call me about some girl you met at your office."

"But, Dad—"

He hangs up, leaving me with the weight of his dismissal. There's no use trying to call him again.

I stare at the blank screen, anger bubbling within me. He could have allowed me to finish. He could have listened to what I had to say.

Anger is not the only thing I feel as I get into bed. There's a fierce determination brewing inside me. Now, more than anything, I am committed to helping Charlie. Together, we will create an app that helps Ronny and others like him.

During my lunch break Monday, I'll go to the bank to explore the possibility of getting a loan.

CHAPTER 10
Charlie

I lie in bed, gazing up at the ceiling, pondering whether I should get up. The morning sun is filtering through my blinds, but I roll over. As I'm drifting off to sleep again, my phone rings. I grab it from the nightstand and glance at the caller ID. *It's Jimmy!*

I sit up. "Hey, what's up? Miss me already?" I tease. Last night's date was wonderful. I hope he has the same feelings I do.

"You awake?" he asks. What is that playful tone I hear in his voice?

"Well, if I wasn't, I am now," I laugh, glancing at the time. "It's seven o'clock."

"I've been up for hours," he says.

"Yeah?" I tease. "Are you looking for an award?"

"Of course, I am. But that's not why I called," he says, his voice trailing off.

My heart sinks. The last time we shared a romantic moment, Jimmy asked to take things slow. *What's he going to say this time?*

"What's going on then? Is something wrong?" I ask, my voice trembling slightly.

"Well, I don't know," he replies.

I can't take it anymore. "You don't know? Did you leave something at the restaurant?" He called for *some* reason, so why isn't he saying?

He laughs. "No, nothing like that, but I think you'd better look out your front window," he says, his voice low and sweet.

I jump out of bed, my curiosity piqued, and race to my bedroom window. As I peek out, I see Jimmy standing on the sidewalk, his right hand extended toward me, his phone in his other hand.

"Care to dance?" he asks, his voice low and sexy.

His smile is captivating, and his messy hair makes him look even sexier. I can't help but think how lucky I am to wake up to such a magnificent sight.

"I'll be right down, crazy," I say and hang up my phone.

Jimmy's eyes light up as I bounce down my front steps, carrying Ronny's monitor. He talks before I reach the bottom stairs. "I've just been thinking a lot about what you said. And I have a bunch of amazing ideas," he blurts out.

"Okay... and what exactly did I say that has you so excited?" I ask, laughing.

"You know, you wanting to build apps to help people like Ronny." He pauses. "The more I think about it, the more it makes sense to me, which is crazy because there are so many people whose lives these apps would change."

"I know," I say. "I need to get them out there, but I've been so hesitant about sharing my plans with other people. I know nothing about patents or legal stuff. I just want to make sure I'm protected from someone stealing my ideas."

Jimmy scoffs. "I hope you don't think that I would ever do that. I certainly don't need—" He stops, leaving his sentence hanging in the air. He looks like he swallowed a balloon.

"Don't need what?" I ask, hoping he'll finish his sentence. *What doesn't he need?*

He looks down at the sidewalk, avoiding my gaze, and it makes me feel uneasy. I sense that something is wrong. "I don't need to steal your ideas. That's all," Jimmy says. He looks up at me. "Besides, I would *never* do that."

Despite his reassurances, I sense that there's something he's not telling me. But I don't push it. He's clearly interested in my project. He's even come to talk with me about it in person, at seven in the morning!

"Come on," I say, leading him to the gazebo in the far corner of my wooded backyard. It's a beautiful structure that my Uncle Ed had built for my Aunt Debbie when he was alive. It's got a picnic table in the center, and I take a seat on one side. Jimmy sits across from me.

"It's nice out here," he says, looking around. The early morning sun is filtering down through the trees, causing a warm glow over everything.

"I can't stay outside long," I tell him. "Ronny will need me." I hold up the monitor.

"That's fine. I have to get to work, anyway."

"On a Sunday?" I say. "That's dedication."

"Yeah, I have an extensive project I'm working on, and I just want to go in for a few hours and prepare a few things for tomorrow, but let's talk about your app ideas."

Jimmy talks quickly, his words tumbling out like a rushing river of thoughts. I'm so excited that I've found someone who cares about all the people whose lives my app could change and understands the mechanics of it.

But then, I remember the reality of the situation. The money to develop such a product, let alone *multiple* applications, seems impossible. Marketing funds alone would pose a significant financial barrier.

"I think there's a lot of potential here, Charlie," Jimmy

continues. "But I don't want to be too forward. It's still *your* brainchild, after all. But I'd love to work with you on this. I meant it when I said you can count on my support. Besides the programming, I'm also a *wiz at biz*."

I laugh at his silliness, but I'm at a loss for words to express my gratitude. I'm excited to hear Jimmy's ideas, but I also feel apprehensive and tell him so. Even though my gut tells me I can trust him, we did only just meet recently.

"We'll have a lawyer draw up the paperwork," Jimmy says, "and we can put in clauses that will protect your rights to the patents. I'm not trying to steal your thunder. I need to build a business for personal goals, and I'd love to do it with you. We could help each other."

"Personal goals?" I ask.

"Yes. I have a personal goal to build a successful business within the next year. Your ideas for the app are the motivation I need to help create something meaningful. We can do this, Charlie, I'm telling you."

"Well, then, James Winslow, I accept your help." His energy is infectious, yet terrifying. I feel it drawing me in. I want to believe him and trust him more than anything.

"Should we shake on it or something?" I put out my hand.

He shakes my hand. His grasp is firm, but when I try to slide my hand away, he grips it tighter. My eyes widen as I look at him.

"I have one request, though," he says, still gripping my hand. "I would like to meet Ronny, Charlie. I know it's an unusual request, and we're trying to take things slow. But I'd love to speak with him. Get to know him?"

He stops talking and examines my face. I must admit, he's winning points wanting to meet Ronny, but I'm hesitant.

Still clutching my hand, he places his other hand over the top of mine, sandwiching my hand between his. Looking into my eyes, he says, "He's the subject of what you — *we* — are going to create. You've personally witnessed how your apps could make a real difference in people's lives. I need to experience it as well. I want to feel the passion like you do, Charlie. That's what will drive me."

"Oh, Jimmy," I say. "I don't know. Ronny rarely leaves the house anymore—"

"Then I could come in," he says, cutting me off. "Not right now, obviously. How about I bring lunch tomorrow? Does Ronny like pizza? Just a simple lunch, Charlie. I get to meet Ronny, and we get to talk a bit more about the apps."

"Wow... you're serious?" I struggle to wrap my head around the sincerity of a man who wants to meet my handicapped brother.

"And determined. So, tomorrow? Pizza?"

"Ronny likes pizza," I reply. "Alright. What time is your lunch break?"

He releases his grip on my hand. "I can be here at 12:30. Does that work?" He gets up from the table. "Meanwhile, I'll contact a lawyer friend and ask him to draw up some preliminary contracts so you can see how they work. We can talk specifics tomorrow."

He strolls through the yard toward the front, and I follow. Before he gets back in his car, he turns and asks, "What kind of pizza should I get? What do you and Ronny like?"

It is a seemingly simple question, but it means so much. Mark had always been dismissive of Ronny, treating him like a nuisance. What a refreshing change this is.

"We both like pepperoni," I say.

He leaves for work, and I'm left pondering tomorrow. He's eager to meet Ronny, a gesture that truly touches my heart. But I can't help but worry that Jimmy won't like my brother or will find him too challenging. More than that, I'm anxious about Ronny's reaction to Jimmy. Ronny's comfort and well-being are paramount, and I can't let anyone who makes him uncomfortable in our lives.

I head back into the house to check on Ronny and let him know my friend is coming by tomorrow with lunch. Ronny has had very few visitors since his accident, and I'm uncertain about how he'll react to me bringing a friend over. I guess I'll find out when he gets up.

As I prepare Ronny's breakfast of strawberries and whipped cream, he sits in his wheelchair in the living room. I set his food in front of him on a tray, along with a big glass of chocolate milk — his favorite. I haven't broached the subject of Jimmy yet.

"Where did you take off to?" he asks through a mouthful of strawberries.

"I was outside for a few minutes. How did you know? I thought you were asleep."

"I heard you go outside, and it took a while for you to come back," he says.

"I was talking to my friend Jimmy."

He raises a brow. "Have I met Jimmy?" He dips another strawberry into the whipped cream and stuffs it into his mouth.

"No, but he asked if he could bring us pizza for lunch tomorrow. Is that alright with you?"

"I don't know," he says. "Depends if I like him, but it wouldn't hurt if he brought *pepperoni* pizza." He laughs.

"Alright," I say, joining in his laughter. "I'll make sure he brings pepperoni pizza if you give him a chance."

"As long as he's not mean like Mark, we should be fine."

"He's not mean at all," I assure him.

I certainly *hope* Jimmy's not a jerk like Mark. I didn't think Mark was a jerk at first, either, until he was.

I guess time will tell.

Jimmy arrives right on time today, and as I open the door, he presses an enormous bouquet of daisies and baby's breath into my hands. "Did the pizza come yet?" he asks.

"It's here," I say. "It just came a few minutes ago." I look at the flowers, warmed by the thoughtful gesture. "Thanks for these. They're beautiful."

"Not as beautiful as you, gorgeous!" Jimmy wraps his arms around my waist and pulls me to him. "Is Ronny alright with meeting me?" He leans close to my ear. "I've been so nervous."

"He is, and he can't wait to dive into the pizza. I told him we had to wait for you."

"Well, we'd better get in there, then." He leans in for a quick kiss, and I lead him into the house.

Ronny is waiting in his wheelchair in the living room when we enter. Jimmy walks right up and shakes his hand, introducing himself. I grab a pitcher from the kitchen, fill it with water, and arrange the flowers before placing the pitcher in the center of the coffee table.

I had shared all about Jimmy with Ronny, who seemed genuinely excited for the company. However, I can't help but feel a whirlwind of nerves as I had worried all morning about their meeting.

"I've heard so much about you," Jimmy says to my brother. "Your sister's quite proud of you."

Ronny glances at me, a soft smile gracing his lips.

"You know it," I say, smiling back at Ronny.

"Glad to meet you, Jimmy," Ronny says to him. "It's Charlie we should be proud of. She's the best." Ronny and I exchange another smile, a testament to the deep bond we share.

"She *is* the best," Jimmy says, his gaze locking on me. I blush at his compliment.

Turning his attention back to Ronny, Jimmy asks, "You ready for some pizza?"

I'm taken aback by how seamlessly Ronny and Jimmy get along. They're loud and animated as they discuss gaming, camping, and even skydiving, of all things. I'm embarrassed to learn Jimmy is as much of a gaming enthusiast as my brother and me, something I should have known. To my surprise, he's been skydiving over thirty times, another interesting tidbit I'd missed.

"Yo, sis. Check this out," Ronny says when he spots me walking back into the living room after clearing the empty pizza box and plates. "Jimmy is a badass in Pirates of Starcrest. I was just telling him how we're a gaming family."

"No way!" I say, stepping forward. "That's our favorite game. What's your username?"

"Oh, wow!" Jimmy says. "My username is Cha—"

"Do I smell pizza?" Aunt Debbie says from the doorway, interrupting Jimmy. Looking at him, she asks, "Charlie, who's your handsome friend?"

I chuckle and blush at Aunt Debbie's unexpected visit during her lunch break. I had told her about Jimmy coming for lunch, so she made a "coincidental" appearance. "This is Jimmy, Aunt Debbie." I turn to Jimmy. "Jimmy, meet my aunt Debbie."

Jimmy stands from the couch and approaches her. "Ah, the guardian angel Charlie talks about all the time." He hugs her warmly, as if he's known her forever. She hugs him back and smiles. Wow! Mark couldn't stand Aunt Debbie. He said all she did was meddle.

Jimmy follows her over to a chair by the couch where Aunt Debbie sits down. "Would you like some pepperoni pizza?" he asks.

Aunt Debbie places a hand on her chest. "He's handsome,

and he has manners, too? Charlie, where did you find this one?"

We spend the next half-hour talking, laughing, and trading stories while Debbie has pizza, and we munch on cookies for dessert. Ronny seems bonded to Jimmy, and Aunt Debbie is definitely in love.

We don't have time to go over any plans for the new app venture, but it doesn't matter. I feel a flood of relief that not only does Ronny like Jimmy, but it's clear that Aunt Debbie does, too.

"Thank you for introducing me to your family," Jimmy says as I walk him out to his car. "They're awesome." He looks down at his shoes, a habit he seems to have when he's deep in thought. His brow furrows, but before I can ask what's wrong, his charming smile and pleasant demeanor return.

"Thanks for bringing lunch," I say. "It was nice to see Ronny laugh. You're pretty funny when you want to be."

He wraps his arms around my waist, and I place my hands over his shoulders. "You think I'm funny, eh?" he says.

"Sometimes," I say, "but don't get a big head."

"Too late," he says, and winks.

I know he has to leave for work, but I just want to stay wrapped in his arms forever.

"You know," he says, "you might have it hard caring for Ronny, but you're fortunate to have such a cool family. I mean that."

I study his face, noting the sadness etched on his features. I wonder what burden he's carrying. "Don't you have a cool family?" I ask. He never talks about his family, and from the sudden ashen look on his face, I regret asking.

"No," he stammers. "I mean, I have a *wonderful* family. I just wouldn't say they're 'cool.'"

I chuckle, but he remains quiet, leaving me feeling

ORDINARY MR. BILLIONAIRE

awkward for laughing. Maybe I shouldn't have mentioned his family.

"Sore subject?" I ask, trying to fill the silence.

He says nothing, so I wait for him to speak. Eventually, he mumbles, "No, yes, sort of... I really can't talk about it."

He sighs heavily and falls quiet once more as he looks at me with a gaze so penetrating that I feel like he's looking into my soul. I feel my face flush. His hand comes up to my cheek, and he brushes it with the back of his hand, softly grasping a loose strand of hair and sliding it behind my ear. I close my eyes at his touch.

"You know what I *can* talk about?" he asks in a low voice, his face only inches from mine when I open my eyes, and I want desperately for him to kiss me again.

Suddenly, Aunt Debbie bursts from the house and comes bounding down the steps. Jimmy lets go of my waist, and I gently slide my arms from his shoulders. My cheeks suddenly feel like they're on fire, and Jimmy's face is as red as a tomato.

"Oh, don't let me interrupt anything," she says as she passes, laughing. "I've got to get back to work."

Jimmy fumbles for his phone, checking the time. "Shoot," he says, glancing at me. "I'd better go, too."

I feel deflated as he starts his car, wishing he wasn't about to drive away.

"Call me later?" I ask, hoping he will.

"I will," he promises before zooming off.

Jimmy was just about to kiss me again, but Aunt Debbie had the worst timing. I make a mental note. Aunt Debbie and I are going to have to talk about that.

"I like him!" Ronny blurts out before I've even closed the front door. He's grinning from ear to ear. "He's so cool and a gamer, sis." His excitement is clear, and I can't help but smile.

I'm relieved lunch is over and that everything went smoothly. Ronny approves. Aunt Debbie seems to like him, and I don't think we scared Jimmy away. Although, he took off in that Prius rather quickly.

I smile. I realize I'm not afraid of Jimmy leaving me. He's not Mark. I have a good feeling about our business venture, too. I think things are finally moving in the right direction for me.

My next memory is Aunt Debbie shaking me awake. I must have dozed off while watching TV with Ronny. I glance over, and Ronny's sound asleep in his chair. His head is back, and he looks uncomfortable. I walk over, pick up a pillow from the couch, and place it next to his head for support.

"You want some of the leftover beef stew from last night?" Aunt Debbie offers, her voice gentle. "Save you cooking dinner."

I nod, thankful for the offer. "What time is it?" I ask, rubbing my eyes.

"Time for you to tell me all about your handsome boyfriend," she teases, her eyes twinkling with mischief.

I let out a deep sigh, feeling vulnerable. "I really like Jimmy, and I'm pretty sure he feels the same about me, but... I'm scared."

"What are you scared of, honey?" she asks, concern on her face.

"I mean..." I nod toward Ronny, who is snoring gently.

Aunt Debbie nods. "I understand. But he seemed to get along with Ronny. He's got a nice way about him, your friend. He knows your schedule with Ronny, right?"

"Yeah, I told him."

"So, *stop worrying*," she lectures.

"I know, but after how things ended with Mark..."

Aunt Debbie places a comforting hand on my shoulder. "Sweetie, you can't let your past dictate your future. You deserve to be happy, and I think Jimmy could be good for you."

I nod, letting her words sink in. She's right. Mark's betrayal won't define me. Even so, a part of me is hesitant, wary of opening myself up to potential heartbreak again.

Aunt Debbie gets up and kisses me on the forehead. "Come grab that stew when you're ready."

"I will," I say. I pick up my controller and headset and do the only thing left to do. Play *Pirates of Starcrest*.

Jimmy's favorite game, it appears.

I wonder what else I don't know about him.

CHAPTER 11
Atticus

"You need to choose a name for the app," I say. "It's a great idea, but it needs a name, gorgeous."

Charlie and I are in a deli close to GamesMade, amidst the city's hustle and bustle. It's our first official business meeting as unofficial partners, and we have much to discuss before Charlie has to clock in for her shift. Despite two cups of coffee and two sandwiches sitting in front of us, we've barely touched either.

Charlie slides her tablet over to me with an open PowerPoint presentation displayed. The words 'ACCESSAID' are on the first page in bold print.

"AccessAid?" I ask. I smile. "Dumb name."

Charlie's eyes widen like flying saucers and her brow furrows. I can tell I hurt her feelings, even though I was obviously kidding.

Before tears can spring from her eyes, I add, "Kidding! Kidding! Geesh." I laugh.

Thankfully, she hits my arm. "Jerk!" she says, but I can tell she's relieved. She narrows her eyes at me, but I can see she's fighting a smile.

"No, I like it. How'd you come up with it?" I ask.

"The idea came to me while I was on a train after Ronny's accident," she says. "Did you know trains and buses in New York have a ton of handicapped capabilities? Not just New York, but all over the country."

I take a bite of my sandwich. "Interesting," I say. "I can see you've done your research."

"I have," she says, sipping her coffee. "But it's more than transportation." She takes the tablet and slides to a new slide, slipping it back in front of me. "Look here." She points to a lengthy list of services displayed on the screen. "People lack the knowledge to access them."

As she picks up her sandwich and takes a big bite, I can't take my eyes off her. *What is it that makes her so captivating to me?*

I take another bite of my sandwich, chewing and glancing through the list of services. "That's an extensive list. I didn't realize all of this was available."

"You have no idea!" she says, laughing. "So, I'm on the train, right, when a wheelchair user boards, but there was no support available for him," she says. "I watched him trying to figure out where to put his chair, getting in people's way, and struggling the whole time. This app minimizes problems like that. I'm designing it to instruct people like him exactly where to enter the train with his wheelchair and where to go once inside. Hence, *AccessAid*."

"That's genius," I say. "I love it!" I feel a genuine rush of excitement. "Let's go over some nitty gritty. My head is buzzing with questions."

Charlie's face lights up with enthusiasm, and we dig into the specifics of her app. After we discussed all my questions, I pull out the preliminary contract my attorney friend had drawn up. Charlie peruses it, her eyes narrow as she asks,

"How do I know he didn't slant things in your favor?" I can tell she's teasing, but her voice has a *hint* of concern.

"Um, read it?" I tease.

She hits my arm again. "You'd better believe I'm going to read it," she says, snatching the contract from my hands. "I assume this is my copy for review?"

I nod. "Yes, take this and review it. Look, you don't have to use this attorney. This is just to finalize the details, and my friend owed me a favor. You should find your own attorney, and I'll pay for it."

"No, I can pay for the attorney, Jimmy," she says.

"Well, let's start with this and go from there," I suggest. I lean back in my chair. "I've been brainstorming about the apps for days. I have a few ideas."

As Charlie looks over the paperwork, I share my vision with her. "It's about the app itself. We could offer a model with basic features available for free and a subscription-based premium version with advanced functionalities."

Charlie's eyes light up with excitement. "Yes, I like that idea," she says, still glancing at the contract.

I continue. "That way, even people with little to no income can still enjoy a range of benefits from the products, increasing the number of downloads we have. That's important for the second phase of revenue generation. It also helps with sponsored content that benefits the disabled community."

Charlie looks up. "Sponsors! Yes, I wondered about that. So, how do we do it?"

"We register a joint LLC," I reply. "As Charlie and Jimmy, we won't make it past the lobby. But as a registered startup, our chances will fly through the roof. You can leave that part to me. But we have to do this together, and I need you to trust me."

"Well...therein lies the problem," she says, looking at me from the corner of her eye.

"What?" I ask. "You don't trust me?"

She sighs and looks down. "I *want* to trust you, and so far, you've given me no reason not to. I'll feel better once we have the contract in place."

"So, you *don't* trust me," I say, trying to get to the root of the problem.

"Ugh," Charlie says, exasperated. She looks me in the eye. "You're misunderstanding my words. I don't want to get into all that right now, Jimmy. That's not the purpose of this meeting."

My skin bristles because now I think I've given her a reason for pause. It's like she knows I'm keeping secrets. It pains me to think she's feeling like this.

"You don't want to get into all of what?" I ask, my frustration brewing. "Look, if we're going to work together, you need to be open with me."

"I'm willing to partner with you, Jimmy, but that doesn't mean I have to be an open book. What happened to taking it slow?" Her tone is defensive, and frankly, pissing me off.

"Don't be *difficult*. Charlie, I'm not expecting you to spill your innermost secrets. I just want to know why you don't trust me." I feel my jaw clench, a habit my dentist continuously warns me about. I'm getting aggravated, but I don't want to cause a scene in the middle of the deli.

Charlie looks at me, and I think she can read my frustration because she wraps up the rest of her sandwich and gets up.

"Where are you going?" I stand as well.

"I've got to run," she says, scrunching up her chip bag and picking up her leftovers. "I'm going to head into work early. I wouldn't want to be *difficult.*"

I can't believe what I'm hearing. "Whatever," I say.

"See ya," she says and heads out the door.

"Yeah, see ya," I say to nobody, because she's already gone.

"Did you miss me?" I whisper into the phone, hoping she says yes.

Her silence in response makes my heart sink. Then she sighs. "I just left you," she says, her voice a mixture of exhaustion and annoyance. "Like, *literally*. Just walked out the door."

"I know," I say. "I thought you might miss me, and I didn't want you to be distressed." I can hear her shuffling around as she gets into her car.

"I didn't miss you at all, actually," she says, her tone blunt. My comedic genius is going unnoticed.

"Aren't you just the flatterer?"

I might as well be performing a one-man show because my attempt at humor is met with silence again.

"Don't be mad at me," I say. I don't want her angry as she heads to work.

"I'm not mad at you, Jimmy. I'm just... tired." She sighs again.

"I hear you. Hey, I thought up a name for our LLC," I say, trying to change the subject and lighten her mood.

"Oh, yeah? What's that?"

"Charlie's Angels, LLC," I announce, proud of my clever idea.

Silence greets my suggestion.

"You there?" I ask. Maybe she doesn't like it?

"Yeah, I'm here," she replies after a long pause. "I...love it... but it's just *my* name. What about you?"

"What about me? The idea for the app came from your brilliant mind, not mine. It's only right the company bears your name. Plus, Charlie's Angels is a pretty cool name, don't you think?"

She chuckles at my words. "It is," she says. "Alright. I like it."

I feel a wave of relief wash over me at her approval. "So, you forgive me?" I ask, hoping to make amends.

"I don't know," she says. "You haven't apologized."

I take a deep breath and swallow my pride. "I'm sorry I called you difficult," I say, even though she can be *so* difficult. "I shouldn't have said that."

We spend the next fifteen minutes discussing the details of marketing our app and our plans for the future as I drive home and she goes to work. I'm impatient as I often am when she heads to that job. I need to remove her from there as soon as possible.

And if I want this to work out with Charlie, I need to think before I speak.

CHAPTER 12
Charlie

With Jimmy's help, it only takes three months for us to finish developing AccessAid and the accompanying marketing and distribution plan. It would have taken me years to accomplish alone, if at all.

Our late nights spent on my living room couch after my night shift and Jimmy's lunch hours at my kitchen table, or local eatery when we could, were all worth it in the end.

While I've been concentrating on ironing out the glitches and firming up the code of the application, Jimmy's been great at helping me with programming issues. He has many skills, but his greatest strength is managing funding, distribution, and marketing.

We finally finished the contract for Charlie's Angels, LLC. Jimmy insisted I hire an independent attorney to represent me. I appreciated his advice, but I couldn't afford it. Despite my protests, Jimmy paid for it himself.

I'm determined to succeed with this project and don't mind the extra hours. Since I'm home with Ronny during the day, I can sneak naps when he's sleeping in the afternoons. Jimmy, however, gets little sleep.

Tonight, while we were working after my shift, I could see the rings around his eyes. When I told him he looked tired, he snapped at me. "Well, if I wasn't doing *all* the work, then maybe I..." He trailed off, mumbling incoherently, and I couldn't make out the rest of what he was saying.

I could feel my face turning red, and he immediately started backpedaling. "Oh, Charlie, I'm sorry. I didn't mean that."

"Well, you said it for *some* reason," I blurted out. "I mean, I know the marketing is intense, but so are all the program tweaks I've been doing."

He just stared at his laptop, feigning concentration to avoid the subject.

"Jimmy!" I said. "We need to talk about this." *Was he kidding me?*

He looked at me then, his shoulders slumped as he admitted he was tired. His usually sharp eyes were bloodshot, and he had me worried.

He ran his hand through his hair like he always does when he's nervous—slow and methodical.

"I have a lot going on, Charlie. It's not just the app." Jimmy had glanced at me before quickly returning his gaze to his laptop.

I couldn't help but feel like he was holding back, but instead of addressing the issue, I let my sarcasm get the best of me. "Oh, do *you* have a lot going on, Jimmy? I wouldn't know anything about that."

"I wasn't insinuating that you don't have a lot going on, Charlie. There are just things you're unaware of."

"Like what?" I'd asked, hoping he would finally open up to me.

He closed his laptop and took both my hands in his. "Alright, look, it's my father. Well, my parents, actually—"

"Guys!" Aunt Debbie had come bounding through the door, interrupting Jimmy mid-sentence. Her face was white.

"What's wrong?" I'd asked, jumping up.

"It's my sink in my bathroom. I can't get it to shut off, and it's filling up. I'm afraid it's going to spill over." She turned to Jimmy. "Do you know anything about plumbing?"

He stood up. "I don't. But I can turn off the water from the main if you show me how to get to the basement."

The two of them left, and I couldn't help but feel frustrated. We never resumed the conversation about Jimmy's parents, leaving me with even more questions. After coming upstairs wet, Jimmy decided to go home. It was getting late, anyway, so he kissed me good night and left.

Aunt Debbie said she would call the plumber first thing in the morning and went back home.

So, here I sit, leaning back on my couch, wondering what Jimmy is holding back and why.

I pick up my phone and stare at it.

CHAPTER 13
Atticus

I step out of Charlie's house, my heart racing and my shirt clinging to my back, drenched in sweat. It feels like I narrowly escaped a firing squad. Sitting in my car for a moment, I try to get my thoughts together.

I know it might sound dramatic, but my heart is pounding in my chest, and I'm gulping down fresh air through the window as if my life depended on it. Leaning against the steering wheel, I struggle to catch my breath. I loosen my shirt collar and draw in more air.

I peel away from the curb, nearly side-swiping a parked car. *Get it together, Atticus!*

Tonight, I had tried to spill the truth to Charlie. It was on the tip of my tongue, ready to pour out of me. But Aunt Debbie's timely disaster saved me. I say 'timely' because I have no idea what I was thinking in there. Telling the truth now could jeopardize the app's development *and* our partnership. And the worst outcome of all would be losing Charlie's affection. *Someone needs to duct-tape my mouth shut.*

I want to come clean with Charlie, but she can be unpredictable. She's also incredibly sensitive and has mentioned her trust issues countless times. Trust means everything to her. What will happen when she finds out I'm not the person I claim to be? That's a big lie to overcome.

I'm not even a block away when my phone rings. I glance at the caller ID, and it's Charlie.

Oh, no!

Normally, I would jump at the chance to answer her call, but tonight, I'm filled with apprehension. I know she's going to want to continue our conversation. I can feel it.

I let the phone ring, staring at it, trying to decide whether to answer. Then it stops ringing, probably heading to voicemail. I pull over to the curb, the engine still running, and stare at my phone.

Everything is such a mess.

CHAPTER 14
Charlie

"Voicemail. Seriously?" I mutter to my phone, looking for sympathy.

When my phone doesn't respond, I resort to talking out loud to myself. "Maybe he just can't answer because he's driving. Yes, I'm sure he'll call me right back."

The evening was so strange. At first, Jimmy looked like he had lost his best friend, and then he snapped at me, basically calling me a slacker. Just when it seemed he was about to share a big secret about his family, Aunt Debbie's plumbing went haywire. This day just keeps getting stranger and stranger.

Now, it seems that Jimmy is avoiding me. I don't want to appear needy, but...

I dial his number again. Three rings. Four rings. "Come on, Jimmy, what are you doing?"

"Hey," he answers. *Could he sound any more nonchalant?*

"Hey," I say back. "You home yet?"

"Yeah, just pulling up."

"Okay, um, when do you want to finish things up?" I don't just want to blurt out all my questions like I'm desperate.

He sits on the other end, and there's dead silence. Was the question that difficult? I say nothing, waiting for him to respond.

"Tomorrow?" he says, finally. "Lunchtime, I guess?" *He guesses?* My neck hairs bristle.

"Oh, yeah, um, lunch tomorrow doesn't work for me," I lie. I'm not looking to force the guy to hang out with me.

Silence. He just sits on the other end. I can hear him breathing, but he's saying nothing.

"Hello?" I ask. "Did you hear me?"

"Yeah, I heard you," he says, his tone icy.

"So...after work tomorrow, then?" I say, tired of waiting for him to answer. He's annoyed that I don't want to meet for lunch, but I need time to think. Besides, he's upsetting me, and I need to cool off.

"Not sure," he responds. "I might have something. I'll have to see if it *works for me.*"

Touché. Before I can speak, he says, "I'll let you know. I've got to get to bed."

"Um...okay," I say. I want to ask a million questions, but...

"Okay," he says before I can finish, and he ends the call just like that.

I sit and stare at my phone for a moment. My stomach hurts, like it does when I'm nervous. Instead of calling Jimmy back, I hurl my phone across the couch.

I try pushing thoughts of Jimmy from my mind as I head into the bathroom to get ready for bed. Yawning, I look in the mirror, hoping I can sleep.

I'll have to just close my eyes and figure things out with Jimmy tomorrow.

CHAPTER 15
Atticus

I don't know what game she's playing, but I don't have the time or the patience for it.

Lunch doesn't work for her? We've been working on the business daily, and she's got Ronny during the day, so why the sudden change? She's toying with me.

I rake my hands through my hair in frustration. I need some rest. I need a strategy to handle the worsening Charlie situation. I feel like I'm on the verge of losing her, and I know I'll regret it.

I'll figure it out tomorrow. My eyelids are begging me to stop overthinking and go to sleep.

The afternoon drags on, and by three o'clock, I decide to take a break. On my way to the men's room, thoughts of Charlie fill my mind. It's funny how every men's room reminds me of her. Only Charlie and I would get that joke. It's our little secret.

I glance at my phone. I should call Charlie and try to smooth things over.

No, I think it's best to give her some space. She must need it if she turned down the chance to see me today.

Looking at my reflection in the restroom mirror, I wonder why I expressed myself in such a way earlier. Charlie works just as hard as I do, if not harder. I guess I'm just feeling overwhelmed. She's been urging me to ease back on my day job, and she's probably right. I shouldn't take my frustrations out on her.

Stepping into a stall, I lock the door and call Archie, the calm in my life's storm.

"You need another suit?" Archie laughs into the phone.

"No, not this time," I say, expecting him to detect something off in my tone.

"Yo, what's wrong?" he says, right on cue. "You sound terrible."

"I'm not getting much sleep."

"Okay, is that why you called? To tell me you're not sleeping?"

I sigh. "No, it's Charlie." I sigh again.

"Ooooh, I should've figured. Trouble in app-land?"

"Hilarious," I say. "Yes, there's trouble."

"Is that why you're not sleeping?" I hear his seat belt warning dinging in the background.

"Where are you going?" I ask. Then I scold him. "And put on your seatbelt." Archie loves to break rules.

He bursts into laughter. "I'm driving to a meeting, and yes, sir." He laughs again. I hear a click, and the dinging stops.

I peek under the stall to ensure no one is nearby. Then I share with Archie that I almost revealed the truth to Charlie but got interrupted midway through my confession. "What should I do?" I ask, eagerly waiting for Archie's words of wisdom.

"I don't know, man," he says. *What? Archie always knows.*

"Get outta the way, pal!" Archie yells. "Sorry, Att, these people in Albany drive like they're from the city. *Geesh*."

"I don't know if I should tell her," I say. "What if she freaks out?"

"Hold on," Archie says. "Dude! You drive like an old lady!"

I wait patiently for Archie to finish his road rage.

"Sorry, Att, now what's the question?"

I want to reach through the phone and strangle him. "Charlie!" I yell. "Should I tell her the truth or not?"

I hear someone enter the restroom. I'm tucked in a stall and remain quiet, hoping they didn't hear me yelling.

"Oh, yeah," Archie remembers. "Charlie! Yeah, sure, tell her the truth. I mean, she's going to find out anyway, right?"

I pause, waiting for the person in the room with me to leave. I hear the door open and close again.

"You there, dude?" Archie asks.

"Yeah, yeah, sorry. I'm worried Charlie may not want to work on the app with me anymore if I tell her now."

"So, this is a business decision?" Archie scoffs like I'm ridiculous.

"No. I mean, yes, but not like *that*." I know I'm stumbling over my words, but it's a complicated situation. It's not for selfish reasons that I'm worried about the app. I'm more concerned that if we don't finish it, Ronny won't be able to benefit from it.

"Yes, but you're saying it's not like that, but not like what? Is this about your parents? Would it ruin your plans to regain your parents' approval?"

He has a point. It's a contributing factor, but not the main one.

"Sure, that would suck. You know I want to get back to my family, but that's not the main reason. I don't want her mad at me. Plus, her brother needs this app, and so do lots of other people." I pause. "Truth is, I'm mostly scared she's going to break it off with me when she finds out."

"Listen, Atticus, only you can know what to do. If it were me, I'd tell her. Besides, I suck at keeping secrets." He laughs. I wish I could find humor in *any of this*.

I know he's right, though, about everything. It's *my* decision, and I *should* tell Charlie. But maybe not just yet? We can finish the app first, and then I'll sit down and tell her what happened with my parents and why I couldn't tell her my real identity.

I'm sure once I explain everything, she'll *completely* understand.

CHAPTER 16
Charlie

I guess Jimmy worked things out because he called me as I was getting ready to leave work, asking if he could come over. I readily agreed. We need to resolve this ridiculous tension between us, and I'm eager for things to return to the way they were.

When I pull up to my house, I see Jimmy waiting in his car out front. I walk over to his window, and he rolls it down. "Get in," he says. At first, I bristle at his bossiness, but the big smile on his face instantly puts me at ease.

I smile back, looking around. "Where are we going at this hour?" I ask, walking around to the passenger side and settling into his car.

"I thought we'd take a break. Let's go to the '76 Diner in Latham for coffee. They've got a killer cherry pie that I've been craving."

"Sounds good to me," I say, relieved that he doesn't intend to work on the app tonight. I think we need a break. We can revisit it tomorrow with fresh eyes after we've cleared the air. I text Aunt Debbie quickly to let her know I'll be home a little later than usual, as I'm going out with Jimmy. She texts back to have fun.

We're both quiet on the ride to the diner. It takes about fifteen minutes to get there from my house. Jimmy reaches over and takes my hand as he drives, his warm touch reassuring me we can work things out. He smiles his distinctive smile, his dimple on full display, and I smile back, squeezing his hand.

As we pull into the parking lot, a Mercedes pulls in front of us, even though we have the right of way. Jimmy beeps his horn. "Jerk!" he says under his breath.

"Rich jackass!" I say in agreement.

I smile at Jimmy, but I'm met with a conflicted look. His furrowed brow and deep scowl are anything but a sign of unity.

After he parks the car, he turns to me. "What do you have against rich people?"

"I know. I'm sorry. I forgot you have rich friends. I just can't stand people who think they're entitled just because they have money."

"I never thought of you as prejudiced," he says.

"Prejudiced? I'm not prejudiced!" I feel unfairly attacked.

"Apparently, you don't know the meaning of the word," Jimmy says. "It comes from two words: 'pre' and 'judge.' It's when you pre-judge someone based on class, race, or whatever. So, yes, Charlene, you hold prejudiced views! There. Is that better?"

Upon hearing him call me Charlene, white-hot stars flash in front of my eyes. The last time he said my full name, it melted my heart. Now, it's lost its charm.

"You know what?" I say. My patience is gone. "I don't feel like coffee. Just take me home." I cross my arms and turn my head toward the passenger window to avoid eye contact. The lesson on the meaning of prejudice felt condescending, and calling me Charlene made me feel like a child.

With a sigh, Jimmy starts the car but doesn't move. Then, he turns the car back off.

"What are you doing?" I ask.

"I'm going in for coffee. If you want to sit here, you can, but I'd really like it if you'd join me."

He gets out of the car and closes his door. I remain seated, refusing to be controlled by his actions.

But, unwilling to give up, Jimmy walks around to my side, opens my door, and extends his hand to me. "Please join me for coffee, Charlie. I'm sorry I got mad."

With reluctance, I relent. "Fine," I say with more than a hint of frustration. "But I can get out on my own, thank you."

Once they seat us in the diner, the waitress brings us menus. Jimmy orders coffee, and I do the same.

When the waitress walks away, Jimmy locks his eyes on me. I can feel his gaze, but I have mine on the menu.

"Can you look at me?" he asks softly.

I sigh and finally meet his eyes across the booth. His dimple twitches as he offers an apologetic smile.

"I'm sorry," he says.

I sigh. "Yeah, me, too," I say. "I don't like rich people, but I honestly don't mean any offense to your friends."

"So, why don't you like rich people?" he asks.

The waitress comes back with two cups and a pot of coffee. I'm relieved for the break as she pours the coffee because I'm unsure how to respond. Mark, with his indifference, is the reason behind my aversion to wealthy people, particularly wealthy men.

When she finishes and leaves, I say, "My ex had a lot of money."

"Yeah, and?" he asks, inquiring further.

I share the painful truth. "Well, when Ronny had his accident, and I had to quit my job, instead of offering to help with hiring an aid so I *didn't* have to quit, he broke up with me because he said my priorities were all wrong."

Jimmy almost spits his coffee on the table. He struggles, coughs, and wipes his mouth. "Are you kidding me?"

"No, I'm not kidding you. Mark came from a wealthy family, and he had a killer business, but apparently, I wasn't worth the cost of an aid."

Shocked by my revelation, Jimmy asks, "How long did you date this bozo?"

I sigh, reflecting on the five-year relationship I now see with newfound clarity. "Five years."

Jimmy's response is a simple "Wow." The waitress returns to take our orders as a layer of understanding mends the rift between us.

"Cherry pie for me with gobs of whipped cream, please," he tells the waitress. Then he looks at me. "What are you having, gorgeous?"

"I'll have the same. I hear it's to die for."

CHAPTER 17
Atticus

I sip my coffee, eagerly awaiting the cherry pie, and glance at Charlie on the other side of the booth. She's seated across from me, a woman who clearly despises wealthy people, sitting with a guy from a family made of money. *Great!*

"Let me ask you something," I begin.

Charlie pours cream into her coffee until it's a pale shade. I can't help but grimace. Black coffee is the only way to drink it.

I take a sip of mine and continue. "If you discovered that my family had billions of dollars, would you hate me, too?"

She laughs softly, her eyes dancing with amusement. "Billions of dollars? That's funny." She stirs her milky drink and takes another sip.

I won't relent. "No, seriously, I just want to know. If I were wealthy, would you still desire me?"

She leans forward and answers with a playful grin. "That depends," she says. "If you weren't selfish with it, and your family wasn't a bunch of rich snobs, then I *might* give you a shot." She shrugs casually, her eyes twinkling.

"Rich snobs, eh?" I laugh a nervous laugh. "You *really* don't like wealthy people, do you?"

She glances toward the approaching waitress carrying our coveted pie. "No, but the waitress is bringing our pie, so let's change the subject. I don't want the thought of rich people spoiling my appetite for this famous dessert."

The pie arrives, but to my disappointment, I'm unable to enjoy it. All I can think about are Charlie's words. It's not just about her being upset that I didn't reveal the truth immediately. It's the looming prospect that she'll despise me for my billionaire status. Not millionaire but *billionaire*, heir to an old fortune accumulated through generations, all destined for me upon my return to the family.

I'm glad that Charlie's enjoying her pie because my appetite has all but vanished.

CHAPTER 18
Charlie

When the app was finally ready to hit the market, Jimmy and I created a business proposal for potential investors, laying the groundwork for Charlie's Angels, LLC.

Jimmy kept his word regarding business development for our AccessAid application and somehow secured the funding to take it to market. Yet, his silence on the source of this funding has made me anxious. As partners, I have a right to know.

I remember one afternoon when my curiosity got the best of me. We were sitting at my kitchen table, scrutinizing company details. Ronny was out with his aid, and Aunt Debbie was at work, providing us with the solitude needed for our discussion.

"So, tell me about the funding," I'd said, my tone more serious than usual.

His response, rather than straightforward, was simply, "You know, Charlie, you're not the only one with a magic wand." He was trying to be funny, but it felt like a stall tactic to me.

"No, really, Jimmy, I'm your partner," I'd persisted. "Please tell me the source of our funding."

Jimmy had leaned back in his chair, his hands behind his head, and a smile played on his lips. "Has anyone ever told you how beautiful you are when you're inquisitive?"

"Jimmy!" I'd said, my patience thin. "I'm serious."

"It's not a secret," he'd assured me. "I have a friend with the means, and he's the one who generously loaned it to us." He stood from the table and walked to the cupboard, looking for glasses. "I assure you, it's all legitimate. Care for a drink?" he'd asked, not bothering to turn around.

"No, thank you," I said. "But I need to review the paperwork. Don't I have to sign something?"

Jimmy had paused for a moment with his back turned to me as he poured iced tea into his glass, his face concealed. "Well, the thing is," he'd begun, "it's not exactly like that. It's more a personal loan between friends."

I'd furrowed my brow, trying to comprehend. "But you mentioned he loaned it to 'us,' meaning you and me, meaning the LLC, right?"

He'd returned to his seat and sipped his tea. "No," he'd said. "I mean, yes, he loaned it for the business, but it was just a handshake. There's no paperwork involved."

"That's a substantial amount of money to exchange on a mere handshake," I'd remarked with concern, uneasy about the lack of paperwork. "What friend? Why didn't you just go to a bank? I would have gone with you." My curiosity was taking over.

Jimmy's gaze had drifted away from mine, focusing on his glass, and he'd hesitated before answering. "My best friend from childhood," he'd said, and his evasive manner had left me feeling even more uneasy. "I tried the bank, but they said we couldn't get a loan."

His reluctance to meet my eyes fueled my growing irritation. "And what's this friend's name?" I'd asked, continuing my interrogation.

Once more, a pause had hung in the air, and I hadn't been able to shake the feeling that something wasn't right. Jimmy's nervousness had become apparent, but he'd managed a laugh as he responded, "You're quite the interrogator, aren't you? His name is Archie, alright?"

Dissatisfied, I didn't back down but continued my inquiry. "I'd like to meet this Archie. Does he have a last name?"

"Archie Bainsfield," he'd replied.

"Well, then," I'd stated firmly."I'd like to meet Archie Bainsfield, if that's alright?"

"Yeah, sure, no problem," he'd said, turning around, but I got the distinct feeling that it *was* a problem for Jimmy if the look on his face and the slight perspiration on his brow were any indication.

Jimmy worked hand-in-hand with Ronny to spread the word around the disabled community to drum up interest in the new app. After months of hard work, the app was ready for launch.

Ronny, being the social media guru that he was, had been actively promoting the app on various social media groups and forums that catered to people with debilitating injuries. He even had a caseworker who was helping him bring awareness of the app's launch to thousands of other caseworkers across the country.

"Thanks for making me feel like a part of this," Ronny said one night.

"A part of it?" I'd said to him, taken aback. "Ronny, you *are* it. Without you, there would be no app."

So here we are, finally, gathered in my kitchen, waiting for the big moment. The app is about to launch live. The air is tense with anticipation as Jimmy, Ronny, Aunt Debbie, and I sit around the table. My palms are sweaty, and my heart is pounding. Jimmy can't sit still, and Ronny is fidgeting with his wheelchair like he sometimes does when he's nervous.

Aunt Debbie is the only calm one. "Relax, you guys," she laughs. "I've been praying about this, and I know it's going to be a tremendous success!"

"You bet it is," Jimmy agreed. "Charlie here is a genius, and Ronny had thousands of connections, so how could we fail?"

"And you did all the marketing," I say to Jimmy, "with help from Archie. Whoever *he* is."

Despite my requests to meet Archie, Jimmy always has an excuse ready. Archie was unwell the first time. Then his car broke down. I think his dog was sick or something the last time. It all sounded like nonsense to me, but I brushed it aside to focus on the completion of the app.

"You'll meet him," Jimmy assures me. "Stop worrying. He really does exist. I promise."

Ronny waves his arms, bringing us back to the present. "Alright, you guys, enough about Archie. We're about to go live, and this app will be life-changing for many. So, let's focus on that, okay?"

"You're right," I say. The app is our focus now, and we can't let anything distract us from it.

Aunt Debbie has brewed coffee, and the smell fills the room as she pours a cup for each of us. Fresh cinnamon rolls are baking in the oven, and a variety of fresh fruit is on a platter with a cream cheese dip in the middle.

"Want a little coffee with your cow?" Jimmy teases, handing me the cream, but I brush him off.

"Focus, Jimmy. We're about to go live!"

Jimmy's finger hovers over the trackpad. "Are you guys ready?"

"As ready as I'll ever be," I say.

"Fire away, boss!" Ronny shouts.

"Here we go!" Jimmy nervously clicks the refresh button on the app's download page. We all hold our breath as the progress wheel spins, waiting for the moment of truth.

Then, suddenly, the numbers appear on the screen.

DOWNLOADS: 1,015

Jimmy's eyes widen, and a broad grin stretches across his face. He leans back in his chair, raises his arms, and lets out a triumphant whoop, which prompts us all to follow suit. In less than a minute, we had a thousand downloads. It's like a dream come true.

Ronny whoops the loudest. "I knew we had something special, Jimmy," he says, holding his arm out to give Jimmy a fist bump. Then he looks at me. "Sia, you're a genius."

Jimmy joins in my praises. "Yeah, she is! All those sleepless nights and hours of coding have paid off!" I feel proud of my accomplishment, and I bask in the praise.

Aunt Debbie walks over and hugs me, and I squeeze her back tight. "You did it, kiddo," she says, her smile broad.

Jimmy returns his attention to the laptop screen, where the download count continues to climb.

DOWNLOADS: 2,906

"Almost three thousand," Jimmy announces.

DOWNLOADS: 5,200

"Over five thousand!" he yells. The atmosphere is electric, and we are all holding our breath.

The count continues to climb. Jimmy can barely contain

himself. He gets up from his chair, comes over to me, and says, "Stand up, will you, Charlie?"

I stand, and he grabs me around the waist and lifts me off the ground. "We did it!" he yells, swinging me around. "*You* did it!"

Everyone laughs as he sets me back on the floor. I expect him to let go of me, but he keeps his arms around my waist. When I look at him, he says, "You *are* a genius, Charlene Welsh. A total genius."

I push him away. "Get back there and refresh the screen. We've got downloads to watch!"

As the day draws to a close, AccessAid has over *thirty thousand downloads*. And within a month, that number skyrockets to half a million.

Six months after becoming an official company and over four million downloads later, we have a team of ten people and five more apps. But I've yet to meet the mysterious Archie. He's always unavailable, and I've given up asking about meeting him.

Despite the happiness I've found with Jimmy, there's always an invisible barrier between us. He carries secrets, and I'm eager to uncover them, but I'm unsure how to do it.

My heart is embracing this incredible, handsome man, but there's a lingering sense that I haven't truly glimpsed his inner self. Every time I try to dig deeper, I'm met with resistance, so I hold back, hoping he'll open up to me in his own time. But, as days turn into weeks and weeks into months, I wonder if he'll ever let me in.

CHAPTER 19
Atticus

I pace anxiously as I wait for Archie's arrival. I called him an hour ago. *Where could he be?*

The buzzer rings, and I race to the door. When I swing it open, Archie saunters in with his usual laid-back demeanor.

"Archie! Where have you been? I called you an hour ago!" My words tumble out in a frantic rush.

"Dude, relax! What's going on?"

I lead him to the living room, where my marred coffee table and worn-out furniture remind me of just how far removed I am from my old life. I put my feet up and take a deep breath, reminding myself I now have the means to replace this furniture. I just need to do it.

"Grab a beer if you'd like," I say, and he goes to the kitchen and grabs two, handing me one before sitting in the chair across from me.

"I'm losing my mind," I say. "I'm literally losing my mind."

"Oh, Att, dude, just tell her," Archie says, his eyes fixed on mine.

I'm taken aback. "How did you know what I was going to say?" I ask.

Archie lets out a loud laugh and takes a sip from his beer. All he says is, "Dude!"

"Yeah, yeah, I know," I say, sighing. "I've been beating this drum for months. I'm sorry, Archie." I slump my shoulders, the weight of my deceit bearing down on me. "It's just gotten to a point where I can't take it anymore."

"Listen, Att, I get it," he says emphatically. "It's tough, but keeping this secret is eating you alive. Charlie deserves to know the truth. She's in love with you, and with good reason. You're a cool dude. She's going to love you no matter what your name is." He leans over and hits my arm playfully. "Right, Jimmy?"

I groan, but a small smile tugs at the corners of my mouth. "You're right. You've been right all along. I should have told Charlie as soon as we launched, but things were going so well, I didn't want to spoil it. Every day that goes by, it just seems harder."

"You've got this, buddy. She won't leave you."

"That's right," I say, feigning renewed courage. "Because you say so."

Archie laughs. He's used to my weird humor. "Besides, dude, I'm sick of hearing about it, and I'd really like to meet her someday."

Sitting with Archie, I decide. I'm going to tell Charlie the truth at dinner on Friday. I had invited her to the all-you-can-eat-sushi bar in Albany that she loves. It's been so much easier since Charlie quit her night job and hired help for Ronny. I hope she'll still love me when she discovers the truth.

CHAPTER 20
Charlie

I stare at my phone, waiting for Jimmy to pick up. It's early in the morning, but I couldn't wait any longer to hear his voice. Finally, after just the second ring, he answers.

"Hey there, gorgeous," he says, using his favorite nickname for me. "You're up early."

I grin from ear to ear as I hear his voice. Despite my constant self-doubt about my appearance, Jimmy makes me feel like the most beautiful woman on earth.

We spent most of the last nine months building Charlie's Angels, LLC. Our kisses are passionate, *more than passionate*, but I yearn for a deeper emotional connection. Jimmy's my best friend, and there is no one I trust more. But there's still a barrier between us I can't seem to break through.

With my financial situation improving, I can now afford proper care for Ronny. And with that burden lifted, I am more inclined to give Jimmy a fair chance. Now, if he'll just give *me* a chance.

"What are you doing tonight?" I ask, trying to hide the excitement in my voice.

"I was going to call you with the same question." He chuckles. "It's Friday night. I'm not planning to work late, so let's get dinner."

He and his work. I can't help but ask him again. "I don't understand why you insist on staying at GGBuff. You know you make way more money now with the business than you'll ever make there, right?"

"What can I say? I enjoy creating video games, and my colleagues are fun," he says, dismissing my concerns. "I love it."

"Right," I say, still unconvinced. "Anyway, I know you've been working extra hard recently, so I'd like to treat you tonight."

"Oooh, nice. Your treat?" Jimmy asks, sounding amused.

"I *am* rolling in the dough now," I say, laughing.

Jimmy laughs. "Yeah, but I bet you miss washing those men's rooms. How are you supposed to meet that 'cute guy' now?"

"Already met him, so I'm all set." I laugh. "Let's go to that Mexican place up on Central Avenue. Marguerita City? They serve big Marguerita towers they set on your table. Think you can get out early? We could ride share home if we get drunk."

He laughs. "I'll finish this project, upload it to the boss, and Bob's your uncle."

"Goofball," I mutter under my breath, laughing. "But great. Meet me there at six. I've got a few errands to run."

I spend the rest of my day daydreaming about my date with Jimmy. I pick out a clingy burgundy dress for the date and pair it with my favorite black boots. I want his eyes to pop when he sees me.

When I arrive at Marguerita City fifteen minutes early, I find Jimmy already seated and poring through the menu. The Marguerita tower is already on the table, and two sugar-rimmed glasses await my arrival.

ORDINARY MR. BILLIONAIRE

He looks *stunning* in his black suit and white shirt, and my heart skips a beat. Two young women sitting at a table nearby are stealing glances at him, probably thinking he's alone. But as I approach him, he stands and gives me a warm hug. He kisses my lips, more than a peck, and I catch a whiff of his cologne, feeling myself getting lost in the moment. What it is about that cologne? It casts some kind of magic spell that makes my toes curl.

"Look at you!" He takes my hands in his and leans back a bit, looking me up and down. "Gorgeous!!!" He whistles, then gives me a look that takes my breath away. I'm sure if I could read his mind, I'd blush.

I squeak out a "Thanks," blushing anyway, and try to catch my breath. When I glance at the two young women who had been gawking at Jimmy, they quickly look away. I smile.

"This is a nice place. Thanks for the invite." Jimmy pulls out my chair, and I sit down.

"Ready for your Marguerita?" Jimmy asks, picking up a glass.

"Sure as night follows day," I say, smiling.

"Sure as a squirrel gathers nuts," he says back, smirking like somehow he'd one-upped me.

He looks especially handsome tonight. Scratch that — he looks downright *hot*. I stare at his jawline, wanting to nibble it. That bit of stubble always turns me on.

"You know," he says, seeming to enjoy his drink, the rim of his glass coated in a delicate layer of sugar. He pauses, taking another sip.

"I know?" I ask, sipping mine as well. The tart flavor leaves a zingy and refreshing sensation on my palate.

He places his glass back on the table. "You know, you don't talk about your parents much. Aunt Debbie is awesome, but is she your mother's or your father's sister?"

"She's my father's sister," I say. I never talk about my

parents, and for good reason. But Jimmy has a way of making me feel at ease.

"So, tell me about them. I know they left after Ronny's accident, but what do they do in Mexico?" he asks, curious.

I take another sip of my drink, feeling the icy deliciousness spread warmth throughout my body. I place my glass on the table. "My parents are semi-retired. Mom sells stuff online, and Dad does consulting work."

"Oh," he says.

"They're not on my good list right now," I say.

He looks at me, his eyebrow arches. "Because of Ronny?"

"Because I just don't understand why they don't help more and never come back to visit. They've got two kids here and my father's sister, yet they just lounge around in Mexico. I'm just disgusted with them, to be honest."

"Do they know about the app and how successful their daughter has become?" Jimmy asks.

"I don't imagine they do," I reply. "I asked Aunt Debbie not to mention it to them, but I'm guessing she may have. Frankly, I don't much care."

I nod in his direction. "What about you? You're not very chatty about your folks either," I say, hoping to shift the attention away from my family drama.

Jimmy clears his throat, and his eyes dart nervously around the menu, not seeming too eager to discuss his parents.

"This is delicious," I say as I place my glass on the table. I feel bad for asking him after seeing the way he's reacting.

"I, uh, so..." Jimmy begins, his voice trailing off as he picks up his water glass and takes a big chug.

"Are you okay?" I ask. I didn't mean to freak him out, but at some point, he just needs to tell me about them.

"Yeah, I...uh..." He takes another sip of water, finishing the glass.

"Geesh, Jimmy, spit it out." I don't want to be rude, but

he's sputtering like a defective sprinkler. It floods my mind with countless scenarios, causing my skin to prickle with anticipation. *What can't he tell me?*

He puts down his glass, but he doesn't meet my eyes. "It's difficult for me, Charlie. I've wanted to talk to you about my parents, and I will, I promise. But right now..." He pauses, obviously flustered. I say nothing and wait for him to finish.

"Why don't we just enjoy our dinner, and we'll talk about them later? Is that alright?" Jimmy suggests.

I nod, but inside, I feel a deep disappointment. I had hoped that this would be the moment Jimmy would finally open up to me, but it seems he's not ready yet.

Looking at him, I wonder what he's hiding. Is his family the mafia? He won't even let me meet the mysterious "Archie" who supposedly funded our start-up. What if it's his mafia family instead? Crazy thoughts swirl through my mind, but I know I need to be patient. I can't force him to open up to me, and I can't let my curiosity consume me.

I take another sip of my drink, trying to shake off the disappointment. I glance at Jimmy, wishing I could read his mind. But for now, I can only wait and hope that someday he'll trust me enough to share his secrets with me.

He smiles at me, raising his glass and taking a sip.

Since he won't tell his secrets, I think I'll just lick the sugar on the rim of my glass and drive him a little crazy.

CHAPTER 21
Atticus

The guilt is killing me.

It's like a relentless punch, constantly poking at my conscience with reminders of my shortcomings and acts of betrayal. I had promised myself that I would tell Charlie everything about my family, my past, and the secrets that threaten to consume me on Friday. But when the perfect opportunity presented itself, my courage abandoned me, leaving me stuttering and stalling. *Again.*

Despite the best intentions, I couldn't bring myself to ruin our perfect evening, but my choice to remain silent had repercussions. Charlie was distant and standoffish over the weekend, and although I didn't see her much, I could feel the suspicion and distrust radiating from her.

Moving into my new place on the outskirts of Albany provided a pleasant distraction. Archie helped me move, but the thoughts of Charlie and the mess I've made kept me up, leaving me exhausted.

It's Monday morning now, and as I sit at my desk at

GGBuff, I take out my laptop for a quick peek at the stats on our new apps. The graphs on my screen show that the new apps we've created are doing well, but even the success of our business doesn't ease my troubled mind.

My father had given me a year to create a business that could gross a hundred thousand. Charlie and I accomplished that in half that time. I can finally go home now that I've met all my father's requirements. But even that seems impossible with Charlie in my life.

The idea of introducing her to my family and the extravagant lifestyle they live makes my stomach churn. I know she'll despise it, and I can't bear the thought of losing her because of it. Even worse, I can't muster the courage to pick up the phone and share my success with my parents. The idea of going back home no longer appeals to me.

At home after work, I appreciate my new "digs," as Archie likes to call my new place. My spacious living room pops with a sleek, modern vibe thanks to its minimalist design and up-to-date features. I'm thrilled about decorating it, especially with Charlie's offer to help.

I glance at the mantel above the fireplace, adorned with a single photograph of my parent and me. It's a framed image I had printed from my Instagram, taken at the Fall Fundraiser two years ago. I bought a rich wooden frame and placed it intentionally where I could see it every day. It's a comforting sight, a reminder of where I come from. I'll be glad when I don't have to think about hiding it when Charlie comes over.

Walking around the space, my imagination runs wild with decorating possibilities. With some effort, I could spruce this place up and make it feel homey. A comfy couch and a simple rug could do wonders in making the living room feel even cozier.

The guilt I've been harboring intensifies. It's become a constant companion, gnawing at my insides like an ulcer. The need to confess feels heavy, like an anchor. But it's not as simple as it sounds. Charlie harbors a deep-seated aversion towards the wealthy because her greedy ex burned her. How will she react when she discovers that I'm the sole heir to a billionaire's fortune? The truth is far from straightforward.

And then there's the part where my family banished me for being a complete slacker. It's all too much to bear.

Atticus Winslow is a wreck, and Jimmy Winslow — the man she's known for the better part of nine months — feels like nothing but a mirage in a tangled web of deception and self-doubt.

As I get ready for bed, I'm flooded with a rush of anxiety. I'm struggling to control my actions, as an unwavering need for honesty drives them more and more. I pick up my phone and punch in Charlie's number, knowing I can't postpone this any longer.

"Hello?" Her voice sounds sleepy, and I realize I may have woken her.

"Hey," I reply, guilt lacing my voice.

Charlie pauses. "What's wrong? It's late. Is everything alright?"

"Yeah, everything is... fine. Listen, I was hoping to talk to you. Are you busy right now?" I can't stand the thought of keeping this secret any longer.

"Um, I was just dozing off, but I'm never too busy to talk to you, Jimmy. What's the matter?" Hearing her say my name feels like a painful twist of the knife, a constant reminder of the deceit.

"Jimmy?" she asks again, and I realize I've frozen up. "Hello?"

"Hey, sorry," I say, clearing my throat awkwardly. "I'm... um, distracted."

"Oh? What's on your mind?"

I can't tell Charlie the truth over the phone. I have to see her in person to gauge her expressions and clarify why I made the choices I did. She may not listen or forgive me, but in person, my odds are higher.

"No, it's late," I say, realizing it would be ridiculous to meet with her now. "Sorry, I'm just tired. What about tomorrow? Can we meet once I'm done with work? Say seven?"

"Is everything alright? You don't sound good."

"Yeah, yeah, everything's fine," I assure her. "I just have a lot on my plate right now. So, seven? My place? I'll make you dinner." I'll show her the picture of me and my parents and tell her *everything*.

"Dinner? Absolutely, I'd love to see the new place," she says, taking a brief pause. "I'm really looking forward to it."

After hanging up, I rush to the bathroom and empty my stomach into the toilet, overwhelmed by the impending revelation.

I drove to the office this morning with a heavy feeling in my chest. Anxiety knotted my stomach all morning, and not even the soothing hot shower could wash it away. Sleep had escaped me, and the thought of tonight filled me with dread. Tonight I tell Charlie everything.

Upon clearing security, I notice Chris, the chief of security, studying me with an unsettling intensity. His smirk doesn't quite hit the mark of sincerity. I shake my head and rush toward the elevators.

When I reach the seventh floor, the sinking feeling in the pit of my stomach returns. Every step I take toward my workstation feels like walking through a gauntlet of piercing stares from my colleagues. Is it mere paranoia, or are they watching me?

My fears heighten when I lock eyes with Phil, a colleague who typically greets me with a lighthearted joke each morning. This morning, he quickly ducks into his cubicle as if he's avoiding me. Turning a corner, I almost collide with the wall, but am saved by a firm hand.

"Watch where you're going, son." Jonathan's arm is strong for a man of his age. "What's troubling you, Jimmy?"

"Thank you," I mutter. "Sorry. I, uh, I'm not feeling too well this morning. I'll be more careful."

"You do that," Jonathan says, patting my shoulder and scrutinizing me. An inner voice scolds me for my evasive behavior with him, the only person who has linked me to my father. Tonight *has to be* the night I reveal the truth to Charlie. I can't live like this.

Heart pounding, I place my laptop bag at my desk and venture to the men's room to freshen up. Despite the office's cool air, sweat beads on my forehead and soaks my shirt. I splash cool water on my face and rinse my mouth, feeling a bit more refreshed and counting down the minutes until I can finally be honest with Charlie. Consequences be damned.

When I return to the bullpen, my heart nearly stops at the sight before me. A group of colleagues huddle around my desk, their expressions saying it all. Panic courses through me as I cautiously approach them, fearing the worst.

They turn to face me, and the truth is clear in their eyes. They all know. But I don't need to guess. Jonathan stands at the center of the huddle, holding a phone with a picture of my father and me, smiling at the camera. It's a photo taken five years ago at a charity event.

"I knew it," Jonathan says as he spots me approaching. "I knew you were Ray's son all along—"

I don't wait to hear the rest of what he has to say. My only thought is of Charlie. I grab my laptop and swiftly head for the exit, all eyes on me. It seems hopeless, but I must get to her before they tell her. The elevator door dings open, and I leap inside.

CHAPTER 22
Charlie

I've been feeling uneasy since talking to Jimmy last night. A pattern of odd behavior's been going on for weeks, possibly months, if I think about it. Lately, though, it'd been more obvious, as if Jimmy was hiding something from me, even though, I have to admit, he's always been guarded. I felt like he had a secret — something big — that he wanted to tell me but couldn't.

Despite my concerns, I try to focus on the positive aspects of our relationship. Jimmy is great with Ronny, my Aunt Debbie adores him, and he's a tech genius. Not to mention, he's smoking hot, a *great* kisser, and incredibly sweet to me.

But this secrecy is wearing on me. I know Jimmy had something important to tell me Friday night about his parents, but instead, he'd hemmed and hawed and promised to talk later. Maybe tonight is finally the "later" he'd promised, but I can't shake this feeling of dread.

As I make lunch for Ronny and me, my mind races with thoughts of Jimmy. Did I make a mistake getting involved with him? I'd promised myself I wouldn't get involved with anyone, but he was too hard to resist, and now, he occupies my thoughts excessively. It's probably not healthy.

I've spent the entire morning working, trying to distract myself, but it was hard to focus. The workload and time commitment of running my own company is overwhelming, especially since I've never done it before. But Ronny loves the business, too, and Jimmy's got him doing social media marketing and other clerical tasks. It's given him a renewed sense of purpose, and that makes me happy. Plus, he loves shopping online with the money he's earning.

When I bring Ronny his lunch, he smiles up at me from his laptop. "Thanks, sis!" he says, and I can't help but smile back. He's come a long way from that troubled kid he used to be. I don't want to say that his tragedy was a blessing, but Aunt Debbie always says that God works in mysterious ways.

As I walk back into the kitchen, my phone buzzes. It's Lindsay. My heart skips a beat — has something happened to Jimmy? When I answer, it's as if Lindsay has become a different person, her voice serious and formal. "I'm sorry to bother you like this, Charlie," Lindsay says. "But we need to have a conversation."

My skin prickles at her tone. She's usually so friendly and outgoing. "What's wrong? Is everything okay?" My heart is pounding out of my chest.

"I'm sorry for calling you out of the blue like this, but I have something important to tell you."

I stay quiet, taking a seat at the table, afraid I might collapse at any moment. When Lindsay notices my silence, she adds, "Charlie, are you there?"

"I am," I manage to say, although talking has become difficult. "Go ahead. You're scaring me."

Lindsay hesitates. "How well do you know Jimmy?" she asks, and my heart sinks.

Why is she asking me that? My face pulses, and I try to

catch my breath. "Look, Lindsay, I don't understand your question. Are you going to speak what's on your mind or not?"

"Well, it seems that while your friend has been going by the name 'Jimmy,' we now know his actual name is Atticus Winslow. His father is *Ray* Winslow, the famous software billionaire. Does the name ring a bell?"

As I listen to Lindsay's words, my heartbeat speeds up. Atticus Winslow? Ray Winslow's son? That makes little sense. My mind races, attempting to connect the bits of information I have about Jimmy's past. Why would he lie to me and pretend he's someone else? And why go through all the trouble of applying for jobs at GamesMade and GGBuff when he can easily land a job at his father's successful company?

An overwhelming sense of betrayal hits me as I struggle to make sense of it all. Jimmy has been deceiving me right from the beginning for months on end? No, that just can't be. It makes me question everything I thought I knew about him.

Something Lindsay says sticks in my mind. Jimmy/Atticus. *At-Jimmy*. And then it all falls into place. I remember our first meeting at GamesMade in the men's bathroom, and I immediately feel dumb.

"I'm sorry, Lindsay. I have to go." I hang up abruptly and begin pacing around the kitchen, trying to sort my thoughts. It can't be true. Lindsay has to be mistaken. I pull open my phone and search for Ray Winslow's son. My worst fears become a reality. There's Jimmy, arm in arm with Ray Winslow — his *father*!

Jimmy has been lying to me this entire time? The whole time I've known him? Months and months? But why go through the stress? Why is he working for competitors to his father's company? He's a *billionaire*, for crying out loud. Why work at all?

As I'm pacing, Ronny calls from the living room. "Hey,

Charlie, can you help me get up the stairs? I want to chill in my room." I walk out, and he sees my face. "You okay?" he asks. I look at him and want to share, but I can't right now. I'll tell him everything after I've spoken to Jimmy. "Yeah, I'm alright. Just tired, is all."

As I help Ronny onto the stairlift and into his room, I realize I can't keep this to myself. I have to speak to Jimmy and confront him about the lies. I need to understand his reasons for lying to me. Is he ashamed of his family's wealth, or is there some other reason at play?

I'm furious that he could deceive me for such a long time. And what about the money he had used to fund AccessAid and start Charlie's Angeles with me? Had it all been a handout from his billionaire father?

I'm seething with anger and betrayal, and these thoughts only stoke the flames that are already burning in my chest.

That explains why he won't tell me where he got the money. It explains why he never wants to talk about home or his family.

Tears well in my eyes as the weight of it all hits me.

Picking up my phone, I intend to call Jimmy for answers, but my hands shake so badly that I can barely hold my phone. Just as I pull his contact up, I hear a car screeching outside and then a car door slams shut, followed by heavy footsteps on the stairs to my porch. My heart is in my throat, and I'm hit by a wave of nausea and dizziness.

I steady myself against the wall, gritting my teeth as the wave passes. I head to the door, knowing it's *At-Jimmy* before I open it. He'd raced over here, desperate to get to me before Lindsay did.

As I open the door, his expression speaks volumes. His face has guilt written all over it. His eyes are wide, and his complexion is beet red. "Charlie," he says. His voice is shaky. "Please, I can explain."

My stomach churns. "Explain? You've got to be kidding

me, *Atticus*! What exactly would you like to explain?" He takes a step back, and I can feel the anger raging inside me. "Go on," I say through gritted teeth. "Tell me what you'd like to explain."

"Charlie, you don't understand," he pleads, desperation in his voice. "Please. Let me come inside so we can talk."

"Talk? That's hysterical!" I'm practically shrieking now. "You lied to me. No, wait, you didn't just lie. You made up a whole scenario and let me believe it. I opened up to you, let you into my life, brought you into my family, and you betrayed my trust, Jim — ATTICUS! Your damn name is Atticus. There is no Jimmy!"

I try to blink back the tears, but they keep coming, streaking down my cheeks in hot rivulets. I bite my lower lip, trying to hold back the sobs that threaten to escape.

He tries to come close, to hold me, but I push him away. He stumbles back against the railing on my front porch. "Don't you dare touch me! Was this a joke to you? Please, just tell me the truth for once, Jimmy!" My voice trembles, and I cover my mouth to prevent a sob from escaping.

He looks down the street and back at me, his eyes full of desperation. "Can we please go inside? *Please*? I'll tell you everything. I promise."

Despite not wanting him in my home, I need to hear what he has to say. I also don't want to continue this spectacle on my porch. I silently turn and head back into the house. I hear his footsteps behind me as I head toward the couch.

Ronny's up in his room, so I lower myself to the couch and motion him to sit in the chair. I can't bring myself to meet his gaze, so I stare straight ahead and wait, my heart heavy with anticipation. I want to hear his explanation, even if I can't imagine any reasonable excuse.

He doesn't waste any time and blurts out a bunch of mumbo-jumbo. He tells me about some ex-girlfriend,

Heather, about his father's friend, and about how she left him. He tells me how his parents threw him out and his father had a bunch of requirements before he could come back. I listen in silence, feeling overwhelmed by the whirlwind of information, barely able to comprehend what he's saying. It's too much to process at once.

"So, let me get this straight. Charlie's Angels? You started that with me to meet your father's requirements?" I struggle to believe it's true, but the pieces are falling into place.

"No, not entirely. I did have a goal of making $100,000 within the first year of business. Yes, it was a motivation to start the business, but it wasn't the main reason. Charlie, you have to believe me!"

I can't help but laugh bitterly. "I have to believe you? That's rich."

He leans forward, his eyes pleading. "Charlie, everything changed when I met you. I would have helped you with that business even if my father hadn't laid out that requirement." He searches my eyes, hoping for a response, but I just glare back. How can I believe anything he tells me?

He continues. "I swear, it was you and Ronny — that's what drove me."

He leans forward, imploring, "I care so much for you. You, Ronny, Aunt Debbie. Please, I need you to trust—"

"Don't you dare talk to me about trust," I interrupt, locking eyes with him. "I don't know who you are. Oh, wait, yes, I do. You're Atticus Winslow, Ray Winslow's son, the renowned billionaire. No wonder you got flustered when I mentioned how much I despise rich people."

I let out a hollow laugh, the absurdity of everything crashing down on me.

"Charlie, please, it's—"

"It all makes sense now. Deep down, I knew you were

keeping something from me. I knew it!" I stand up and pace about the floor.

"Listen to me, Charlie," he says. "It wasn't about my father or the money. It was about you and Ronny, and—"

"Liar," I scream, pointing at the door. "Get out. I have no desire to see your face ever again. I want us to sell off the company and dissolve the LLC. You figure out how to do it, but we're *done*!"

"Come on, Charlie—"

"GET OUT!" I scream again, loud enough to bring the walls down.

Ronny calls down from his room. "You alright down there, Sis?"

"I'm fine, Ronny. No worries," I call back up, trying to conceal the tremble in my voice. I don't know why I bothered, as I'm sure he heard me screaming.

Atticus stands up, a slouch in his posture I haven't seen before, and walks toward the door. When he glances back at me, I cross my arms and turn away. Then he opens the door and shuts it behind him.

I watch through the curtains as he makes his way to the car. I can't believe we're over.

Oh, Jimmy. How could you do this to me? To us?

Images of his face, that charming dimple, and his disheveled hair all play with my emotions, tugging at my heart, trying to crack my resolve. I can picture the way he winked at me that first night in the men's room. He was so funny. So sweet. So good with Ronny.

I sit back on the couch, cradling my stomach, and let the sobs wrack my body.

Jimmy.

CHAPTER 23
Atticus

I'm driving through the streets, my hands gripping the steering wheel tightly, my head pounding with regret. I should have listened to Archie's advice and told her the truth. But I didn't, and now I've lost her.

The weight of losing Charlie crashes down on me like a ton of bricks, leaving me gasping for air. I speed down the streets, faster than I should, trying to outrun the pain, but it relentlessly catches up with me. I'm lost in thought, contemplating my next move.

As I pull into my driveway, my head clear and my speech rehearsed, I call Charlie. My heart races as I wait for her to pick up, but she doesn't answer, and I'm left feeling even more alone than before.

I try again, hoping against hope that she'll answer this time. But it goes to voicemail, and I don't leave a message. Part of me thinks that maybe she'll answer, but I know deep down that she won't. She made it clear that she never wanted to see me again.

I can't face returning to work. The thought of the stares

from my coworkers is enough to keep me away. So I call Archie, hoping he can put things into perspective for me.

"Dude!" he says, his voice cheery and upbeat. "What's up?"

I scoff and tell him everything — the big revelation, the humiliation at work, and Charlie's reaction. "She said we're done, Arch. She said she never wants to see me again."

"Well...I tried to tell you, man," he says, his voice sympathetic. "But that's water under the bridge. Now, you need to focus on winning her back."

GGBuff returned my few personal effects from my desk two days ago. No letter, no note, nothing. Just my belongings in a box sent through UPS. It's not like I care. I'm never going back there again, that's for sure.

I'm sitting in my living room, lost in thought, when my phone rings. I jump, hoping it's Charlie. I pick up my phone, and my shoulders sag in disappointment. It's my father.

"Hello, Father," I answer, unable to imagine what *he* wants.

"Atticus! You son of a gun! Boy, am I happy to speak to you." My father sounds uncharacteristically chipper, his mood a far cry from my own.

I brace myself, steeling my nerves for whatever's coming. "What's up?" I ask to be polite, even though he's the last person I feel like talking to.

If my dismissive tone offends him, he doesn't show it. "Straight to the point, eh? I like that. Anyway, several months ago, I heard about a breakthrough product in medical tech, right? Tons of downloads and lots of amazing reviews." He stops to cough and clears his throat. "Hang on a minute, Atticus." I hear muffled coughing like he's put his hand over the phone. He must have a cold.

He continues. "Initially, I paid little attention, but then I discovered that the company launched multiple other apps. So, you know me, always digging around, trying to keep ahead of the competition. Well, you'll never guess what I discovered. I found that none other than my boy, my own son, is one of the founders and directors. Atticus! Boy, am I proud of you!"

His words bounce off of me, hollow, meaningless. I feel a pang of guilt for not being able to share in my father's enthusiasm.

"Your mother and I see no reason to keep you away any longer. Atticus, it's time to come home."

I don't respond at first, trying to process what I just heard. My parents want me to come home. Isn't that what I've been dreaming of? To go back home? That dream feels like a distant memory.

"It wasn't me," I say.

"What do you mean it wasn't you?" my father asks, confused.

"It was somebody named Jimmy Winslow," I reply.

As a heavy silence lingers between us, I can sense my heart pounding. I can't bear to hear my father's response, so I click the button and end the call. It's a daring move — I've never hung up on my father before in my life.

The phone rings immediately, and I know it's him. But this time, I don't answer. I mute the sound and let the constant calls fade away.

It's been a few days since I spoke with my father. He finally gave up trying to get ahold of me, and it's just as well. I'm not sure how to face him after what happened. But when my phone rings and I see that it's my mother, my heart sinks. I'm shocked that she had waited so long to call me.

"Baby, why won't you come home?" Distress fills her voice, and I feel guilty. "Your father said he called you and welcomed you back with open arms, but you told him the company he heard about wasn't yours. Is that true?"

"What's true, Mom, is that someone named Jimmy Winslow started that company," I say firmly.

"I don't understand. Why would your father think—"

"Mom?" I interrupt, sensing her confusion.

"What, baby?" My mother's concern tugs at my heart.

"I'm not coming home. I love you, and I love Dad, but I'm not coming back."

The sun beats down on me as I ring the doorbell of Aunt Debbie's house. I squint, trying to glimpse Charlie's door, hoping she doesn't come out at this exact moment. I see Aunt Debbie's car parked out front, so I know she's home. Charlie's car is there, too.

When the door opens on the second ring, Aunt Debbie greets me with a warm smile and a tight hug. "Oh, Jimmy — sorry, *Atticus*. That will take some getting used to." She chuckles. "Wow, have I missed you. Please, come inside."

As I step through the doorway, I tell her, "You know, Jimmy's not entirely a fabrication. It's my middle name — James."

"Ah, is it? Then can I still call you Jimmy?" She motions to a chair. "Here, have a seat."

"Yes. I don't mind if you call me Jimmy. I kind of like it," I say, taking a seat.

Aunt Debbie hums pleasantly as she bustles out of the room. When she comes back with a plate of chocolate chip cookies and two glasses of milk, she settles onto the couch. "So, Jimmy. What brings you down here?"

I take a deep breath before replying. "It's Charlie. I can't live without her." The words spill from my lips. "It's been a week, and I'm barely surviving. But I can't do it anymore, Aunt Debbie. I need her. Please. Help me."

She takes a sip of her milk and nibbles on a cookie before saying, "I want to help you, Jimmy. However, there's something you should know about Charlie. She has a strong dislike for wealthy men. And the fact that you hid the truth from her for so long? That was a deal breaker for her." Her face holds concern, but her words are killing me.

I groan and cover my face with my hands. I explain my dilemma to Aunt Debbie, telling her how torn I was between being honest with Charlie and obeying my father. "It may seem straightforward right now, but it wasn't to me," I say, taking a swig of the ice-cold milk and setting the glass back down.

"They forced me out of my old life with only the clothes on my back. My father told me he'd never accept me back into the family if I disclosed my identity to *anyone*. He wanted me to make it on my own. Learning about Ronny's situation and Charlie's plan to help him confirmed I was in the right place at the right time. Charlie's a master developer, but she knows nothing about business."

"That's true," Aunt Debbie says, offering me a cookie. "Charlie made them. She and Ronny. She's been trying to keep busy."

I take a cookie from the plate and have another sip of milk. "I dedicated my efforts to aiding Charlie in the business because she means the world to me. Ronny, too. He and I have become good friends. Despite countless opportunities for me to start my business elsewhere, I made the deliberate decision to lend a hand to *Charlie*."

She's quiet for a moment, chewing her cookies and drinking her milk. It feels good to be here, with her, close to Charlie. I hope she understands what I'm saying.

I continue explaining. "I wanted to tell Charlie so many times, but obstacles kept getting in the way. Then one night, just as I was about to confess, she began ranting about her distaste for wealthy men. I couldn't tell her after that. I just froze."

Aunt Debbie listens intently, nodding, her eyes soft and understanding. "I get it," Aunt Debbie says. "Does Charlie know all of this?"

"She barely gave me a chance to speak before she kicked me out." I sigh and rub my temples. "I know I hurt her, but I never intended to do that."

I blink rapidly, pushing back the tears that threaten to fall. "I need to go now," I say, standing up, still holding the cookie. "If you talk to Charlie, please tell her I'm sorry." I shove the cookie into my mouth and walk to the door.

Aunt Debbie hugs me at the door and says, "I'll talk to her, Jimmy. No promises, though. She's a tough one once her mind's made up."

As I drive back home, I feel *some* peace. At least I'm not living a lie anymore. Aunt Debbie has a lot of influence over Charlie. I'm hopeful she can convince her to at least hear me out. I don't know what I'm going to do if she can't.

CHAPTER 24
Charlie

I didn't get a call from Jimmy today, and for the first time since we broke up, my phone has stayed silent. It's been almost a week that he's been calling multiple times a day without fail. I didn't realize how much I'd grown used to his calls until they stopped. I keep checking my phone to see if he's called, and it's silly, honestly. I guess he gave up.

I set my phone on the kitchen counter and open the refrigerator. Ronny wants hamburgers for dinner, and I'm happy about that because it's nice and simple. I haven't felt like cooking lately.

As I grab the burger and set it on the counter, I stress to think that maybe he's finally over me. And if he is, well, good riddance, then. I won't waste time thinking about someone who was comfortable with me believing he was someone else for *months*. No sense in losing sleep over it.

But I am losing sleep. The truth is, I'm miserable with how things turned out for us. I can't stop thinking about Jimmy, and I need to get him out of my mind, but it's impossible when I see him everywhere. He was amazing to me and Ronny — more than amazing. I thought I'd found someone special. Sometimes when I lie in bed at night, I can smell his cologne. I know it's childish, but it sends shockwaves through my system as if he's still here.

Even when I shower or fold laundry, I find myself lost in thoughts of his dreamy eyes, lush lashes, wild hair, defined muscles, and the dimple that appears when he smiles. My heart beats faster, as if he's right in front of me. Most of all, I can't get those kisses out of my mind — the way he held my face in his hands, gazed into my eyes and made me his. He had a power over me like no other man ever did. The desire to feel his lips on mine once more overwhelms me.

I pound the hamburger until it's paper thin, not even paying attention to what I'm doing. I don't know how to move on. *Again*! What is wrong with me? I need my head examined!

I mash up the hamburger and try again. I used to like to cook, but now nothing is fun.

The mood in our house has been somber. Ronny rarely leaves his room unless coaxed to go out with his aid, Mrs. Alvarez. I think he feels as betrayed by Jimmy as I do. I convinced him to help me make cookies, and that was nice, but Ronny's quieter now. He barely speaks to me, as if someone sucked the life out of him. I feel so guilty. Ronny has so few friends, and he and Jimmy are very close.

While cooking our burgers, my thoughts drift to Aunt Debbie. She's tried so hard to keep us going this week. She was a bright spot through the ordeal with Ronny's accident, and she's trying to be a bright spot now. I don't know what I'd do without her, honestly. If that woman carries any worries — and she's most likely worried about us — she never shows it.

I remember the day when everything changed. The day I discovered that the man I fell in love with, Jimmy Winslow, was actually Atticus Winslow.

Even though he isn't the man I thought he was, I still feel

gratitude toward him. Despite his deceit, he did help me create the app and launch it. The app's success breathed new life into Ronny — for a while — and greatly improved my finances.

After learning his real name, I researched him and read every available article about him and his family. I pored over photos, feeling like I was looking at a familiar stranger. Videos of him at parties and events were all over the internet. He was known as a billionaire playboy with a new woman in every photo. He smiled, but the smiles didn't reach his eyes. His gorgeous eyes didn't have the sparkle that Jimmy's had.

I bring Ronny's food to him in his room. I set down his tray, and he grunts. His fingers are flicking his controller in the middle of the action. When he's immersed in a game, he doesn't hear much. "Need anything else?" I ask in a raised voice to grab his attention.

"No, thanks," he says without looking up from his game.

As I come downstairs, I hear a faint knock. The front door opens, and Aunt Debbie walks in. Smiling, I say, "Hey, what's up?"

She closes the door, sits on the couch, and pats the spot beside her, signaling me to sit. I glance at my burger, visible on the kitchen table, but it can wait.

"My dear," she says once I sit down. "It's important that you listen to me. Think you can manage that?" I feel a lecture coming on. Whenever Aunt Debbie wants to give me sage advice, she always asks me if I can 'manage' to listen to her, as if I ever don't listen to her.

"Of course," I say.

She takes a breath. "He came to see me yesterday," she says.

My heart skips a beat. *Jimmy was here?* He came to see Aunt Debbie? My eyes widen with anticipation, and I try to push down the excitement building up inside me.

"Jimmy? But, what—"

"Now, before you say anything, hear me out."

I nod, trying to contain my emotions. I bite my lip as my stomach churns.

"Good," she says. "When Jimmy came to see me, he had a lot to say, and I listened as he poured his heart out, Charlene. I can't tell you everything he said verbatim, but there's one thing I *can* tell you from all he said. That man cares for you, Charlie. He truly does, and he *adores* your brother."

My heart is slamming around in my chest as I try to process what Aunt Debbie just said. I can't believe Jimmy came over, sat down with Aunt Debbie, and poured out his feelings. I'm not sure what to do with this. It seems surreal.

"Trust me, sweetie, I'm not at all pleased about the lies and false pretenses, but I believe everything else he shared with you — and us as a family — was genuine. That doesn't excuse his mistakes, but I believe he never set out to hurt you."

I look down at my hands in my lap. "Well," I say, "He *did* hurt me."

"I know he did," she replies, patting my knee. "But he was in a tough spot. He's his parents' only son, and did he tell you they kicked him out of the house with nothing? His father said he couldn't return until he proved himself, and he threatened Jimmy that if he told *anybody* who he was, he would disown him. That had to be terrible. Jimmy loves his parents and was just trying to please them."

I had thought about all that, and I could understand if he kept it from me initially. But he lied to me for almost a year, and deep down, I knew he was hiding something. It's impossible to get satisfaction from being right when I wish I were wrong.

Aunt Debbie pulls me tight and rubs my arm. "Look, I'm not saying you should just forget what he did. I'm just suggesting that if you consider everything else you've seen in this man, maybe you should give him a chance to explain what was going on in his mind and his heart." She offers a warm smile. "Just talk to him."

I continue to sit on the couch, my mind whirling. Aunt Debbie's arm feels warm around me, and I'm trying to process what she just said. If Aunt Debbie had come over here to plead Jimmy's case, then maybe there's something worth considering.

"Also," she continues, "I'd like to add that you've been miserable without him. So, I don't see what you stand to lose by hearing the poor boy out. Ronny's been upset, too, as you know. So, what do you say…Hmmm?"

She smiles, knowing she's gotten through to me. Leaning over and hugging me again, she says, "Got any more of those cookies?"

"Ugh… I hate it when you're right," I groan, getting up to get her the cookies.

"No, you don't," she replies, giggling.

CHAPTER 25
Atticus

"Hello?" I answer. It's my mother, and I frown as I pour myself another cup of coffee.

"Hi, baby," she greets me warmly. It's eight o'clock in the morning, and I carry my coffee into the living room.

"Hi, Mom," I say as I brace myself, knowing that this call is likely about her trying to convince me to come back home. Again. I set my coffee down, sink into the couch, and get ready for the impending discussion.

"I had a long talk with your father," she begins. "He'd like it if you came here in person to discuss things."

I sigh, already sensing the familiar push to return home. I take a sip of my coffee, wincing as the scalding liquid stings my lips — one peril of drinking it black. "I have a lot on my plate right now, Mom. I'll have to check my calendar."

"I can hold on," she offers.

"No, I mean, I've got to go look at it. I don't have it with me," I say.

"Atticus James, I know *full well* your calendar is on your phone. Please, your father wishes to see you... and so do I."

Frustration wells up. "What's this about, because if it's about me moving back home, I told you, I'm not—"

"Atticus. Your father's not well," she interrupts, her voice quivering. My heart sinks.

"What do you mean not well?" I ask, my throat tightening with dread.

"He's got cancer, baby. I didn't want to say it over the phone, but you need to come home to see him."

"Oh, Mom," I say, tears welling up unexpectedly. Despite the recent estrangement, I still love my dad with all my heart. Growing up, he was a hundred percent invested in everything I did with unwavering support. I lean back on the couch, trying to steady my nerves and catch my breath.

I mute the phone and grab a tissue from the end table to blow my nose and wipe my eyes. When I unmute the phone, I ask, "What kind of cancer?"

"We can talk about it in person. Can you come by today?" She sounds so sad that I can't say no.

"Of course, Mom. I'll leave here shortly. I'm about forty minutes from you."

"That's my boy. Thank you, Atticus. I'll see you when you get here."

"I'll see you then. Love you, Mom."

"Love you, too, baby."

I hang up and sigh heavily, staring at the ceiling. Just when I thought things couldn't get any worse, BAM! I get thrown this bombshell. Thoughts of my dad and the memories we've shared flood my mind.

As I get ready to leave, my mind recalls when I got into trouble in high school for getting into a fight. I stepped in when a big bully started pushing around a smaller kid. My dad had been called to the school, and I remember sitting there next to him, shivering with fear as the principal gave his speech. Dad had worn a stern expression and nodded in agreement as the principal spoke. He assured the principal it would *never* happen again.

When we got to his car, I had expected him to tell me he was grounding me for six months, but my dad had turned to me and said, "So tell me *exactly* what happened." I sat there, shocked. I hadn't expected him to care about what I had to say. But I'd poured my heart out to him, telling him everything that had happened.

When I finished telling him what went down, he'd smiled at me like he was proud of me. "That's my boy," he'd said, and then he scoffed. "You should've *punched* him."

I remember being taken aback by his words, my eyes as big as saucers. "Really?" I said. In my infinite wisdom, I had entertained the thought of going back and punching the guy, now that my father approved. But my dad had chuckled and said, "No, not really. You know I don't condone violence, but I am proud of you for defending the little guy. You'll go far doing that, son."

That memory hurts now because I might lose him. I can't bear the thought of it. I rush out the door and into my car. As I drive north on I-87, my mind bounces between my dad and Charlie. The business crosses my mind, too, as I need to check on the marketing team. Jake, the manager I hired, left several voicemails, but I haven't had the energy to return his calls. I haven't even asked Ronny about the progress on the social media marketing. I can't afford to let things slip like I did after Heather. I want to believe I've progressed since then.

The traffic is manageable as I speed north to Saratoga. I have this powerful sense of urgency to see my father *and* my mother. She must be devastated. How long have they known, and why didn't they tell me? They probably didn't want to impede my *progress*.

Just then, my phone dings, and I pull it out to see a

message notification from Aunt Debbie. Heart beating fast, I open the message, expecting the worst, but as I read the text, a brief glimmer of light appears at the end of my gloomy tunnel.

Congratulations, we are a go. -Aunt Debbie.

CHAPTER 26
Charlie

"Did you inform Jimmy I'm open to talking to him?" I look at Aunt Debbie, hopeful she's contacted him to let him know.

"Yes, I texted him at nine-thirty this morning. Why? Have you not heard from him yet?" She appears taken aback. "I thought you were going to tell me he called you."

"No. He hasn't, and I've had my phone on me the whole day." I worry when she says she texted him hours ago.

"That's strange," she says. "Jimmy seemed so eager to talk to you...Hmmm." She mulls it over, her brow knitted together. I think it's strange, too, given the way he acted the last time I saw him. I thought he would jump at the chance to resolve things with me, or at least try to.

We're sitting in the gazebo in our backyard, surrounded by luscious greenery. The special ramp Aunt Debbie had put in after Ronny's accident allows him to join us for dinner outside, which Ronny enjoys. Before his accident, he was what I would call an 'outdoorsman.' He would camp and hike and find any excuse to be outside, especially by the ocean. It was hard to keep up with him sometimes.

Aunt Debbie has prepared her 'world-famous-pack-it-with-meat lasagna.' I serve Ronny a large helping and pass some silverware to him.

"You don't think he's changed his mind, do you?" I ask, scooping some lasagna onto Aunt Debbie's plate.

"No, of course not," Aunt Debbie says. "Don't be silly. The man was in tears when I spoke to him. There's no way he would change his mind."

Ronny speaks up. "You weren't very nice to him," he says, cutting into his meal and stuffing a gigantic piece of lasagna into his mouth. He narrows his eyes at me as he chews it.

His words startle me. I knew he was upset, but not with *me*. Is he taking Jimmy's side in this?

"What do you mean?" I ask, stopping in the middle of cutting a piece of lasagna for myself.

Ronny looks me straight in the eye. "You don't give people a chance. You're quick to just discard people at the first sign of trouble."

I scoff. "That's not true. Why would you say that?"

"What about Janice?" he asks, taking another bite.

"What about her?" I roll my eyes, picking up my fork and knife to cut into my meal.

Ronnie continues, "She was your *best friend*, but you wrote her off when she said one dumb thing."

"Are you serious?" I pause with my forkful of lasagna in mid-air, trying to believe what I'm hearing. "She told me Mark made a pass at her, but when I confronted him about it, he told me *she* was the one who had been flirting with *him* all along."

"And you believed him? How do you know he wasn't the one who was lying?" Ronny says. He picks up his glass of milk and chugs almost the entire thing.

"Because she'd lied to me before. *Repeatedly*. She told me she couldn't go on our trip to Lake George because she wasn't feeling well. Remember that? I found out she was feeling fine. She went out with that Frank guy she met on that dating app and blew me off," I say, feeling frustrated at Ronny's accusations.

"Okay, but you guys were friends for like *forever*. She was a cool chick. Now you won't even take her calls," Ronny says. He scowls at me with what looks like contempt.

I throw my fork onto my plate, followed by the napkin I had placed in my lap. My lasagna is untouched. "That has *nothing* to do with Jimmy lying to me, Ronny. He withheld his true identity from me and started a business with me under a false name. Do you see no problem with that? Jimmy made me think he had feelings for me. That's not how you treat someone you supposedly care about."

"Alright, you guys," Aunt Debbie interjects. "Ronny," she says, "Charlie has agreed to talk to Jimmy, so let's give her the benefit of the doubt. She's willing to hear what he has to—"

"No, actually, I'm not," I say. I get up from the table, pushing my plate away. I look at Ronny. "Why don't *you* talk to Jimmy since he seems to be *your* best friend? I'm going in and taking a bath."

"Oh, come on, Charlie!" Ronny says.

"Charlie!" Aunt Debbie scolds. "Don't take your aggression out on Ronny. He was merely—"

"He was merely telling me that this is all *my* fault!" My voice cracks. "And you want me to talk to Jimmy, but gee, I don't see my phone ringing, do you?" I hold my phone up and wave it in the air. "Yeah, I didn't think so."

"I'm sure he'll call you. Maybe he's busy," Aunt Debbie says in her never-ending attempt at positivity.

I laugh a cynical laugh, standing but leaning on the table with my hands. "That's hysterical. Jimmy's *busy*. Busy doing what? He lost his job at GGBuff. He hasn't even checked in with the marketing team in — what — *days*? So, tell me, what's he so busy with?"

"I only texted him this morning. It hasn't even been 24 hours," Aunt Debbie says.

"It's been over eight hours, Aunt Debbie. *Eight* hours! Apparently, I'm not *that* important." I'm so upset that I storm toward the house without looking back.

As I climb into the tub, guilt consumes me. I can't believe that Ronny is mad at *me* for the Jimmy situation. The *Atticus* situation is more like it. I know he misses Jimmy, but it hurts that he blames *me*. I'm not the one who lied. Ronny expects me to forgive him, just like that?

My phone still hasn't rung. If it does, I'm *not* going to answer it.

He can call *Ronny*.

CHAPTER 27
Atticus

I feel like I'm walking on air when I receive Aunt Debbie's text message. My excitement and nervousness are bubbling over. She did it! Aunt Debbie convinced Charlie to talk to me! I want nothing more than to dial Charlie's number right away, but my mind is swirling with thoughts of my father, and I can't afford to mess up my conversation with Charlie. So, I know now is not the time to have it, especially when I'm not thinking clearly and driving like a madman on I-87.

As I pull into my parent's driveway, Billy, their gatekeeper, greets me. He smiles when he sees me. "Atticus! Your mother rang and said you were on your way. How are you?"

"I'm good, Bill. How's Mandy doing?" I inquire about his wife.

"Oh, she's good. Enjoy your visit. Hope to see more of you." He puts in a code, and the large metal gate slides open.

"You will," I assure him, and drive down the long driveway, through another open gate, and up to the house.

As I approach the grand mansion that has been my childhood home, a lump rises in my throat. It's been nearly a year since I've been here, and the memories come flooding back to me.

I remember the countless family gatherings and the long summer evenings spent in the garden. I can picture my father and me playing catch in the yard, him yelling at me to keep my eye on the ball. He never had much patience, but at least he tried.

My baby blue Prius looks ridiculous parked next to my parents' cars in their circular driveway. I swallow my anger that they put me into a car they knew full well I would hate. If I hadn't been so busy with everything, I would have bought myself a new car by now.

The front door swings open before I reach it, and my mother rushes out and hugs me. "Atticus! My baby! Oh, I've missed you so much." She puts her arm through mine. "Come on, your father's in his study. He's expecting you."

We walk through the halls of the house that had been my home my entire life. Something that was once so familiar now feels foreign.

Before we reach the study, my mother stops and turns to me. "I told your father that you know about his condition. He'll explain in more detail about it, but it thrilled him to hear you were coming to visit today."

"That's good," I say, smiling at her. "But just so we're clear, Mom, it is *just* a visit. I'm not planning to move back in."

"We can talk about that later, baby. Let's go see your dad." She puts her arm back in mine, and together, we make our way to the study.

My father rises from his seat when he sees us enter. He sets aside his newspaper and steps forward to greet me. I put my hand out to shake his, but he pulls me in for a hug, something I was not expecting. "Atticus, my boy, I am *so* proud of you."

"Come, sit down," my mother says, and we sit in the oversized, plush leather chairs that encircle the large mahogany coffee table. It's a cozy room, dimly lit in this massive house, and my father's favorite place to be. Floor lamps cast a soft glow, illuminating the carved furniture that the staff keeps meticulously polished.

"Would you like something to drink, dear?" my mother asks me once I'm seated.

"Yes, a glass of water, please." My throat feels like sandpaper.

She rings a small bell, summoning Michael, our butler, who's been a constant in our lives for as long as I can remember. He comes over with a friendly smile, and I stand up to shake his hand. "Atticus!" he says. "It's so good to see you again."

"Likewise, Michael," I say with genuine affection. Michael and I have always had a wonderful friendship. He would cover for me as a child whenever I would break a rule, and as an adult, he always looked out for me.

"Please get Atticus a bottle of water, Michael," my mother asks.

I gulp down the cold liquid, nearly emptying the bottle. The drive here left my throat as dry as a desert, and my nerves are ablaze as I wait for my father to speak. I clear my throat and empty the bottle.

My father breaks the silence, acknowledging what my mother had revealed. "Your mother told me you know about my condition."

I nod. "Yes, but Mom didn't give me any details. She said you have cancer?"

My father meets my gaze. "Yes. I'm afraid that's correct." He glances at my mother, and she smiles at him. "It's stage four, I'm sad to say — lung cancer."

I gasp in response, shocked by the weight of his words. "Stage four?"

"Yes, son, stage four." He says it so matter-of-factly, his demeanor unwavering. I search his face, expecting to find signs of fear or sadness, but instead, I see a resolute acceptance of his circumstances.

I turn to my mother, who reaches for a tissue from the end table. When she looks back at me, her eyes glisten with tears.

"So, what are they doing for you?" I try to keep my voice steady and control my emotions *and* my voice. I wonder if my father is doing the same or if he's truly handling it so well.

"There's not much they can do, I'm afraid. Doctors tell me I've got six months. You and I both know that means three."

My mother bursts into tears, and my father gets up and walks over to her, offering her a tender embrace. "It's alright, Carol. It's alright. We all have our time, don't we? You've got Atticus here. He'll take care of you." He turns his head and coughs, making me realize how fragile his health is.

Tears well up in my eyes, but I brush them away, not wanting him to see me cry.

"I'm so sorry, Dad," I say.

My father sits back down and clears his throat. "Son, I know you tried to deny your successful application business, but I know it was you. You do realize I have connections, so I've seen all the paperwork. I can't for the life of me understand why you would deny it. Can you explain that?"

I pause, unsure *how* to explain. "I'm sorry, Dad. Yes, it was partly me. I partnered with a lady named Charlene Welsh, and we developed the app together. I—"

"Welsh. Welsh," my father muses. "Do I know her family? It doesn't ring a bell."

"No, Dad, you wouldn't know her family. She lives in Albany with her brother and her aunt."

"Oh, then surely, I would know her aunt. What's her name?"

"You wouldn't know her aunt, Dad. They don't run in the same circles as us—as *you*."

Curiosity fuels his next questions, and he leans in. "What does this Charlene do for a living?" My heart rate picks up as I anticipate his reaction.

"Well, she used to be a game developer, but then her brother had a debilitating accident, so to care for him during the day, she took a job as a night cleaner. But now she's—"

"Wait, did you say a night cleaner?" my father interrupts, his eyes wide.

"Yes, but it was out of necessity because she—"

His coughing interrupts my explanation. My mother leans over and grabs a tissue, handing it to him. He takes the tissue and coughs into it, wheezing in between coughs. I feel sweat burst on my forehead as I watch. Michael rushes in with an oxygen tank. My father accepts it and inhales, his complexion shifting from ashen to a healthier hue.

After Michael removes the tank, I ask my father, "Do you need oxygen all the time?"

He dismisses my question and redirects the conversation. "Tell me, Atticus, you're not romantically involved with this woman, are you?"

I bristle at the implication. "We're friends," I say, "but I have feelings for her and want to pursue a relationship. I care about her a lot."

My father wipes his mouth with the tissue, an exasperated look on his face. My mother, sensing his dismay, leans over and puts her hand on his knee. "Hear the boy out," she says.

Unswayed, my father stands up, brushing her hand off his knee. "I don't have to hear the boy out, Carol. I have to ask the boy to leave."

I stand and face him, my anger flaring now. I can't believe he's about to kick me out *again*.

He looks at me, his face steady and serious. "Atticus, I am

thrilled that you met my requirements and pulled your life together. For over a year, I've been living with the knowledge of my cancer and the limited time I have left. Watching you wallow in self-pity, I knew you would squander our family fortune upon my death. Your mother and I made a rash decision to help you."

My father's face grows red, and he's beginning to sweat. My mother tries to console him, but her efforts prove futile. "Don't get riled, dear," she says, trying to soothe his anger.

Pointing his finger at me, my father says, "It appears you've learned nothing. I'm telling you right now that you won't inherit *a single penny* of our money until you've learned how to act. Allowing a cleaning woman to lay claim to your inheritance is unacceptable. Now, either tell me you'll forget this ridiculous behavior with her, or you can walk out of here right now and make your own way."

My mother won't look at me, a silent witness to my father's will. I can't deny my love for my parents, but the choice is clear. I face my father head-on.

"I'm sorry, Dad. I love you and Mom more than anything. I do, and I'm not in any way trying to disappoint you or cause you pain. But Charlie means the world to me, and since you wouldn't allow me to use my real name out there, she only *just* found out who I am. So how could she be a gold-digger, huh?"

A bitter laugh escapes my father. "Ha! Oh, I don't know, son, let's see. Your last name is *Winslow*, right? You were going by Jimmy? You said this young lady — Charlene, was it? — was a programmer? Do you seriously think she never heard of Ray Winslow? Anyone with a bit of common sense can make the connection. Would you have me believe she didn't look me up and find your face splashed across magazines and social media? If that's true, and she didn't know, well, she might not be a gold digger, but she's not the brightest."

"That's enough!" I shout. "You're *impossible!* I did everything you asked. I built a successful business in less than six months, paid all my bills, and improved my life. All to what end? So that I can inherit your fortune? I don't need your fortune or anyone else's. I'd rather be poor with Charlene than wealthy without her."

"You don't mean that," he says.

"Oh, yes, I do."

I look at my mother. "I'm sorry, Mom," I say. Without another word, I turn around and storm out the door.

I hear my mother's voice call after me, but I don't look back. Exiting the house, I jump into my Prius and drive away.

Once I'm home, I'll have a beer, settle down, and reach out to Charlie.

Charlie — I need to talk to her.

CHAPTER 28
Charlie

It's seven-thirty at night when the phone finally rings. I reach for it, my hands trembling with a strange mix of anticipation and anxiety. The caller ID flashes "Jimmy." My heart pounds in my ears, and I can feel my blood pressure rising.

Should I answer it? The desire to do so is overwhelming. My finger hovers over the answer button. I ache to hear his voice, to offer him the opportunity to clarify things. A simple swipe to the right.

But what can he possibly say to justify nine months of deception? Is there any explanation that can explain it? His daddy told him to? That's hardly worth the breath to say. So, I let it go to voicemail, where it belongs.

I don't want to be with a liar, not again. Mark was a liar. I blamed poor Janice for saying Mark was making advances, and I did cut her off, just like Ronny had said. But now, I wonder if it was Mark, after all. I am overwhelmed with guilt over how I treated her.

I should have known it was Mark who was lying. Mark's eyes roved over other women every chance he got, checking out their curves as they passed by. I can't afford to give my heart away again to someone I can't trust. I just can't do it.

I get Ronny into bed, and a heavy silence envelops us. He answers my attempts to engage in conversation with curt, monosyllabic responses, causing me to abandon my efforts. I place the remotes and a glass of water within his reach and say, "Goodnight, Ronny."

"Uh-huh," he mutters, and my heart sinks as I close his door and head to my room.

My phone rings again, and I rush to pick it up. It's Jimmy again. I'll give him points for persistence, but this time, I hit ignore. Maybe he'll get the hint. But before I can even put the phone down, it rings again.

With a sigh, I answer, irritation seeping into my voice. "Stop calling me," I say firmly.

"Charlie," he says. "I need to see you. It's important."

His voice! Uh! *His voice!* I can feel my resolve melting, but I can't let it sway me.

"No. I—"

"I'm not taking no for an answer, Charlie," he interrupts, his voice unwavering. "I need to see you. So, here's the deal. I can either come to your house, scale your wall, and climb in through your window, or you can let me in when I arrive. The choice is yours."

I want to laugh. Jimmy can be amusing. But I hold my breath and say nothing. I need to stand my ground, to resist being pushed around by someone who seems to think he owns me.

But I want him to own me, don't I? To hold me in his arms and make me his own? I am left with a question I can't seem to answer. *What do I do?*

After a tense minute of silence, I hear the unmistakable sound of his car door slamming. Then his voice, laced with an urgency — but barely above a whisper — says, "Charlie?"

I remain silent, hesitant to answer. Afraid to give in, to cave to my desire for him.

"You need to open your door. I'm standing in front of your house." I gasp, although I don't make a sound. I can feel the sweat on my brow.

"I never said you could come over," I say, standing up from my bed and racing to look out the window. There it is, confirming the truth that sends me into a panic. Jimmy had parked his blue Prius across the street. I feel a rush of butterflies when I see it. I guess he's on my porch because I can't see him from here.

"I told you, Charlene," he says, his voice unwavering, "that I'm going to scale the wall and climb in your window, or you're going to let me in on your own. It's your choice, but either way, I *am* coming in to talk to you."

I sigh. I feel so conflicted. I want to run downstairs and fling open the door, but I can't let him think he can control me. "You can't just boss me around. You don't own me." I say. I try to use a voice of authority, but it cracks, giving my nervousness away.

"I'm not trying to own you, Charlie. Please. Just let me in. I won't touch you. I promise. Not if you don't want me to. I just want to talk. That's all. A simple conversation, and if you ask me to leave when the conversation's over, I'll walk out the door and leave you alone."

Leaving him standing on my porch in the cool night air doesn't seem like an option. He's so stubborn, and I suspect he would fulfill his promise to scale the wall or, at the very least, wait indefinitely on my porch.

"Alright," I finally relent. "I'll be right down."

When I open the door, my heart skips a beat. Jimmy's more handsome than ever. Although it hasn't been that long since I've seen him, it feels like forever. He's leaning on the front porch post, his hands in his pockets. My heart melts like chocolate on a hot summer night.

"Hi," he says, his smile tentative. "Can I come in?"

"Well, you didn't give me much of a choice, did you?" I say, stepping aside and motioning him in. He walks in, and I close the door behind him, drawing in the scent of his cologne. It gives him an unfair advantage.

"Have a seat." I gesture to a chair near the couch. He complies, taking a seat while I settle onto the couch. "Alright, I'm listening." I sit up straight and place my hands in my lap.

He draws a deep breath, his eyes filled with remorse. "First, I want to tell you how sorry I am for keeping you in the dark. Believe me, Charlie. I hated keeping my family a secret from you. I wanted to tell you so many times, but I was afraid this would happen."

"What would happen?" I ask.

"This! You breaking up with me. I couldn't bear the thought of it, and it became harder to tell you as time went by."

"Alright, I get that, I guess, but why didn't you just tell me when you first asked me to have a relationship with you? We hadn't known each other that long. I would have understood."

I search his face, and he looks so uncomfortable that I feel bad. I want to understand why he did what he did. I want to forgive him. I'm just not sure I can get past everything.

"I wasn't sure you would understand. I wanted desperately to tell you with everything in me, but at that time I was determined to show my parents I could meet the requirements and earn my father's approval back. He cut me off from the family, Charlie. Completely. I couldn't call or text them. *Nothing.* They tossed me out like garbage. If I wanted to go back home, I had to do exactly as my father instructed. He made it clear that I was to tell *no one* who I really was — Ray

Winslow's son. If I did, that was it. He'd never let me come home."

"So, you admit that because you weren't sure I would understand, you decided I wouldn't, and so you just kept lying to me. You thought that was okay...because...? Oh, wait, don't answer that. It's because you had no faith in me."

I don't let him answer. Instead, I continue. "*You're* the one who asked me to be in a relationship with you, knowing you were lying to me. You should have waited until after you told me the truth, don't you think? What's that, like misrepresentation?" I'm frustrated, but I smile to myself because I realize I sound like a lawyer.

He sighs. There's a sense of resignation on his face. "Well, when you say it like that..."

"Listen, Jimmy," I begin, wanting to make sure my thoughts come out right. "It's not that I don't want to forgive you. I genuinely like you, but I just got out of a terrible relationship with Mark. It's too much for me to process, and I've got Ronny to think about. He's already all pissed off at me because of you. "

"I've missed Ronny," he says. "He's my bud, but I'm sorry he's mad at you because of what I did."

"Yeah, well, maybe you should have thought about that before you pretended to be someone you're not. It makes my stomach hurt to think about it. I keep going back over everything in my head. " I don't like being vulnerable, but he needs to know what he did to me.

"I know." His face is pleading. "I need you to forgive me, Charlie. I'm so sorry. I promise you, I *never* meant to hurt you. I made the wrong decision when it came to telling you or not telling you. I wanted to tell you forever, and hate myself for not having the courage."

He looks down and then his gaze meets mine again. He appears to be searching my face for understanding. "You have to believe me that everything else was real with me. Everything! My feelings and our connection. You know it was real, Charlie. You and Me? That was *very* real."

Although his voice is sincere, as well as his eyes, I can't help but be skeptical. I can't read his mind to know what his true motivations were. I want to believe him and run into his arms, but I don't know if I can. He gained his parents' approval by starting the business with me and by lying to me.

"It was real to *me*." I scoff. "But then, I didn't have a hidden agenda. You, on the other hand, were out to please your parents and get back in their good graces. I bet they're so proud of you now that you're so successful." My sarcasm oozes out, fueled by my despair. I hate it when I'm like this.

"My parents are proud of what *we've* accomplished." He points his finger back and forth between us, emphasizing *we*. "I saw them today after almost a year."

"How nice for you," I say, the bitterness seeping through my words. I don't want to be bitter and sarcastic, but the mere thought of it — Jimmy, lounging at his parent's probably massive estate, sipping champagne and celebrating the prodigal son's return. *How sweet!*

"Well, it was 'nice' seeing them, but things weren't 'nice' for me," he says. He makes air quotes, his brow furrowed. I don't think he appreciates my sarcasm, either.

"I don't understand. I thought you did what your father wanted?"

"I did, but..."

"But, what?" I say.

"I wish there was a way for you to understand my parents. They're really good people. I know you don't like 'rich people,' and I understand why after what Mark put you through. But that was Mark. My parents are hard-working, decent people. But, the thing with my dad is, he has experienced the pain of being burned on several occasions. Before my mother, he had girlfriends who played him for his money and people he thought were good friends who also used him for his money. My mom said it changed him and made him overly cautious."

"I mean no disrespect to your parents, Jimmy. I don't even know them, and I'm sorry for what your dad went through. But what does any of that have to do with him taking *you* back into the family?"

"I'm telling you this because he's always forbidden me from dating anyone who doesn't come from money. I know that sounds callous and probably strange to you, but he made that rule to prevent me from experiencing the same trauma. He didn't want me to get hurt."

My gut knots at his words. "You told him about me, didn't you?"

"Yes, I did."

"And...what? He told you not to see me?"

"No, not exactly." He looks at his hands and rubs them together as if gathering his thoughts. *He's going to tell me he can't see me anymore.* I want to cry. He could have simply made a phone call or chosen not to contact me. I'm praying that's not what he's going to say.

"Then what?" I say. I'm not trying to be callous, but he's beating around the bush. "Spit it out, Jimmy. *Please.*"

He looks up at me. "What happened was I told him you were my business partner and that I have feelings for you. When he balked at that, I told him you weren't some gold-digger after my money. I told him you just learned who I was."

"Okay, so what did he say?"

"He suggested you most likely found out my identity by searching for my name, Winslow, and that you discovered I was Ray's son. He's convinced you only took an interest in me after you found out."

My face feels like it's going to explode as I sit and take in his words. If it's one thing I can't stand, it's being accused of something I didn't do. "Is that what you believe, too?" I try to keep my voice from quivering without much success.

His eyes get wide. "No, of course not. It's ridiculous. I tried to tell Dad, but he told me he would never leave his money to someone who would let a *cleaning lady* take half of it." His voice trails off at the end of his sentence, and I'm not sure he said what I thought he said.

"Wait. You told him I was a cleaning lady?" I feel my face flush at the thought of him telling his father that. *Why would he do that?*

"Charlene, I'm going to tell you something about my father," he says, looking at me intently. "He has the resources to learn your name, date of birth, and social security number. He would have found out on his own. Believe me."

"Oh, so now it's Charlene, is it? That's twice you called me that. Are you my father now, scolding me? You know I hate that."

He sighs. "I didn't mean it like that. I'm sorry. Look, Charlie, I can't change who my father is, or what he believes. But I did tell him I don't want his money if it means I have to stop seeing you. I said I'd rather be poor with *you* than wealthy *without* you. And I meant it."

I blink and my mouth falls open. I'm trying to process Jimmy's words, but I'm failing miserably. Did he just say he chose me over billions of dollars?

I close my mouth and glance at Jimmy. His face looks so sad, and my anger fading as I see the hurt in his eyes. I've been so consumed by my own feelings and so blinded by anger that I haven't truly looked at *him*. My heart pinches.

"I...uh...," I stammer, at a loss for words, so many conflicting emotions swirling inside me and no idea how to sort them out.

CHAPTER 29
Atticus

I wish I had opened up to Charlie months ago. Her face, now looking at me with a hint of understanding, gives me hope. She's just sort of staring at me, her silence making me nervous. I wish I could read her thoughts. A twitch at the corner of her cheek hints at a suppressed smile.

"Did you honestly say that to your father?" Charlie finally says. "You'd walk away from your inheritance for me?" Her eyes, wide and searching, hold a glimmer of delight, or at least it seems. Is she trying to hold back a smile, or is it just my wishful thinking?

"I did," I state, realizing the importance of maintaining transparency with Charlie from now on. "I told him, but it hurt me to defy him. I learned some bad news today that complicated things." I shift in my chair, sweat forming on my forehead.

The concern appears in her expression as her brows furrow. "Can I get you something to drink, Jimmy? You don't look good." The unease evident in her eyes makes me realize I must look terrible.

"I'm alright," I say. "It's just been a trying day."

"So, what's the bad news?" She's staring at me so intently, but I take a minute to phrase my thoughts.

"Alright." I clear my throat. "My father has stage four lung cancer. He only has a few months left." My voice quivers slightly as I speak, but I keep it from cracking. Just saying the words out loud makes my stomach churn uncomfortably.

Her mouth drops open, and her eyes get wide. "Oh, Jimmy, I am so, so sorry." She reaches over and places her hand on my leg. I lay my hand over hers, grateful that maybe she's forgiven me.

"What are the doctors doing for him?" she asks.

I sigh. "Not much. Pain meds. Oxygen. It's not treatable at this stage."

"Oh, Jimmy, I feel terrible. How's your mother taking it?"

"Not good, and all this stuff with me isn't helping."

"No, I'm sure it's not."

"My father was hopeful I'd be around to help my mother. Now, he's telling me to get out again. I don't know what to do."

She withdraws her hand from my leg and sits up. "What do you mean, you don't know what to do? You just said you told him you—"

"No, I did," I say, realizing my mistake in saying that. "I told my father I'd rather be poor than—"

"I know what you told him, but it sounds like you're not convinced it's the right decision," she says, and I can see the hurt and anger flashing in her eyes.

"That's not true," I say. "I made my decision, Charlie."

"No, you literally just said, 'I don't know what to do,' which means you *haven't* decided what you're going to do."

I try to speak, but she raises her hand to stop me and stands up. "I think it would be best if you left now."

"Charlie!" I say, but she interrupts me again.

"You said you'd leave when I asked, and I'm asking you to

leave, Jimmy. I'm sorry about your dad. I truly am. You're a great guy, and I care a lot about you, but your family is pulling you in a direction in which I am not welcome to accompany you. I won't have you living with regrets because of me. I will *not* be the reason that you and your father don't speak, especially now."

"It's not like that," I say. "Not at all."

"Your father is dying, Jimmy. How are you going to feel after he passes, and you distanced yourself from him because of me? You wouldn't get to spend his last months on this earth with him? You wouldn't be able to comfort your mother? No. No. No. I'm sorry. This can't work out. You need to go now."

Charlie walks to the door and opens it. My heart sinks. This is not how I wanted this to go.

I rise from the chair and move toward the door, pausing before I leave. "What about our business? What about Ronny?"

"We can talk about that tomorrow. Right now, I need to get to bed. Good night, Jimmy."

CHAPTER 30
Charlie

I collapse onto the couch and let the sobs wrack my body. It feels like Jimmy has torn my heart out of my chest. Again. The possibility of us being together now seems utterly impossible.

Suddenly, a gentle knock on the door startles me. Could it be Jimmy again? I can't bear to see him right now. I quickly wipe my face with my shirt and approach the door. "Who's there?" I ask.

A familiar voice from the other side of the door says, "It's me. Aunt Debbie."

I open the door, and Aunt Debbie greets me with a broad smile that quickly fades as she observes my tear-streaked face. Concern replaces the smile. "Oh my goodness, what's going on?"

I walk back to the couch as she closes the door, and she follows me, taking a seat right next to me. Her arm wraps around my shoulder, offering comfort as I lean into her, letting my tears flow freely once again.

"Oh, honey, what happened? I saw Jimmy's car outside

and was so excited that you two kids were talking. Why are you crying?"

"It's over," I sob. "It's really over."

Aunt Debbie's concern deepens. "Oh, sweetie, tell me everything. Could you not forgive him?"

"It's not that, Auntie. His father has cancer." Fresh tears fall from my eyes. Aunt Debbie reaches over, grabs a tissue from the end table, and hands it to me. I blow my nose and wipe my eyes. She takes her arm off of me and walks to the kitchen.

"I'm going to get you a drink of water," she says.

I sit on the couch, playing with the rings on my fingers, my breathing slowly returning to normal. Aunt Debbie returns with a glass of water and hands it to me.

Taking a sip, I glance at her. She sits down and gently cups my face in her hands.

"I hate seeing you so distressed. What does Jimmy's father's cancer have to do with you two?" she asks.

I set the water down and blow my nose again. "His father doesn't want him to be with me. He thinks I'm a gold digger just after his money. Jimmy told him he would walk away if his father couldn't accept me, but now he's having second thoughts."

"He's having second thoughts? Because of his father's illness?"

"Yes," I say, sobbing into my hands.

Aunt Debbie wraps her arms around me. "There-there, sweetheart. It's going to be alright. We'll figure this out."

I sit up. "There's nothing to figure out. Even if Jimmy was fully committed to me, I can't possibly be the reason for his estrangement from his father. Not now. Given his short life expectancy. He'd resent me. Don't you think?"

"Well...maybe you two could wait until—"

"Don't say it!" I say. "Oh, don't you see? Jimmy thought

he wanted me and was willing to do anything to be with me, but now he's having second thoughts. I can't handle this. I can't play second fiddle to his family, and I can't make him choose me. It's just not going to work!"

I'm feeling hysterical and exhausted. I want to pace the floor. I can't keep hashing over this.

I stand up. "Please don't be offended, Auntie, but I think I need to go to bed. My head hurts, and I don't want to talk about this anymore."

Aunt Debbie stands and gives me a warm hug before returning to her side of the duplex. I turn out the lights and head upstairs. Passing Ronny's room, I peek inside. He's sound asleep, his controller in his hand, and the TV is still on. I kiss his head as I take his controller from his hand, turn off the TV, and go to my room.

At least I know Jimmy cares about me. He cares enough to forsake billions of dollars, so he says. I would never allow him to do that. But he's torn, unsure about what to do. I can't be with someone who's unsure. What a mess!

What a tangled, absurd, heartbreaking *mess*!

CHAPTER 31

Atticus

I hardly slept at all last night. I glance at the clock. It's only six a.m.

After leaving Charlie's last night, I reached out to Archie and spilled my guts. He was full of advice, as always. "You need to talk to your parents again," he'd told me. "It sounds like Charlie's hesitant because of your dad's cancer."

"She doesn't want my father and me to be estranged because of the relationship I have with her."

Archie's voice, warm and understanding as always, had countered, "So talk to them again, then. I'm sure you can convince your dad." Forever the optimist.

"I don't know, Archie, but I'll try. I don't plan to stay away, no matter what, anyway. My father doesn't have long, and I won't let him push me away for the time he has left."

Good ol' Archie, I think as I drag myself out of bed, yawning and stretching. There's no point in pretending that sleep will return to me now. I might as well get up.

As I make my way to the bathroom, guilt pokes at me. *The business.* It's something I've been neglecting, and it pricks at my conscience. It's not fair to Charlie or to Ronny. Ronny's played a crucial role in our marketing endeavors, and I feel negligent leaving him and Charlie holding the bag. They're more than capable of running the business without me, but I owe it to them to do my part.

I call Jake, our marketing manager, to check in. He reassures me that Ronny is still handling the social media marketing as scheduled and that everything is running smoothly. After tying up a few loose ends with Jake, I end the call.

Almost as soon as I set my phone down, it rings with a call from my mother. Dread tightens in my chest as I answer. "Mom? Is everything alright?"

She quickly eases my worries. "Oh, yes, your father's fine, baby, don't worry. I didn't call about that."

I catch my breath. "What did you call for, then?"

She takes on a hushed tone as if sharing a secret. "I don't want you staying away because your father doesn't like your choices, Atticus. It would help if you spent as much time with him as you can." Her voice gets lower. "Look, I *know* he's difficult, and you don't always agree with his opinions, but he *is* your father, and you know he loves you."

"I know he does," I say. "I didn't plan to stay away, anyway. I can promise you that."

My mother, still in her secretive tone, adds, "So...tell me about this, *Charlene*, you're interested in. *Just between us.*"

I imagine her tucked away in her sewing room, whispering so my father won't overhear.

"Well, that's done and over with, it seems." I sigh, opening the fridge to grab a bottle of water and heading to the living room. It's only seven a.m., but I need to sit down.

Mom, ever perceptive, prods further. "You left her because of Dad?"

"No, it wasn't *my* choice. I love Dad, but I won't allow him to dictate who I care about."

She asks about the breakup, and I recount last night's events. "Charlie ended things with me last night. I went to her house to have a conversation. She was upset with me because I lied to her about my identity. She thought I was *Jimmy*, and now she's told me she wants nothing to do with me."

My mother murmurs, "That's not good."

"I know! I tried to tell Charlie I was just doing what my father required and could she give me another chance."

Her voice drops even lower, making it harder to hear. "So, what happened?"

"I'm pretty sure she forgave me, but when I told her about Dad and his cancer, she backed away. She said she couldn't be the reason that Dad and I don't speak to each other."

"Oh," she says, "I see."

My head throbs as I recline on the couch and place the cold water bottle on my forehead, closing my eyes while still holding the phone to my ear. My mother remains silent for a while, and I sit up, taking a big gulp of the water.

Finally, Mom says, "I'm sorry about your girlfriend, honey. I know how hard it was for you when Heather broke it off. I don't want to see you fall back into a slump. You really like this girl, Charlene?"

"I really do, Mom. She's amazing. She's so smart — she developed that app by herself — *and* she's funny. She's a good person. Do you know she takes care of her paralyzed brother every day and never complains? She even gave up a great job to stay home with him and worked nights cleaning to make ends meet."

"Wow, she sounds like a *delightful* girl," Mom says. Then she sighs. "Let me talk to your father, Atticus. I'm sure I can convince him to change his mind. Maybe if he just meets her."

I chuckle softly, realizing the hurdles ahead. "Well, it will be hard for Dad to meet her if she won't talk to me."

My mother, full of determination, encourages me. "I think

if you really like this girl, keep trying. It sounds like she likes you, too."

I sigh, understanding the effort it'll take. "Alright, if Dad is agreeable, I'll try to convince Charlie to come and meet you guys."

She suggests I come and visit this afternoon and promises to talk to my father before my arrival.

"Okay," I say.

"And does your Charlene live near you?"

"Yes, she lives in Albany on New Scotland Avenue. My new place is on Sawyer, just a few minutes from her. Why?"

"I was just curious. It's nice that you live near each other. I'd love to see your place sometime."

"Sure, Mom. I'd love that. Absolutely. I'll see you this afternoon," I say, the weight on my shoulders somewhat lightened by her support.

"Love you, baby. See you this afternoon."

As I approach my parent's front door, my pulse races with dread. I'm not sure of the cause. It's not that I'm afraid of my father. I'm not. But I've *always* wanted him to be proud of me. I've always sought his approval. He's a powerful man, and everyone's assumed I would follow in his footsteps. But when I messed up, when things got so bad that he'd kicked me out of the house, well, it felt like everything went spiraling out of control. I guess I'm not sure I can fix this, but I *have to* fix this.

As I step into the front hall, my mother greets me with a warm smile. She's been waiting for me. "Hey, baby, come on. We're just having lunch in the dining room," she says, putting her arm through mine. As we make our way down the long hallway, she whispers, "I think I made some headway with the situation."

I stop and raise my brows, intrigued. "Really?"

"Yes, come," she says with a smile.

We enter the dining room. My father sits at the head of the long table, looking every bit the powerful man that he is. I know he's sick, but his outward appearance would never give it away. My mother takes her place on one side of him, and I on the other.

"Hello, son," he says when I pull out my chair.

"Hey, Dad," I say, feeling nervous but glad to see him. He'd greeted me, so maybe Mom's gotten through to him.

He takes my hand and shakes it, grabbing my elbow with his other hand, as is his custom with me. His grip is firm, but I can feel his affection, and I relax a little. The room appears even more magnificent than I recall, with its high ceilings and elegant chandeliers casting a warm, inviting glow.

"How are you feeling today?" I ask him, wanting to make sure he's doing okay.

"Don't start asking me how I'm feeling every time you see me. I'm fine," my father says. I'm not trying to annoy him, so I make a mental note to avoid that question in the future. "Mildred is bringing out the food shortly."

I adjust myself at the table, and my father immediately speaks. "I spoke with your mother today," he says, clearing his throat. I glance at my mother, who smiles at me, giving me a knowing look before looking back at my father. "It seems I may have misjudged your lady friend."

Relief floods through me at his words. "I'm glad to hear you say that."

"Your mother told me your friend broke off the relationship with you to avoid complicating things between you and me. That's admirable," he says, nodding.

I wait for him to continue, hoping this is leading where I want it to.

"I'd like to meet her, son, if that's alright. Sooner rather than later, I'd suppose."

I clear my throat. "I don't know if Charlie will want to do that, Dad. She broke it off with me."

"Well, Atticus, if I know you, and I think I do, I'd say you'll find a way. Tomorrow for dinner would work the best. Please don't disappoint me," he says, his tone leaving no room for argument.

Mildred arrives with the food, greeting me and making me stand for a hug. My parents and I eat and talk about everything but Charlie. I know better than to bring it up again. I'll take what I can get. I don't want him to change his mind.

After we finish our meal, my mother tells us she needs to leave for a while to take care of some things. My father smiles at her as she kisses him on his head. "Don't be too long, dear," he says as she goes.

My father and I head to his study. "What do you say we play a game of chess?"

My competitive side takes over. "You got it, Dad, but I'm not going easy on you."

I glance at him from across the chessboard and realize how much I'm going to miss my dad.

CHAPTER 32
Charlie

I don't know how to do this. These men who break my heart — how am I supposed to move past this? I've tried so hard, but nothing works out for me. I know I'm wallowing in self-pity, and I hate myself for it, but I'm just so broken. I feel so lost.

Jimmy. I have to admit he tried. I'll give him that. But deep down, he couldn't fully commit to me. Was I expecting too much? Men like Jimmy rarely fall for girls like me, anyway.

Standing in front of my mirror, I pick apart every aspect of my appearance, as I often do. It's even worse now. I compare myself to the rich model-type women Jimmy's probably used to. His last girlfriend went to Hollywood or something. She was probably drop-dead gorgeous, too. Then there's me. My nose is too big, and my hair refuses to cooperate no matter how hard I try.

Jimmy's a *billionaire*. I've seen the pictures and the glamorous women he's been seen out with in public. The ones with the perfect figures, perfect hair, and perfect *everything*. He's so far out of my league that it makes my head spin. During his exile, I provided a convenient escape. Maybe he developed feelings for me, but they can't compete against his parents, his inheritance, or the myriad of women in line to date him. If I think they can, I'm fooling myself.

A tear escapes, and I quickly wipe it away. *Suck it up, buttercup! You ended things with Jimmy, and now you have to live with that decision!*

As I stand before my mirror, Ronny calls from the living room. "Charlie, someone's at the door!"

I hurry down the stairs, wiping my eyes and straightening my hair. I open the door, and I'm taken aback. On my porch stands an elegantly dressed older woman, the kind you'd expect to see on a magazine cover. Her clothes are impeccable, and she swept her hair into a perfect, ornate bun. She's remarkably beautiful.

For a moment, I'm lost for words. I'm pretty sure this woman isn't a salesperson, but I can't imagine why she's standing on my doorstep. Her smile is warm and kind, reminding me of my late grandmother.

"Can I help you?" I say.

"Yes," she says. "Are you Charlene?"

"I am."

"Oh, you *are* lovely! No wonder my Atticus is so smitten with you. I'm Atticus' mother, Carol, and I was wondering if I could have a word with you. I won't take up much of your time."

I have trouble swallowing, but I manage. "Um, yes, of course. Come on in." I usher her inside and introduce her to Ronny, who greets her with a handshake.

She turns back to me. "I wasn't sure which side was yours. I had to check the mailbox." She chuckles nervously. "I hope you don't mind me just dropping in on you like this."

"I'm going into the kitchen and give you two some privacy," Ronny says, wheeling himself out to the kitchen.

I gesture for Carol to sit down. "It's fine. Please, have a seat."

"Thank you," she says, taking the chair at the end of the couch. I sit down on the couch and wait.

"I'm sure you know why I'm here," she begins, making my heart race. *Is she going to tell me to stay away from Jimmy?*

"Well, I'm sure it's about Jim—uh, I mean Atticus."

"It is. I hope I'm not overstepping, and I'm sure Atticus would be upset if he knew I was here, but I just felt I had to speak with you."

"Okay," I say, and then remember my manners. "Would you like something to drink?"

"Oh, no, dear, no thank you. I'll get right to the point."

I hope I can hear what she says through the blood rushing in my ears.

"Atticus is a very nice young man. I'm sure you've already figured that out. He's devoted to his family and his friends. He's sitting at my house with my husband right now. I made excuses to leave and come to talk to you because I can't bear to look at his face one moment longer."

"What do you mean?" I ask. My palms feel sweaty, and I attempt to wipe them discreetly on my pants.

"I mean, he's heartbroken, sweetheart, over *you*. You *do* know he defied his father and told him he'd rather be poor with *you* than wealthy without you, right? Did he tell you that?"

"Yes, he told me that, but—"

"Well, his father has changed his mind."

I'm sure my shock registers on my face. "He has?"

"Yes. When my husband learned from Atticus that you broke up with him to save his and Jimmy's relationship, he realized you were not after the money. You have to understand, dear, my husband has had a lot of heartbreak in his life because of his wealth. When one has been blessed with money, it becomes difficult to form genuine human relationships. He just didn't want Atticus to go through the same agony, especially after his recent experience with Heather."

"Yes, I heard about Heather. That's what put... *Atticus* into his depression and caused his father to kick him out."

Carol scoffs. "I hate that phrase, 'kicked him out.' It wasn't like that. We merely gave Atticus a push to pick up the pieces and get on with his life. He was wallowing, and we couldn't stand to watch it any longer."

"I didn't mean any disrespect," I say.

"Look, Charlene, my son cares about you, and you will be hard put to find another man like him. He's truly one of a kind. I'm here hoping you will give him another chance."

I look at Jimmy's mother, and my heart squeezes. She must love him so much to come all this way to talk to *me*.

"Alright, Carol, I'll talk to Atticus." It's so strange to call him by that name.

She puts her hand to her heart. "Oh, thank God! I prayed all the way here!" The relief and smile on her face make me glad I agreed.

As I walk her to the door, I realize that maybe not all wealthy people are jerks. Carol seems genuine and kind.

"Thank you, dear," she says at the door, taking both my hands in hers and squeezing them. "It was lovely to meet you."

Glancing outside, I spot a long silver limousine parked across the street. That thing could easily accommodate ten people. I hadn't noticed it when I first opened the door for her.

"It was nice to meet you, too," I say.

Back in the house, I enter the kitchen, where Ronny sits at the table, eating a sandwich.

"Alright, sis!" he exclaims. "You're getting back with Jimmy!"

"Don't count your chickens yet. I still need to talk to him."

"Charlie's getting back with Jimmy — Charlie's getting back with Jimmy!" he chants like an excited child.

"You're silly," I say.

"And you're getting back with Jimmy," he says, a huge, goofy smile on his face.

CHAPTER 33
Atticus

When the phone rings, I see Charlie's name flashing on the car's Bluetooth screen, and my heart drops to my stomach. Taking a deep breath, I answer the call, my voice trembling. "Hello? Charlie?" I breathe.

I can hear her breathing on the other end of the line. "Yes, it's me," she says. "Can you talk?"

I try to sound casual as I reply. "With you? Always, gorgeous." But I know she can hear the excitement in my voice. I'm driving back from my parent's house and quickly pull off the Northway at an exit ramp. I need to focus on this conversation without the distraction of the surrounding traffic.

"Can we meet up?" Charlie asks.

My heart skips a beat. "Yeah, sure. When? Now?" I pull into a local Stewart's shop and throw the car in park.

"Well, no, not this minute, because it's going to take me a while to get Ronny into bed. How about in an hour? Say nine at Ship's Pub? Do you know where that is?"

I can't believe what I'm hearing. Charlie wants to see me?

My mind is racing as I agree to meet. "Yes, I know where Ship's is. I'll be there. Nine o'clock."

"Alright, then. I'll have Aunt Debbie turn on the monitor, and I'll see you then."

Getting back on the Northway, I head home, my mind filled with thoughts of Charlie. I've got to shower and get ready to meet her. This could be the start of something amazing. Or it could be the end of everything.

Ship's Pub is bustling for a Thursday night. They packed people shoulder-to-shoulder, but amidst the chaos, I spot a couple leaving a small table in the corner. I walk over and sit down once they leave and wait for Charlie. My brow is moist, and my nerves are on high alert. I can't believe she's asked to meet with me. I arrived twenty minutes early because I had too much anxiety to sit and wait at home.

Looking up, I see Charlie walk through the door and I rise, waving. She looks stunning in form-fitting jeans and a peach colored top with delicate straps. I long to embrace her, but I resist the urge. After all, I don't even know what she wants to talk about.

"Hey, you look great," I say, smiling my most charming smile.

"Thanks, Jimmy," she says. She gives what I can only call a forced smile.

I pull out her chair for her, and she sits down. As I take my seat on the other side, I study her face, wishing I could read her mind. The suspense is killing me.

"Would you like me to get us some drinks?" I ask.

As I say it, a waitress approaches us. "Hi," she says. "My name's Felisha, and I'll be your server. Can I start you off with some drinks?" She hands us each a menu.

I wait for Charlie to order. "I'll have a White Russian," she says.

"I'll have a Blue Moon with a slice of orange."

"You got it," she says and hurries off to get our drinks.

"So, what did you want to talk about?" I ask. All I can think about is kissing her ruby lips.

"Your mother came to see me today," she says.

I almost choke. "My mother? What?"

"Yes. She came to see me today at my house. Did you tell her where I live?" Charlie asks, her tone unreadable.

"Uh, yeah, well, sort of. I told her you lived on New Scotland Avenue. Wow. What did she want?"

"She wanted to plead your case. Your mother's worried about you and wanted to ask me to give you another chance." Wow. So that's where she went today after lunch.

"Oh, I'm sorry, Charlie. She shouldn't have done that," I say, feeling a little embarrassed. "I didn't know."

"No, it's alright, Jimmy. She was sweet. I was glad she came. She told me how your father's changed his mind about me?"

"He did!" This gives me the perfect opportunity to ask her to come to dinner tomorrow to meet him. So I go for it. "He actually would like you to accompany me to their house for dinner tomorrow night." I hold my breath.

"Um...tomorrow? At their place?" she says, barely audible. I can see the shocked — maybe worried — look on her face.

"Yes," I say, but I don't want to push her. "But we don't have to go if you're not comfortable." I feel like I'm fumbling the ball. "I mean, we can do it some other time." The last thing I need to do right now is upset her.

"No, no, just let me gather my thoughts," she says, taking a moment to think.

I try to be patient, but the silence is killing me. "You've already met my mom," I say, "and you know me, so that's *two* out of three." I smile, trying to convince her it'll be okay.

"But your *father*," she says.

I laugh. "You act like my father's some scary monster. I can assure you, he's not."

"I know, but—"

"Let's put my father aside for a minute. Does the fact that we're even talking about this mean we're getting back together?" I can't stand not knowing. I don't want to push too hard, but patience is not my strong suit.

Charlie smiles. "I'd like to give us another go, yes. But on *one* condition."

I sigh a tremendous sigh of relief. "Alright, what's the condition?" At this point, I don't care what it is.

"That you *never* lie to me again, Jimmy. I mean it. I honestly understand why you did what you did, but it's a lot to forgive. So please, promise me, no matter what, that you'll always be honest with me, even if you think I'll be upset." She locks her gaze on me intently as she waits for my response. I don't delay.

"You've got it," I say. "I promise with *everything* that's in me. Give me a stack of Bibles, and I'll swear on them, too." Standing up, I practically knock my chair down as I push it back. "Come here."

She glances around but stands up, and I take her in my arms. "Thank you, baby, for giving us another shot," I say, pressing my lips to hers.

As soon as our lips touch, she melts into my embrace. It's like her body was crafted to fit exactly with mine. We meld together perfectly. The world fades away. All that matters are her and me, *together*. Mimicking a scene from the old-time movies, I lean her back and plant another tender kiss on her lips. As we lean, she gracefully lifts her leg.

Suddenly, an outburst from the surrounding people interrupts us. Bringing her back up, we see the crowded bar, people clapping and whooping loudly, all looking at us and smiling, and we both burst into laughter at the absurdity of it all. I take a bow, holding Charlie's hand, and she follows suit, which only makes the crowd cheer louder.

The waitress is standing there with a tray and our drinks, a huge smile on her face. "Well, you guys just got the Customers of the Year award," she says, laughing.

Charlie and I take our seats, and the waitress sets down our drinks, shaking her head and laughing as she goes. I raise my beer to Charlie. "To total honesty," I say.

"To total honesty," Charlie repeats, raising her drink. We clink our drinks together.

"Does this mean you'll come to dinner tomorrow night?" I ask, hoping she says yes. I'm working so hard at mending the fences with my father, and I don't want to ruffle his feathers again.

"Yes, Jimmy, I'll come to dinner," Charlie says, sipping her drink and setting it down. "What do I wear?"

"Dress nice," I tell her. "It doesn't have to be formal. I'm going to wear a pair of slacks and a sweater. Just be comfortable."

"Alright," she says. "I'm so nervous."

"Don't be nervous, *gorgeous*. He's going to love you."

CHAPTER 34
Charlie

"What about this one?" I twirl around in front of Aunt Debbie, the skirt of the dress flaring out around me. My heart is racing with excitement and nerves.

Aunt Debbie studies me for a moment, then shakes her head. "I like the blue one better," she says with a smile.

I nod, feeling a little deflated but trusting her opinion. I'm not used to dressing up like this, and I want to make a good impression on Jimmy's parents. But I also want to feel confident and attractive, especially around Jimmy himself.

As I slip out of the dress, my hands shake a little. I can't help but think about what the evening will be like — meeting Jimmy's dad, trying to make conversation, trying not to spill anything on myself.

But then Aunt Debbie's voice breaks through my thoughts as if reading my mind. "Oh, sweetie," she says with a chuckle. "They put their pants on one leg at a time, just like you do."

I can't help but laugh, feeling a bit better. Aunt Debbie always has the funniest expressions, and she can always read my mind. "Alright," I say. "The blue one it is." It's a little longer than the flowered one I had tried on, and it's not as low cut. It's not exactly what I had in mind, but it's a bit more conservative and probably a smarter choice.

Ronnie calls from the living room. "Charlie! Your phone is ringing." I must have left it downstairs.

"Coming!" I call down, throwing my robe on and bouncing down the stairs.

I pick up my phone and look at it. *Janice!* I had called her and left her a message, and she's calling me back.

"Janice!" I say, excited she returned my call. "Thank you for getting back to me."

"It surprised me to hear from you. Is everything all right?" It's a legitimate thing to say since I haven't spoken to her in a few years now.

"It is. No worries. I was just calling to apologize to you."

There's silence on the other end, so I say, "I just wanted to say that I treated you unfairly and called you a liar, and I'm so sorry, Janice. You were a good friend, and I've missed you terribly. I hope you can forgive me."

Silence again. I wait this time. Finally, she says, "What made you finally believe me?"

Again, it's a legitimate question. I feel like an idiot. But I tell her. "Mark is the liar," I say. "He was always ogling other women, and I was wrong to believe him over you. I just didn't want it to be true, so I thought it would be easier to accuse you of lying instead of believing what you said. I am so sorry."

Janice sighs on the other end. "Wow. I never thought I'd hear from you again."

"I know," I say, feeling so stupid. "I was wondering if you might want to do lunch sometime? I mean, if you can't forgive me, then I totally—"

"No. I forgive you, Char, and I'd love to do lunch. Nothing's been the same since we stopped hanging out. I don't have another friend as cool as you." She chuckles.

I laugh. Good ol' Janice. Ronnie was right, and I owe him a hug for making me see my error.

"Great," I say. "I'm in the middle of something right now, but can I call you tomorrow? We can set up a day to get together. I can't wait."

"I'd love that," she says, "And I can't wait, either."

"Charlie! He's here!" Ronny's voice rings through the house from the living room.

Shoot! I'm not ready yet. I quickly slip on my heels and add another coat of lipstick. Downstairs, Jimmy, Ronny, and Aunt Debbie are laughing, making it feel like I'm off to prom. I wonder if Aunt Debbie is going to have us pose on the stairs for pictures.

As I make my way down the stairs in my heels, Jimmy turns to look at me. "Wow, Charlie! You look *great*!"

I blush a hundred shades of red. "Thanks, Jimmy. You look nice, too."

He looks more than nice. The sight of his broad shoulders in that white sweater tempts me to run my hands along them and feel their strong, masculine presence. My heart races with anticipation because I know he's going to kiss me as soon as we get into the car. I've been thinking of little else the entire time I've been getting ready. I can't wait to run my fingers through his gorgeous hair and get lost in his warm and protective embrace.

"You ready to go?" he says. "We don't want to be late."

Aunt Debbie hugs me and plants a kiss on my cheek. She whispers in my ear. "Don't be nervous, dolly. You're going to do just fine. Just relax and *be yourself*."

Ronny puts his hand up to give me a fist pump. "Knock 'em dead, Sis!"

As we walk to his car, Jimmy takes my hand in his. "I can't wait for my dad to meet you, Charlie. I know he's going to love you."

"I hope so," I say. "I just can't wait for this to be over."

His face falls from the beaming smile he had. "Don't say that," he says. "He's awesome. You guys are going to hit it out of the park. All you have to do is to be yourself, and Bob's your uncle."

I laugh. I adore the way he adds a little British accent when he says that phrase. Being with Jimmy is so easy. "Alright, I'll trust you on that," I say.

He opens my door and I climb in, nervously adjusting my dress over my knees. I hope it's not too short. I'm glad I listened to Aunt Debbie and chose the blue one. Jimmy closes my door and walks around.

Jimmy glances over at me once he's settled behind the wheel. "Here we go," he says, starting the car.

My heart sinks a little. I was hoping he'd kiss me, but I'm sure he will later. He probably doesn't want us to be late.

He puts on the radio, and music fills the car. It's a pleasant distraction because I'm such a ball of nerves I'm having trouble thinking of anything to talk about. I glance at Jimmy, and he glances back and smiles as he reaches over and takes my hand in his.

The house exceeds all my expectations. I wonder what they even do with all those rooms. It feels like the place goes on forever, and I've only seen the front from the driveway.

Before we even get out of the car, the grand front door swings open, revealing two figures waiting for us. One is

Jimmy's mother, Carol, and the other is his father, whose face I recognize from the countless articles I have read about him. Seeing him in person, I can see the resemblance between him and Jimmy. In fact, Jimmy looks way more like his father than he does his mother.

My feet wobble a bit on my heels as I walk, but Jimmy takes my arm, steadying me. I take a deep breath, and we walk up the steps and stop at the doorway. I inhale deeply. *I can do this!*

"Hello, Charlene!" His mother greets me warmly. "Welcome!" She takes my shoulders and kisses me on each cheek like we're old friends. "I'd like you to meet Atticus' father, Ray." She turns to Jimmy's father. "Honey, this is Charlene."

Ray extends his hand, and I offer mine. He takes my hand in his and places his other hand on top of it, giving it a warm squeeze. "Atticus has told me all about you, young lady. It's a pleasure to meet you. Come in. Come in. Mildred and the staff have prepared a feast to die for."

I glance at Jimmy, and he smiles. We follow his parents down a seemingly endless hall that leads to a room that could easily house a small town. Is this their dining room? They must entertain a lot to have a room this enormous.

Ray takes his place at the head of the table, and Jimmy's mother sits to one side. Jimmy motions for me to sit on the other side of his father and pulls out my chair for me. Once I'm seated, he sits down next to me. I observe the others and copy their actions as they place napkins on their laps.

I look down at my plate, three forks on one side and three spoons on the other. My stomach churns with nerves. I have no appetite, and the thought of eating a lavish meal makes me feel queasy.

"So, Atticus tells me *you're* the brains behind the famous AccessAid app," Ray says with a warm smile.

"Yes," I reply, clearing my throat. "I developed it to help my brother."

"Atticus told us your brother had an accident and that you are his primary caregiver. Family's everything, isn't it? We believe that strongly, here." Ray looks over at Carol, and they smile at each other. He turns back to me. "I think it's admirable that you take care of him."

"Thanks," I say. I look from Ray over to Jimmy, and his face is beaming.

"How's Ronny doing?" his mother asks. "He seems like a nice young man."

"Oh, he's good," I say.

A waiter comes to the table and asks for our drink orders. It feels more like an upscale restaurant than someone's home. I order my usual White Russian while Jimmy orders a beer. His mother rolls her eyes. Then his parents order a wine I've never heard of.

"Did Jimmy tell you he's a professional chess player?" Ray asks.

I glance at Jimmy, noticing his slightly red face. "I'm not a *professional*, Dad," he laughs. "I'm just a master." His parents chuckle.

"I didn't know you played chess," I say. "I played a little in college."

"Oh, where did you go to college?" Jimmy's mother asks. The waiter brings our drinks, and I want to gulp mine down and ask for another.

"Hudson Valley," I say. It's a small community college located across the river in Troy. It's probably someplace they would never have considered sending Jimmy.

His parents glance at each other. "Oh," his mother says, smiling politely. "That's a nice little school."

I feel awkward suddenly. I should've just said "Yale," or "Harvard," but knowing his father, he'd probably check.

Suddenly, Mr. Winslow coughs and gasps for air. His mother, her eyes wide, rings a bell, and someone, presumably a butler, immediately rushes in with an oxygen tank. Ray breathes through the mask for a moment before handing it back.

"Thank you, Michael," his mother says. Then she turns to Ray. "You know, sweetheart, the doctor would like you to keep that on all the time unless you're eating."

"I know, Carol. I'm well aware of what the doctor said. But we're eating now, aren't we, so let's just enjoy our meal."

Ray turns to me. "You know, Charlene, my grandmother was injured in an accident when I was just a small boy. I watched my grandfather care for her, and it was no simple task. They didn't have all the gadgets they have these days, either. He had to lift her constantly to get her around. I've got to say, I admire you for doing what you do."

"Well, like you said, he's family," I say.

"Here's to that," Ray says, looking at Jimmy's mother. "My Carol here has been a God-send to me during *my* ordeal. I'd be lost without her."

He raises his glass, and we all follow suit. "Here's to family," he says. "And to Atticus for finding this wonderful girl during his adventure."

I flush, surprised that Ray had toasted to me. Relief washes away all the angst I had been carrying. We all clink glasses, and my appetite suddenly returns as Mildred brings out the first appetizer — scallops wrapped in bacon.

"My favorite!" I exclaim.

"I know," Ray says. "Atticus told us."

CHAPTER 35
Atticus

"I believe that went rather well," I say to Charlie as we exit the driveway. "Goodnight, Billy," I call to the guard at the gate.

Charlie sighs and puts her head back on the rest. "Ugh. I'm relieved *that's* over."

"You don't think it went well?" I ask.

"No, I think it went wonderfully. I liked your dad. He made me feel welcome, and of course, your mom is amazing. I was a bundle of nerves, that's all."

I chuckle. "I was, too, to be honest, but I knew he would love you. I was just unsure if you would like him." I glance over at her.

"Well, I do, so you can relax."

I veer onto the Northway, heading north instead of south.

"Hey, where are you going?" Charlie sits up and looks around.

"Oh," I say, "I thought we might get a drink. The night is still young."

"I have to ask Aunt Debbie," she says. "I told her I'd be home after dinner."

I smile and look over at her. I reach over and take her hand. "It's already taken care of."

She laughs and playfully hits my arm. "You're too much," she says.

Lost in thought, I drive in silence while Charlie gazes out the window. "Where the heck are we going?" she says as we pass yet another exit.

"You'll see," I say slyly, not wanting to spoil the surprise.

We reach Exit 23, and I put on my blinker. The exit sign reads "Lake George Village."

"Lake George!" she exclaims. "I love Lake George!"

"I know you do," I say.

We pass through the village. My family has a pontoon boat docked at our camp, which sits directly on the lake, many miles up from the village. I say 'camp,' but it's more of a summer home. It's one of my favorite places. I turn the car down a long, winding road that leads us along the lake. We drive for quite a while before I pull into the driveway of our house. "Here we are," I say.

Her eyes widen. "You have a house on Lake George?" She looks around as if I've taken her to a magical kingdom.

"Yes, we do, and a *boat*." I flash her a smile, and her face lights up even more. "A pontoon boat. Want to go out on the lake? Traffic on the lake is light at this hour. It's very peaceful. And *private*." I give her a knowing look and wink at her.

She smiles. "I'd love to." We walk to the dock, and I help her onto the boat.

The view from the lake is enchanting, with clusters of tiny islands, and the stars illuminate the sky, their brilliance enhanced by the absence of any light from Lake George Village, miles away and hidden from view.

Whenever I want to relive the nostalgia of my youth, I head to a secluded cove where my parents and I spent countless hours swimming. It's paradise, nestled amongst towering pines, with no camps in sight. It's perfect.

I anchor the boat in the cove. "Want to swim?" I ask her.

"Swim? I don't have a suit."

"My mother has a bunch of them in that drawer over there." I point to a drawer. "Use the cabin at the back of the boat to change."

"Alright, sure. That could be fun. You're going to swim, too, right?"

"Of course. You go ahead and change, then I'll follow. I'll get the tubes out so we can float around."

The water is cold when we get in, but Lake George is always cold.

"Brrrr," Charlie says. "It's freezing."

I push my tube over to hers so we are facing each other. "I can come over to your tube and keep you warm."

I don't wait for her response. I duck under my tube, immersing myself in the cold water, and push the tube aside, letting it float away. Then I come up through the center of her tube, squeezing my way in.

She laughs. "You're squishing me."

"Oh, am I?" I say. "Too bad for you. You don't want me to drown, do you?"

She tries to adjust herself, but I say, "Turn around."

"I can't turn around. It's too squishy." She's struggling to hold the side of the tube.

"Charlie," I say, "Just turn around. I won't let you fall through."

She turns around, putting her arms over my shoulders so she doesn't fall into the center.

"Now that's a good girl," I tease.

As our bodies press together, her skin feels so warm compared to the icy water.

"Is this better?" I ask. "Are you feeling warmer?"

"I am," she whispers, seeming to have difficulty speaking.

"Alright, good," I say, savoring the closeness between us. "So, what should we do now?"

"Oh, I don't know. Look at the stars?" she says, glancing up at the night sky.

"I've got a better idea," I say, staring at her. It's so dark. We're just shadows to each other, but I can hear her breathing picking up pace.

"What's your idea?" she says.

"Oh, I think you know very well what my idea is," I say.

Holding the tube to prevent us from falling, I place one hand behind her head. She knows what I'm about to do and gasps in anticipation.

"What's the matter, gorgeous?" I say, running my fingers through her hair. "You seem to be having trouble breathing."

"I hate you," she pants.

"You hate me?" I say. "That's too bad because I had such big plans for us."

"Are you going to tease me all night?" Her hands are on my shoulders, gripping tightly, and I feel her tremble.

"Not *all* night," I say.

I wait for a moment before wrapping my fingers through her hair. Her breathing quickens even more as I bring her toward me. I have a desire to tease her, but my need is too great. All I could think about was kissing her all night. I can't wait any longer.

I brush my lips against hers. Charlie tries to press in harder, but I yank her head back by her hair, denying us both what we want. Then I set her free and grin. Her eyes get wide, and she's about to speak when I bring my face close and lick her lips. She moans, igniting a fierce desire in me. There's a minty sensation on her lips, and when I kiss her again, our lips glide together perfectly. I can't get enough of her. I want to consume her, and my passion is surging more than I've ever experienced before. I press my lips harder, more urgently, and a gasp escapes her. I pull away. Oh, how I delight in tormenting her.

Her wide eyes are visible even in the dark. She's panting, and so am I.

"I've missed you," I say, meaning it with everything in me.

"Me, too," she says. "So much." She's breathing rapidly. "I need you," she pants.

I pull her hair, bringing her head back until it's leaning on the tube behind her. She cries out as I do, but I hold her there. Even in the water, I can detect her fragrant scent, like fresh air and flowers. It's almost too much to bear. My desire for her consumes me, leaving me barely in control.

I groan as I kiss her neck and make my way up toward her face, lifting her head off the tube as I move to caress her ear with my lips, pushing her wet hair aside with my fingers. I lick her ear, and she moans louder. I exhale a hot breath into her ear as I utter a low, guttural moan filled with lust.

"Oh, Jimmy," she gasps, and goosebumps burst to my skin.

I bring my mouth back to hers and indulge in my pleasure. "I knew you'd come back to me," I say. "How could you stay away?"

"I couldn't," she says. "I couldn't."

We kiss for what seems like a long time, but the kisses always leave me wanting more. I feel her shiver again, so I reluctantly release her.

"Come on," I say. "Let's get out of the water."

I kick my feet, feeling the cool water rushing past my toes as I bring our tube back to the boat. We'd drifted a considerable distance from it, lost in our own little world.

Once on the boat, we change back into our clothes. When I come out from the cabin, I find Charlie waiting for me, her smile radiant even with her hair all wet and stringy. I reach under the cabinet and pull out an ice bucket, revealing a bottle of champagne and two glasses on the tray beside it. Tiny white lights illuminate the boat in a romantic glow, and I can't help but feel like this moment is perfect.

"What's all this?" she asks, her eyes widening in surprise.

"It's a celebration," I say, holding up the bottle of champagne. "For *us*."

I pop the cork, and we laugh as it lands who knows where in the water. I pour us each a glass, and we sit with our feet over the edge of the boat, the dark water rippling against its side. It's a peaceful, serene moment, leaving me grateful for everything in my life.

I make a toast, raising my glass. "To us, Charlie. To our business, to Ronny, and to Aunt Debbie, too."

"And your parents," she says, her voice soft. "Don't forget about them."

"And my parents," I add.

I pause for a moment, thinking about my parents and our complicated relationship, one that I rarely like to dwell on. But right now, I have a peaceful feeling about them. About everything.

We clink our glasses and take a sip. The champagne is cold and bubbly, its sweetness dancing on our taste buds under the sliver of the moonlit sky, casting a serene aura across the cove.

"I've got another surprise for you tomorrow if you're game," I say casually.

"Another surprise? You're full of it, aren't you?" She giggles.

"If you're curious, come with me tomorrow."

She says nothing for a minute, and then she turns to me. "You know," she says, "you don't have to work so hard, Jimmy. You don't have to *buy* my affection."

I stop short. Buy her affection? *Is that what she thinks I'm doing?*

"I'm not buying your affection, Charlene, I'm merely—"

"And there you go with the 'Charlene' again," she says, her tone sharp.

"Oh, come on, that *is* your name, isn't it?"

"Yes, *Jimmy*, that's my name, but you know I don't like it."

"What's with the sarcasm?" I ask, puzzled by the sudden tension. We were having a great night. Everything was perfect.

"I just hate having to call you *Atticus* in front of your parents when your name is Jimmy to me. It was so awkward trying to remember not to call you Jimmy tonight. It's just so ridiculous, and yet I ask you a simple thing, not to call me Charlene, and you do it anyway. It's bad enough I had to listen to them call me Charlene all night."

"I'm sorry. I won't call you Charlene anymore. Promise." I hold up my hands.

She scoffs. "You make a lot of promises, don't you?"

"Are you going to hold my mistakes over my head forever? I've apologized like a hundred times. I thought we were past this?" Now I'm getting frustrated, which is clear in my tone, and I regret displaying it when I see her face.

She gets up, walks to the bar, sets her drink down, and picks up her phone. She looks at it for a minute. "I think I should get going now. Aunt Debbie is going to wonder where I am, and I'm not getting any service out here."

I get up and go to her. I put my hand on her shoulder and turn her around. She doesn't fight me, but her pout shows me she's not entirely receptive.

"I'm sorry, Charlie. Can I say it again? I'm *sorry*. I mean it. I'm not looking to fight with you. We've had a nice evening, and I don't want to go home knowing you're mad at me."

She sniffles. "I've got a lot of emotion right now, Jimmy. This is just a lot for me. I don't mean to keep bringing stuff up. I'm sorry, too." She wipes a tear from her eye and sighs.

I lift her face to look at me. "I'm here for you, gorgeous. *Always*. I am as committed to working on us as you are. I promise you. Let's go home and get a good night's sleep. It's been a long day."

"Alright," she says. I lean in and kiss her softly, pressing my lips to her but not moving as I savor the sensation of her lips on mine and the warmth of her touch. I part her lips slowly with my tongue and enter her mouth. The meeting of our tongues sets off an electrifying pulse, gradually intensifying as desire takes over. Our tender embrace has erupted into an intoxicating whirlwind of yearning again.

My heart is crashing into my chest again when I release her. I *need* to release her. My urge is too great. "Let's head home," I say.

I can see her brow furrow, so I take her hand. "Come on. I'll let you drive the boat."

As we stand at her door, my arms wrapped around her waist, I ask her, "So, you haven't answered me about tomorrow. You up for another surprise?"

"Why not," she says, smiling. "I'm sorry that I was rude about it earlier."

I put my finger to her lips. "Shhh. It's alright. So, I'll pick you up at ten, then?"

I take my hand down and lean in for a kiss, but she moves her head back, out of reach. "In the morning?" she asks, looking surprised.

"Yes, in the morning. And Ronny, too. Make sure you're ready at ten o'clock."

She looks at me with raised eyebrows. "Ronny, too? Really?" Her face breaks into a huge grin.

I nod and say, "Yes, and dress casually and comfortably. We're in for a fun day."

I kiss her good night and walk down the steps, turning to watch as she opens her door. "Good night, gorgeous," I say, standing on the sidewalk.

"Good night, Jimmy," she says. She pauses at the door, looking out at me, and then closes it gently.

As I walk to my car, I stop and gaze at my baby blue Prius. I still haven't gotten a new one, but somehow, this one is growing on me.

CHAPTER 36
Charlie

I'm pulled out of my thoughts by a knock on the door. It's exactly ten a.m. I get up from the couch and head to the door. When I open it, I see Jimmy leaning against the front porch rail, looking as handsome as ever in a blue polo shirt and khaki shorts, his smile making my heart skip a beat. I take a moment to savor the sight of him.

Behind him, where his car should be, is a silver van. He leans forward and kisses me, and I savor the taste of his hot lips.

"Hi, are you guys set?" he asks when we break apart.

I raise an eyebrow and smile. "As set as we can be. Where are we going?"

"Great," he says, ignoring my question.

"Hey, Jimmy!" Ronny comes wheeling out, his smile so big it melts my heart.

"Hey, buddy. It's been a minute," he says to Ronny as he extends a fist towards him. They bump fists, and Jimmy adds, "I hear you're doing great things with the marketing. Jake tells me you've created a bunch of new marketing pieces. You're quite the artist."

Ronny's face lights up with pride. "Yeah, I did a lot of computer graphics in high school."

"It shows," Jimmy says, taking the handles of the wheelchair. "Come on, buddy." He gently glides Ronny down the ramp situated at the side of our stairs.

The van has a lift, clamps, and a belt to secure Ronny in place. It's a comfortable luxury van, not one of those cargo vans used by UPS. I've wanted something like this since his accident. Getting Ronny in and out of his wheelchair for car trips has always been challenging. And his wheelchair is heavy, making it difficult to put it in the trunk.

Jimmy opens my door, and I climb into the passenger seat. When he's seated behind the wheel, he turns around to Ronny. "You ready? Here we go." His energy is infectious, and before long, I'm bristling to get to our destination. *Where on earth is he taking us?*

The massive Ferris wheel in the distance, as we turn off the highway, gives our destination away. *We can't be going there!* But as we get closer, with nothing else in sight, it's clear that we are. I turn to Jimmy, concerned. "The amusement park? Are you kidding?" I glance at Ronny, who's looking out the window, then turn back to Jimmy. I whisper to Jimmy, hoping Ronny can't hear me over the music playing, "There are usually too many people, and I don't feel it's safe. That's why I don't take him."

Jimmy glances at me, grins, winks, and turns back to the road, nodding along to the song on the radio. He can be so infuriating.

The morning sun bathes the amusement park in a warm, golden glow as we pull into the parking lot. To my surprise, the lot is practically empty except for a grouping of cars near the entrance. Jimmy pulls up into a handicapped spot. My heart flutters with anticipation, and I glance over at my brother Ronny, who's sitting in his wheelchair, a wide grin on his face as he looks around.

As the van comes to a stop, I turn to Jimmy, who's sitting in the driver's seat with that mischievous twinkle in his eyes that I love so much. "Why is the park empty?" I ask.

He flashes me a smile. "Well, Charlie, I made a little arrangement. My dad knows the owner, so I called him, and well, Bob's your uncle — We've got the entire park to ourselves today except for a few other special guests the owner knows. He sets a few days a year aside for things like this."

My jaw drops, and my eyes widen in disbelief. "Wow, that's amazing." I can hardly contain my excitement. Ronny's eyes light up, too, and my heart bursts to see him so happy. Jimmy wasn't lying when he called himself a magician. "Did you have to pay a lot of money?"

"Let me worry about that," he says. "You worry about having a great time. This is all about you and Ronny."

Glancing at him, I see his dimple on full display. I say, "I've missed you."

"Ditto," he says, planting a kiss on my lips.

Jimmy opens the van door, and we maneuver Ronny out, carefully easing his wheelchair down. As we make our way into the park, I can't help but notice the dozens of assistants scattered throughout. They're all dressed in matching uniforms, ready to assist with anything we might need. They greet Jimmy by name, "Mr. Winslow," with a nod and a smile.

"This is incredible," I whisper to Jimmy. He's pushing Ronny, and I have my arm through his. "I can't believe you arranged this for us."

"I wanted Ronny to experience the amusement park again. You said it was one of his favorite places. I wanted to create a special day for you *both*."

Tears well up as I realize my deep affection for Jimmy. He's shown me kindness in ways I couldn't have imagined.

As we walk along, Jimmy pushing the chair, he says to me, "Remind me to buy Ronny an electric wheelchair. It's the least I can do for his hard work on the app. We'll call it a bonus."

"Oh, yes," Ronny says. "That would be great. I'd be able to buzz around the house and chase Charlie."

"Hilarious," I say, hitting him on the arm.

"Ouch," he yells, feigning pain. "That's brother abuse."

We all laugh.

As we approach the first ride, Ronny's excitement is contagious. Jimmy and the attendant help him onto the ride, and I take a seat next to them. The ride starts, and the wind rushes past us as we soar through the air.

Ronny's laughter fills the near-empty amusement park, and I can't help but join in. I've missed that sound for so long, stifled by the accident that left him in a wheelchair. But today, thanks to Jimmy, that laughter's back.

We go on ride after ride, and Ronny's smile never fades. Jimmy is right by us, taking care of Ronny's well-being at every step.

When lunchtime comes, we enjoy a picnic under the shade of a massive oak tree in the center of the park. Jimmy thought of everything, from Ronny's favorite sandwiches to the cool lemonade that quenches our thirst. He even had a package of Tootsie Rolls just for me. I must have told him they were my favorite at some point. He stores everything I say, like a computer. It's sweet.

As the sun dips below the horizon, we find ourselves back at the entrance of the amusement park. Ronny looks exhausted, but the contented smile across his face warms my heart. Jimmy looks at me, his eyes full of affection, and says, "Ronny hasn't stopped smiling."

I nod, tears of gratitude in my eyes. "You've given us a day we'll never forget, Jimmy. I don't know how to thank you."

Jimmy leans in and kisses me softly, his lips warm and tender. "You don't have to thank me, Charlie. I'd do anything to see you smile."

Ronny makes a grunting noise. "Eww, get a room, guys." I look at Jimmy, and we burst out laughing.

Jimmy takes hold of my arm before I can climb up into the passenger seat. I stop and turn around to see him holding up the keys to the van and jingling them.

"What are you doing?" I ask, laughing.

"I thought you might want to drive your new van," he says.

Just when I thought the day couldn't possibly improve, Jimmy surprised me yet again. I tell him I'm too tired to drive, even though I'm beyond excited about the van. It is going to improve our lives dramatically.

As we head back to my house, I glance back to see Ronny asleep in his chair.

"I had a blast," I tell Jimmy. "It looks like Ronny's sleeping, so I guess he did, too." I nod toward him.

Jimmy takes my hand, and I gaze out the window, feeling tired. Maybe I'll take a nap, too. Before I do, though, I turn to Jimmy. "I guess your mom was right," I say.

He cocks a brow. "Oh, yeah? About what?"

"You're a keeper, James Winslow."

CHAPTER 37
Charlie

Today will forever be ingrained in my memory. It was a whirlwind affair that left me feeling alive and rejuvenated. I haven't enjoyed myself this much in a long time. But it wasn't just me who had a good time. Ronny did, too. I can still hear his laughter ringing in my ears, echoing through my mind whenever I close my eyes.

There is a bittersweet feeling, too, watching him struggle every day, yet able to find happiness despite it all. He has a way of rolling with the punches and not feeling sorry for himself. Today, his spirits were high, and it warmed my heart and filled me with joy.

Jimmy left for home a few minutes ago, declining my offer to stay for dinner. I can't say that I blame him. We've all had a long day, and I can only imagine how exhausted he must be.

I mull over everything he's done for us, and Aunt Debbie's words ring in my head. She was right. Jimmy is a great guy.

Now, several hours later, I'm helping Ronny get ready for bed. "Hey, have you played Pirates of Starcrest lately?" he asks.

"No," I say. "I haven't felt like it."

"Oh, sis, you gotta get on. They're doing some crazy new stuff in there."

"Really? Maybe I'll jump on tonight."

"Yeah, you'll *love* it," he says. "Jump on tonight and let me know how you like it. Alright?"

"Sure, Ronny," I promise.

I'm exhausted as I slip into my pajamas, but Ronny's enthusiasm about Pirates of Starcrest is contagious, and I kind of promised him I'd check it out, so I log on to play.

I find *ChaosMaster518* waiting for me in the lobby when I enter the game, and he sends me an invitation for me to join.

"Seems like you've been waiting for me," I tease. "Did you miss me?"

"Oh, you know I did," he replies. "This world is hopelessly boring without you in it. I've been checking to see if you're on. Where have you been?"

"Awww, sucks to be you. I've been busy, but I'm here now." The game starts, and as usual, *ChaosMaster518* takes point, shooting enemies I can only see after their bodies drop.

"So," I say, cutting through an alien sentry who's backing my avatar, "Figured out how to beat the level yet? I hear there might be some new tools. It's getting boring watching Rozak wipe the floor with our butts week in and week out."

"I have a plan," he says. "Come on, this way."

He veers off the usual map towards a hidden passageway I recognize from internet walk-throughs for the level. A new map pops up on the screen that leads us away from the enemy encampment we would have otherwise tried to cross on previous attempts.

"Hey," I say, impressed. "You had to break into the cryptic vault to find this map. Where did you find the vault? Forget that. How did you get into it?"

He laughs, amused. He sets C4 on a dam at the top of the mountain, and we climb higher up the mountain. When he detonates the bomb, the dam is going to flood the valley, washing away the enemy encampment and giving us a free run at their warlord, Rozak.

"I told you before, sweetheart. I'm awesome," *ChaosMaster518* says as he sets off the bombs.

"Don't be cocky now. What happened to being partners?"

"Fine, fine. It was quite simple, actually. I found a rhythmic wand in the tools, so I used it, and Bob's your uncle."

I freeze, confused. "What did you say?"

"I said Bob's your uncle, Charlie." *ChaosMaster518* laughs.

My controller falls to the ground. "Oh, my... are you serious? *Jimmy?*"

Hearing movement behind me, I turn around to find Jimmy, his headset still in place, on one knee with a ring box extended. Aunt Debbie and Ronny are there, too, holding Jimmy's laptop.

"If I give you a rhythmic wand so *you* can get into the cryptic vault, will you marry me?"

Tears pool inside my eyes as I whisper, "How did you know it was me?"

Jimmy's smile widens. "In my conversation with Ronny, we got to talking about the game, and I found out your handle," he says. "They helped me plan this and get you on the game. So, Charlie, will you marry me?" He looks so anxious, but so handsome, kneeling there with his headset on and the ring box extended toward me.

I feel like my heart is about to burst out of my chest. Aunt Debbie is clutching her hand over her heart, crying and laughing at the same time. Ronny is by the door, his smile lighting up the room. He nods at me, and that's all the push I need.

I take a deep breath and set down my headset, taking

Jimmy's hand. "Yes," I say, the tears falling freely now. "Yes, I will marry you, and *Bob is indeed your uncle.*" We laugh as he hands Aunt Debbie his headset and takes me into his arms, placing the most beautiful ring I've ever seen on my finger.

I walk Jimmy out to his car, admiring the enormous diamond ring he'd bought me. Under the street lamp in front of my house, it sparkles brilliantly.

"Oh, Jimmy," I say, my voice filled with wonder. "You really want to marry me?"

"I've never wanted anything so badly in my life. I love you, Charlie. I think I've loved you since the moment you took ten years off my life in the men's room."

I laugh, feeling the warmth of his presence. "I thought you were pretty hot yourself."

"Oh, did you, now?" He grabs me around the waist and pulls me closer. "You sure gave me a run for my money."

I smile, feeling the electric chemistry between us. "That's how we do it. Don't think the trouble's going to end just because you're marrying me."

"Oh, you're a feisty one, aren't you? I might have to teach you a lesson."

"Oh, yeah, how's that?" I tease.

He takes me by the shoulders, pushing me up against the car. "Like this," he says, and then he pulls me to him, his lips capturing mine, a promise that I'm his.

Then he releases me and steps back. "See what I mean?"

I stare at him, my desire ignited. "Jimmy!" I scold. "Get over here."

I grab the front of his shirt and pull him towards me, my lips ready for his kiss.

He laughs. "Oh, no, no, no. I don't think so," he says, tugging back from my grasp.

"What?" I ask, pouting playfully.

"So, you're going to give me trouble, Wifey-to-be?" he teases.

"No, I won't give you *any* trouble." I bat my eyelashes.

He steps forward once more and wraps his arm around my waist. "I didn't think so," he says. His voice is low, and my heart flutters at the sound.

He grabs my hair, pulling me toward him, and our lips collide once more. I moan loudly as he bites my bottom lip.

"I'm glad you parked away from the house," I say between kisses. "Aunt Debbie and Ronny are probably looking out the window."

"Shhhh," he says. "I thought you weren't going to give me any trouble."

"Oh, you—" I start to say, but his lips silence my words with another passionate kiss.

I part my lips, and he takes the cue. His tongue enters, and he explores my mouth, stoking the fire already ignited within me. "Mmmm," he says as we become lost in each other's embrace. I feel myself melting into his arms, overwhelmed by his scent, his presence, and the intensity of his love. I've never loved anyone more in my life, and I hope it's always like this.

We remain that way for what feels like an eternity. If Ronny were here, he'd tell us to get a room.

"I love you, Charlie, so much," Jimmy whispers. "I'm always going to be here for you. For Ronny, too. I'm going to get us a big house that we all can share. You're never going to worry about anything ever again. I promise."

He holds me tight, and I relish in the warmth and security of his embrace, burying my head into his chest to soak in his scent and his love.

"I love you, too, Jimmy," I say, my heart overflowing. "More than you know."

I call out to Ronny from the living room. "Ronny! Are you coming or not?"

It's been over a year since Jimmy proposed, and tomorrow is our big day. Right now, we're heading to the rehearsal dinner, which is taking place at Jimmy's parents' house since his father's health has made travel difficult. We're so thankful he's still with us to witness our union. He's a remarkable man. As sick as he is, he's still as sharp as a tack. He's been actively showing Jimmy how to manage his businesses for the past year. Ray has a virtual empire, but Jimmy's been able to hire the right people and delegate wisely so he can focus most of his energy on Charlie's Angels, LLC.

Aunt Debbie and I are standing in the living room of our new home in Saratoga Springs, waiting for Ronny to emerge from his study. It's not a mansion by any means, but Jimmy had it designed with Ronny's needs in mind so he can easily get around and have his own space. Aunt Debby has her own apartment that connects to the main house, and Jimmy had Aunt Debbie work with the architect to design it just the way she wanted it.

Aunt Debbie laughs as Ronny finally comes zooming out of his study and down the hall in his electric wheelchair.

"Geez, Sis, relax," Ronnie says, coming to a stop in the living room. "You'd think you were getting married or something." He laughs.

Aunt Debbie scolds us. "Come on, you two, let's go," but a slight smile graces her lips. She's been beaming all week about the wedding. She was a big help with the wedding, as was Jimmy's mother, Carol. Aunt Debbie and Carol have hit it off after spending so much time together planning the wedding.

My parents have flown in from Mexico to0 for the big day, and my father is going to give me away. After a long soul-searching journey, I've released my resentment toward my parents. Life's too short to hold a grudge, as I've learned from Jimmy's grief over his father's illness.

I never thought I'd call my mother again after she left us years ago, but Jimmy convinced me to reach out to her after our engagement. Mom had sounded so excited over the phone, and it made my heart ache. She and my father came to visit a month later, and Ronny surprised us all by being the most welcoming of the bunch, laughing and reminiscing with my dad and Aunt Debbie about our childhood memories.

My mother thanked me before she left, tears in her eyes. "I'm so glad we came. I don't know why we stayed away so long." I think my mother was just scared. Not everyone handles tragedy well. I knew if I wanted to have a relationship with her, I had to forgive her.

When we said our goodbyes on their last visit, Mom had given me a warm embrace. "I love you guys. I hope you know that. We'll be back for the wedding," she'd said. She kept her word.

I'm very excited that Janice agreed to be my maid of honor. Reconnecting with her has been such a blessing. I never realized that the reason Ronny was so angry about my treatment of Janice was because they actually get along well, him and Janice. I'd almost say they flirt, but I don't want to jump the gun. It might be wishful thinking on my part, but sometimes I feel like she comes over to see Ronny more than me.

As we head to Jimmy's parents' house for the rehearsal dinner, my heart is full, and I can hardly believe that tomorrow I'll be Charlene Winslow. It's a name that sounds regal, and I'm not so sure I mind *Charlene* after all.

Our house is only minutes from Jimmy's parents. He wanted a place in Saratoga to be close to them. His father's illness requires a lot of attention, and he didn't want to let that fall on his mother's shoulders alone. We spend a lot of time there, giving his mother a chance to get out and giving Jimmy time with his dad.

My phone rings, and it's my husband-to-be. My stomach somersaults at the sound of his voice. "Hello, handsome," I say into the phone. We're all in the van on the way to the Winslow house. Aunt Debbie's driving, and Ronny's in his chair in the back. My parents are meeting us over there.

"Hello, gorgeous. On your way?" Jimmy asks.

"No, we've decided not to come. Rain check?" I joke.

He laughs. "Hilarious. You'd better be on your way, or I'm going to eat all the bacon-wrapped scallops."

"They're looking good," I hear Archie yell in the background. "I'll make sure Atticus saves you a few."

I smile to myself, feeling incredibly lucky to be marrying Jimmy. "Alright, fine," I say to Jimmy "We'll come, but don't think just because I'm marrying you that you get to boss me around. We've talked about this."

He chuckles. "Woman, you'll do as you're told."

I roll my eyes, even though he obviously can't see me through the phone. "We'll see about that," I say playfully.

Aunt Debbie gives me a sideways glance, her eyebrows lifted. "What are you two talking about?"

"Oh, just being silly, Auntie."

"Oh, so the usual, then."

Ronny pipes up from the back. "Tell Jimmy not to eat my pizza!" It's a running joke between them as they always fight over the last piece.

"Tell him I won't," Jimmy promises over the phone.

"He promises he won't," I tell Ronny, and he laughs.

"Are you ready for this?" Jimmy says to me, getting serious suddenly. "Are you ready to marry me, Charlie?"

"I've decided I want to be *Charlene* now," I say.

He bursts out laughing. "You're kidding me, right? After all the times you scolded me for calling you that?"

"Yeah, but I like the sound of Charlene Winslow. It sounds...classy."

"Alright, Charlene, my *darling*. Are you ready to marry me?" He sounds so sexy on the phone that I can't *wait* to marry him. "Because I'm not taking no for an answer."

"I've never been more ready for anything in my life," I say.

"Good. I'll see you soon."

"I'll see you soon, *Atticus*."

He laughs again. "Oh, Atticus, is it now?"

"Well, you don't expect me to have a husband named Jimmy when my name is Charlene, now do you?"

"No, I guess not."

"Alright, I'll see you soon. We should be there in a few."

"Wait!" he says.

"Yes?"

"Have I told you I love you today? Because I do, you know."

"No, I don't think you have, but I love you, too."

"Partners forever, *Charlene*?"

"Partners forever, *Atticus*!"

Epilogue

Seven Years Later
Aunt Debbie

"Young man, when your parents get back, they're not going to want to find out you didn't do your homework." I scold Raymond, my great nephew, and the cutest, sweetest boy on the planet. If I do say so, myself.

Raymond may only be six, but the school gives them homework every night, which he's not too fond of. His mother typically works on it with him, but today is Charlene and Atticus' wedding anniversary, and I agreed to babysit for them and help Raymond with his homework. I'm retired now, but I was a teacher my entire adult life, so I enjoy helping Raymond.

"Mommy lets me have a snack when I do my homework," he complains. "Can you give me one? Please, Aunt Debbie?"

"Sure, baby. What would you like?" How could anyone say no to his sweet face?

"I want cookies," he says, and I laugh out loud. Maybe I can say no. His mother would kill me.

"Not cookies. We haven't had dinner yet. You can have fruit or some veggies and dip."

He grunts. "Okay. Strawberries? With whipped cream?"

I chuckle. He's just like his Uncle Ronny. He loves strawberries and whipped cream, too. I miss Ronny, even though he's only going to be gone for a couple of weeks. He's just so good with Raymond and always helps out whenever I babysit.

Ronny's taken multiple vacations with Janice over the past couple of years. They're on some kind of cruise this time. The two of them are world travelers. The AccessAid application makes it a lot easier for Ronnie to travel, and since Janice is a travel agent, she gets deep discounts. I'm happy for Ronny. I never thought he'd find a girlfriend given his situation, but apparently, Janice always had a crush on him.

Atticus is having another house built on the property for Ronny and Janice when they finally get married. Ronny proposed to her, but she wants some big fancy wedding, so it's going to take a few years to put it all together. Ronny doesn't care. He would rent the Taj Mahal for Janice if he could, and if she wants a big wedding, that's what he'll give her.

The phone rings, and it's Charlie, calling to check in on Raymond. "Hello?" I say.

"Hey, Auntie. How's it going?"

"Well, Raymond didn't behave, so I had to drop him off at the zoo." I glance at Raymond. His mouth is full of strawberries, and whipped cream covers his face. We smile at each other.

Charlie laughs. "Put him on speaker." I'm grateful she doesn't want to FaceTime with him.

I put the phone on speaker and set it in front of Raymond. "Hi, Mommy. I'm in with the lions," he says, and we exchange a giggle.

"Well, you'd better have your homework done when we get home," she scolds, and his face gets a pout. He rolls his eyes.

I whisper, "See? I told you," and he hands me back the phone. Apparently, he doesn't feel like talking about his homework anymore.

I take the phone. "He's getting it done, don't worry. How's the date going?"

"Oh, Aunt Debbie, this place is so cool. Atticus reserved a table for us in one of those igloo tents I was telling you about. It's right by the lake with white lights all inside. It's so romantic and cozy. I'm having a great time."

"You feeling alright?" I ask. She's expecting their second child in about a month, and she'd had some back pain earlier today. I thought they might postpone, but she said she was feeling better.

"I feel good," she says. "I'm having too much fun to feel any pain."

Atticus had hired her a pre-natal massage therapist who comes to the house whenever Charlie needs her to. Charlie thought about having her come today, but Atticus had planned a whole day's adventure at Lake George for their anniversary, and Charlie didn't want to miss out. Their business has been so busy with the development of the new apps Charlie recently created, and with Ronny gone a lot, they can't afford to miss too much time from the business.

Since most of their work is done from home, Charlie will still be able to work when the baby arrives. However, Atticus emphasized his desire that she focus on the new baby and not stress about work. They're having a girl, and they're naming her Veronica. Charlie thought it would be cute to call her Ronny like her brother, and Atticus left the entire decision up to Charlie. He likes to act like he's in charge, but he'd give her the world.

The doorbell rings, and I say goodbye to Charlie, promising to get Raymond into bed on time. I've been expecting a visit from Carol, Atticus's mother. She's coming to have dinner with us and see her grandson.

"Hey Carol," I say, as I open the door. She's carrying several bags as she comes into the house.

"Here, let me help you with those," I say, taking two bags from her hands. We head to the kitchen, and when Raymond sees her, he runs to her arms. "Grandma!" he yells, giving her a big hug.

Carol spends a lot of time here at the house with us. Ray's passing was tough on her, but I've got to say, she's been a trooper. Atticus and Charlie spend a lot of time with her, and she and I have become good friends over the years. After Ray died, Carol got bored being in her big house alone, so Atticus gave her a large department to manage at one of her late husband's companies. She loves working there, and she's a superb manager. It's given her a new lease on life.

She sets the bags on the counter and starts pulling items out of them. She's brought her usual ice cream sandwiches with the strawberry filling for Ronny and Raymond. Those are their favorites. She's got a package of scallops and a package of bacon for Charlie. She brought me my favorite cut-and-bake chocolate chip cookie dough rolls. She got Atticus a package of sushi.

"You didn't have to do this," I say, laughing, as she pulls everything out of the bags.

"I enjoy doing it, Deborah!" she says, narrowing her eyes at me and smiling. She always calls me Deborah when she's scolding me.

I laugh. "Alright, then, Carol." I say. "What's in that bag?" I point to the last bag that's still sitting on the counter.

I see Raymond's eyes light up as he listens to our conversation. He knows there's something special in that last bag because there always is.

"In this bag," she says, turning to Raymond. His eyes are enormous. "We have...the Nintendo game you've been wanting." She holds the game up in the air in a grand gesture.

Raymond squeals, runs over to Carol, and practically knocks her over, grabbing her around the waist and hugging her. His excitement is over the top as he looks at me and asks, "Can I play it now, Aunt Debbie?"

Oh, brother. I just promised his mother he'd have his homework done. "Alright, you can play, but only until dinner. Then you need to do your homework before bed. Okay?"

"Okay, I promise," he says, taking the game from Carol and running toward his bedroom to play it.

Carol selects a cup from the cupboard and helps herself to a cup of coffee on the counter. "Have you talked to the kids?" she asks. She's referring to Charlie and Atticus.

"Yes. They're having a great time," I say.

She sits down at the table, setting her coffee cup in front of her. "It smells so good in here. Are you making lasagna?" I try to make my lasagna for her at least once a month. It's her favorite.

"You guessed it," I say.

She smiles and sips her coffee. "I can't wait for that baby," she says, getting a dreamy look on her face.

I open the refrigerator and take out a bottle of water. Thinking about the baby, I say, "I can't wait, either. Did you know Atticus painted that entire baby's room himself? I told him to hire someone, but he said he wanted to do it. He did the same thing for Raymond's room, remember?"

"Yes, he enjoys working with his hands," she says. "Didn't Archie come to help him?"

"No, Archie offered, but he has a new girlfriend, and she had to travel to Pittsburgh for her sister's wedding, so Archie went with her. Atticus didn't want to wait for him to get back. You know how babies are. They can come early."

"Nice girl?" Carol asks. "Archie's girlfriend?"

"Oh, yes, a sweetheart," I tell her.

Archie practically lives at our house. He feels like a member of the family. He's here so much. His girlfriend Chris fits right in with the bunch. He had a few girlfriends previously who were jealous of how much time Archie spent with Atticus. Silly girls. But Chris is different. She loves it here.

"I wish Ray was here," Carol says, a sentiment she often expresses. She's told me how sad it makes her that her husband never got to meet his grandchildren.

"I know," I say. She's handled Ray's death with grace, but I know she's lonely.

"I'm just glad that he and Atticus mended their relationship before he passed," she says, her smile returning. "He really grew to love Charlene, and at least he got to see his son get married."

"He did. He seemed to have a good time that day, too," I say, remembering how much fun their wedding was and how full of life Ray had seemed.

"We all did," she says, getting a faraway look in her eyes. Then she takes another sip of her coffee, glancing at me and smiling. I smile back, and a comfortable silence envelops us.

I sip my water, waiting for the lasagna to bake, thinking about how thankful I am for the way things turned out.

Life is unpredictable, and we don't know what tomorrow will bring. But today?

Today, I think we're doing alright.

Let other readers have your thoughts!

(It helps them and the Author!)

REVIEW LINK:

https://amzn.to/48vHKoH

 **Thanks!**

Your next Gigi Sloan read: https://amzn.to/3Qaokvo

"Hike with me to scout the property, Samantha, or look for another job."

Matthew Hale, billionaire CEO of Hale Properties, is *drop-dead gorgeous*. I mean **hot**, but he demands obedience from his employees. I'm his brand new assistant, and I'm no exception.

When Mr. Hale instructs me to pack for a three-hour hike to a remote cabin, I know I have no choice. **Go or be *fired*.**

The snow pours from the sky, stranding us in the cozy, secluded cabin in the middle of the mountains. As the snow deepens, so do our feelings. He opens up to me in ways I never thought possible. I'm playing house in my head, and I need to **stop**.

Forced to cohabitate with no end in sight, we strive to suppress our fiery attraction, but the raw intensity threatens our resolve. It would be so easy to just…

No! I can't! I *need* this job, and an office romance is *strictly forbidden*.

Read Your Next Gigi Sloan Novel For FREE

Limited Offer - Receive a free copy of My Fake Billionaire Boyfriend

Sign up for Newsletter, Contests and Giveaways

GET YOUR FREE COPY

If you like passionate but clean romance, this adventure is for you. Join Isaiah and Diane on this journey. It will leave you craving more.

Grab your copy, a cozy corner, and let the passion begin.

Magnetic billionaire, Isaiah Wentworth, made me a tantalizing offer.

Pretend to be his girlfriend for the world to see.

He had to prove to his powerful grandfather that he was a man who could settle down. I yearned to show my cruel ex that I was more than the plain Jane girl he'd dumped.

What could go wrong? We were perfect strangers and it was a perfect plan. Except…

As we ventured deeper into the deception, I wondered if Isaiah's attention was more than just a performance.

But someone like him could never have genuine feelings for someone like me… Right?

With my heart still reeling from my past heartbreak, I had to keep my emotions in check. He was gorgeous and wealthy, every girl's dream.

Was his affection and attention just part of the act or could it be more?

https://t.ly/MyFakeBillionaireBoyfriend

Also by Gigi Sloan

The Billionaire Romance Collection

 **My Fake** Billionaire **Boyfriend**

Available in eBook and Paperback

https://amzn.to/3tGfxwg

 **Stranded with** Mr. Billionaire

Available in eBook and Paperback

https://amzn.to/49Mo8OD

 **Ordinary** Mr. Billionaire

Available in eBook and Paperback

https://amzn.to/3TwCSvx

 **Snowbound with** Mr. Billionaire

Available in eBook and Paperback

https://amzn.to/3Qaokvo

Acknowledgments

A heartfelt thank you to my cover designers,
my editor, my formatter and everyone else
who was a major contributor in making
this book a reality.

Special thanks to Victory Ehikhametalor, who was
instrumental in helping me in the creative process.

I also want to thank Fiction Profits Academy for sparking my creativity and teaching me the mechanics of publishing a novel.

A special shout-out to my most amazing teachers, James Scott Bell, and Victorine Lieski.

Thanks,
Gigi

Cover Designers: Mia Kiely@MiaKDesign and Anees Ahmed@Aneesdesigner7
Editor: Lisa Sargent@Upwork
Logo: Flower Image by jcomp on Freepik.com
Chapter Image: Easel Painting by Anees Ahmed@Aneesdesigner7
Format Designer: Dawn Baca

About the Author

Gigi Sloan
Romance Author

Gigi Sloan is a Contemporary Romance Author who specializes in Clean & Wholesome Billionaire romance novels. This book is part of her Billionaire Romance Collection. Gigi writes wonderfully entertaining and exciting romance stories that will get your heart pounding for more.

Gigi's first love is her family. Her four children (two sets of twins) and her five small grandchildren are the driving force of her success. Gigi is a full-time author who has been writing her entire life.

Gigi writes most of her words in the great outdoors. Sitting by the river or a mountain lake, her fingers dance across her keyboard to create heartwarming love stories that are sure to excite.

If you would like to connect with Gigi, you can email her anytime at Gigi@gigi-sloan.com.

You can find her on Facebook, Twitter or here at her website: https://gigi-sloan.com

- facebook.com/Gigi.Sloan.Writes
- x.com/GigiSloan
- instagram.com/gigi_sloan_writes

Made in the USA
Monee, IL
25 February 2025